The climb up to the farm was spectacular. Mile after mile of wonderful hills piling one on the other with amazing views at every turn of the road. The farm itself stood tightly nestled into a hill, looking as though it had grown there rather than been built over two hundred years ago, and one didn't come upon it until the turn into the farm gateway. There it was, grey-stoned, solid, secretive almost, but inviting at the same time.

And there she was, Megan Angharad Jones, waiting in the kitchen doorway for him to arrive, arms outstretched, her whole face filled with a smile. Half the house was in shadow but the sun still shone on the back door, highlighting the glints of red in Megan's hair, the sparkle in her dark eyes, and he thought, not for the first time, of the wonders of the world and that surely it must be the eighth wonder that she loved him.

Educated at a co-educational Quaker boarding school Rebecca Shaw went on to qualify as a teacher of deaf children. After her marriage, she spent the ensuing years enjoying bringing up her family. The departure of the last of her four children to university has given her the time and opportunity to write. *Country Lovers* is the third novel in the Barleybridge series from Rebecca Shaw, author of the bestselling Turnham Malpas books. In the Barleybridge series she has created an enchanting cast of characters, recreating the warmth and humour her readers have come to love and expect.

Visit Rebecca Shaw's website at www.rebeccashaw.co.uk.

By Rebecca Shaw

TALES FROM TURNHAM MALPAS
The New Rector
Talk of the Village
Village Matters
The Village Show
Village Secrets
Scandal in the Village
Village Gossip
Trouble in the Village
A Village Dilemma

THE BARLEYBRIDGE NOVELS
A Country Affair
Country Wives
Country Lovers

Country Lovers

Rebecca Shaw

ORION

An Orion paperback

First published in Great Britain in 2003
by Orion
This paperback edition published in 2003
by Orion Books Ltd,
Orion House, 5 Upper St Martin's Lane,
London WC2H 9EA

A CIP catalogue record for this book
is available from the British Library.

ISBN 0 75284 258 7

Typeset by Deltatype Ltd, Birkenhead, Merseyside

Printed in Great Britain by
Clays Ltd, St Ives plc

COUNTRY LOVERS cast of characters

THE BARLEYBRIDGE VETERINARY PRACTICE

Mungo Price, senior partner, his wife *Miriam*, and his dog, *Perkins*

Colin Walker, partner, and his wife *Letty*

Zoe Savage, partner

Dan Franklin-Brown, partner, his wife *Rose* and son *Jonathan*

Rhodri Hughes, Practice vet

Graham Murgatroyd and *Valentine Dedic*, Practice vets

Joy Bastable, Practice Manager, and her husband *Duncan*

Senior nurse *Bunty Bird* (née Page) and nurses *Sarah One (Cockcroft)* and *Sarah Two (MacMillan)*

Receptionists *Kate Howard*, *Stephie Budge* and *Annette Smith*

CLIENTS AND OTHER VILLAGERS

Lloyd Kominsky, Rose Franklin-Brown's stepfather

Idris Jones, farmer of Beulah Bank Top, and his daughter *Megan*

Callum and *Nuala Tattersall* of Tattersall's Cop

Miranda Costello, an eccentric animal lover

Bryan Buckland, manager of Chesham Chicken Farm

Mike Allport and *Graham Hookham*, officers of the State Veterinary Service

Phil and *Blossom Parsons*, of Applegate Farm, and their foster boy *Hamish*

Billy and *Adele Bridges* of Bridge Farm, and sons *Gabriel* (Gab), *Gideon*, *Ben*, *Simeon*, *Joe* and *Joshua*

Inspector Richie Jamieson, uniformed police

Declan Tattersall, Callum's cousin, and his seven children

Bert Featherstonehough, ex-army dog handler

Lord Askew, the local squire and stud-owner

Bernard Wilson, puppy breeder at Badger's Lot and his sister *Hannah*

Tad Porter, farmer at Porter's Fold

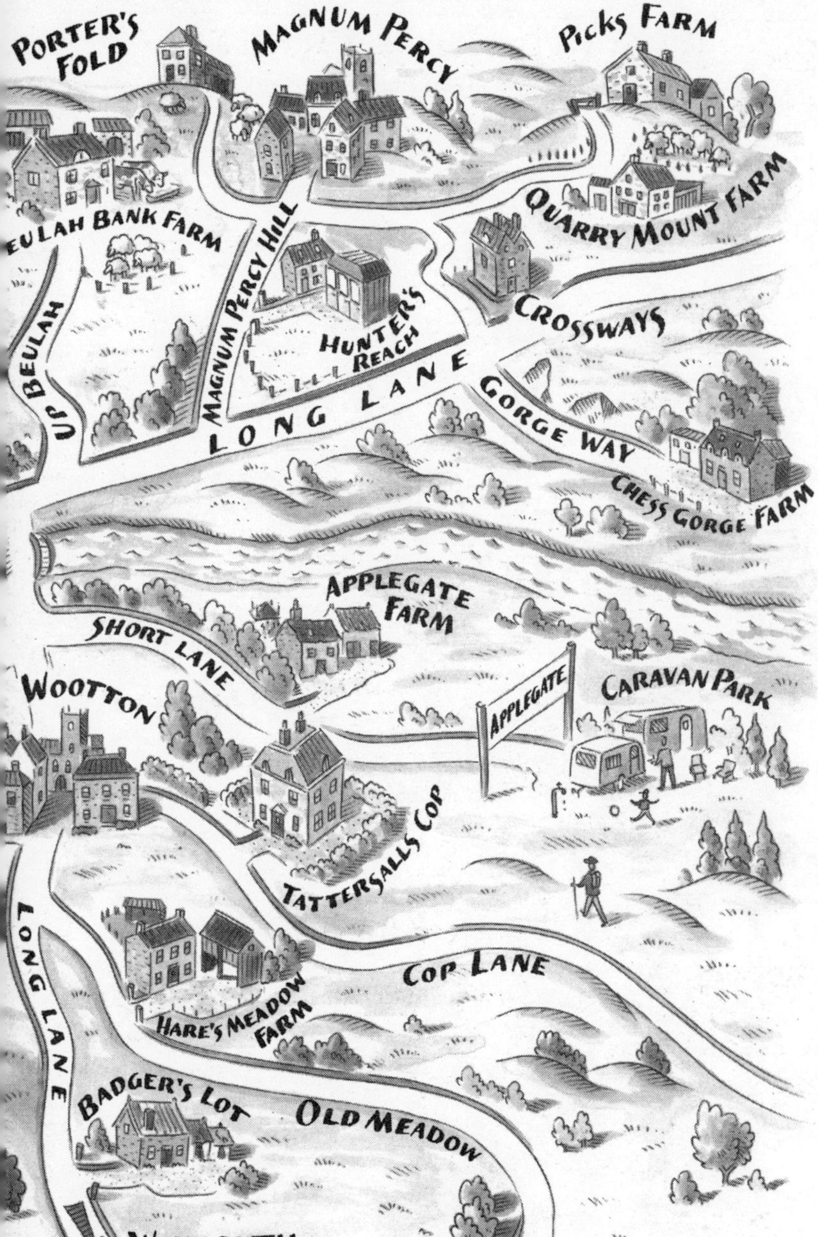
PORTER'S FOLD
MAGNUM PERCY
PICKS FARM
EULAH BANK FARM
QUARRY MOUNT FARM
MAGNUM PERCY HILL
HUNTER'S REACH
CROSSWAYS
UP BEULAH
LONG LANE
GORGE WAY
CHESS GORGE FARM
APPLEGATE FARM
SHORT LANE
WOOTTON
APPLEGATE
CARAVAN PARK
TATTERSALLS COP
COP LANE
LONG LANE
HARE'S MEADOW FARM
BADGER'S LOT
OLD MEADOW
WEYMOUTH

Chapter 1

It was Joy, as Practice Manager, who struggled with the staff rota every month and with Graham Murgatroyd off with flu, and Dan hovering distractedly waiting for the birth of his son and likely to be off for at least a week, and Rhodri behaving like the lovelorn chap he most decidedly was, it was proving more than usually difficult to plan June's staffing. She sat in her office in the last week in May, planning and replanning until her head spun. It was no good, she'd have to get Duncan to take a look. Joy rested her head against the back of her chair and closed her eyes. Briefly she dropped off, drained by a long, busy day. Moments later, someone clearing their throat disturbed her.

'Sorry, Joy, to disturb you but . . .'

'My fault. I've developed a splitting headache trying to plan the rota for June, it should have been done days ago.' She rubbed her eyes to refresh them and saw Mungo looking down at her with sympathy. Her heart raced, though not quite as wildly as it had at times during the last twenty years. She sat upright. 'What can I do for you?'

'Just to say I've finished operating for today and I'm going up to the flat. I know you're shorthanded, so Miriam and I are not taking this weekend away we promised ourselves, just in case.'

'That's wonderful. Thanks. If things get any worse I shall be doing the operating myself!'

'You've had plenty of experience assisting me in the past. I've no doubt you'd do an excellent job.'

Joy laughed. 'I don't think so, things have moved on since I first helped you. New techniques, new equipment. No, no, our reputation would go straight down the pan! As they say, you're only as good as your last operation.'

Mungo leaned across the desk and placed a kiss on her cheek. 'Thanks for all you do and thanks for being such a good friend to Miriam. She does value your friendship.'

Joy's eyes slid away from his face. 'And I hers. Must press on. I'm taking this rota home to Duncan. He'll sort it for me. There's a solution somewhere but I can't see it.'

'Don't hesitate to ring if you need me. Any time, and I mean it. It's just a difficult patch and we have to gut it out.'

'I'll ring, you can bet on that.' Joy allowed herself to watch him leave, to smile at him when he turned to say, 'Be seeing you,' to enjoy his handsome bearing, his restless energy, those splendid eyes and the gentleness of his mouth. She swallowed hard. There I go again, she thought, just when I'd begun to think he didn't matter any more. When he'd closed the door behind him she clenched her fist and banged it on the desk in anger. Would she never learn he loved elsewhere? That his kiss was that of a comrade and not a lover and never would be.

Duncan. Duncan. She focused on Duncan's face as she'd seen it that morning when the alarm had gone, making no impression on him at all. He lay snugly tucked in right against her back, one arm laid carelessly across her waist. When she'd tried to get up, he'd held her down and grunted his contentment. But she'd managed to turn over so she could look at him. She was always surprised how young he looked first thing. Which he was, all of nine years younger.

Joy said, 'Got to get up. Let me go.'

'Five more minutes.'

'No.'

'Please.' It was more of a command than a request. The arm across her waist had tightened and kept her there.

Joy tolerated the five minutes and then pushed off his arm and sat up on the edge of the bed. But he followed her and was kissing the back of her neck and his arm was round her waist again, gripping her.

'Duncan. Please. I'm going to be late.'

Duncan turned away from her without a word.

She'd stood up and headed for the bathroom and a shower and for an assessment of her allure in the bathroom mirror. It hadn't made good viewing. That mood had stayed with her all day and was still with her as she parked her car and went into reception the following morning and found she was five minutes late.

Ordinarily she would have apologised for being slightly late, but this morning, instead, she could find fault with absolutely everything. In reception, Stephie and Annette came in for a few broadsides, Sarah Cockroft for leaving dirty, blood-streaked operating sheets out on the laundry worktop instead of putting them immediately in the washing machine, and finally Mungo for arriving late for his first appointment. 'You should know better than to leave your first client waiting.'

'Sorry.'

Mungo saw the way the wind blew and escaped Joy's office as soon as he could, salving his conscience by being as charming as he possibly could to his client. 'Please, forgive me. Do come this way.'

'Don't worry yourself, Mr Price, we know how busy you are.'

3

Joy saw the owners of the dog shake his hand and smile and she thought he could charm the devil himself, he could.

He ruffled the head of his patient and asked, 'This is Teddy, is it? Hello, old chap.' To the owners he said, 'Now, tell me in your own words what the problem is.'

Joy watched him lead them into his consulting room, and smiled grimly to herself. It really wasn't fair for one man to have so much charm and such good looks. She saw Annette putting her empty coffee mug down on the reception desk. 'You know how much Mr Price dislikes empty mugs standing about in public view. Take it away. Please.'

Duncan had organised the rota to her satisfaction and after she'd pinned it up on the staff notice board and made sure everyone of the veterinary staff had a copy in their pigeon hole she put her own copy on the noticeboard in her room and sat down to think.

But not for long. Dan Brown came in to see her.

Dan had lost weight these last few weeks and was not looking quite as stocky or well-built as he used to. But the craggy face and the penetrating brown eyes were still there and so too was his in-your-face-energy, which sometimes caught one on the raw, but not now, not since he'd won her over. She greeted him with warmth and affection. 'Dan! You're soon back, is everything all right with Rose, you know?'

'She's fine, we got there early and they're delighted with her and we've to go back next week same time if the baby hasn't happened in the meantime. She's furious that she can't drive herself any more.'

'Have they said she shouldn't?'

Dan gave the happiest laugh he'd given since she'd known him. 'No. The truth is she can't get behind the wheel and reach the pedals.'

'Oh, well! Go have a coffee or something and take a rest. You've no calls for the moment.'

'None?'

'None whatsoever.'

'Right. I will.'

'You do that, it may be your last quiet day for some time!'

'We can't wait for the baby, you know. Just can't wait. Rose's stepdad has arrived and is out buying every item of baby equipment he can find. We wanted to wait . . . not tempt fate, you know.'

As Dan went off to take his break, Joy said quietly to herself, 'I can understand that.' She had just finished speaking when she heard the most terrifying sounds coming from reception. The papers on her desk flew in all directions as she squeezed out of her chair and raced to see what was happening.

Joy was appalled at the scene that met her eyes. A very large, heavily built dog of uncertain ancestry had a cat in his mouth. The cat was hanging upside down, yowling and trying to swing itself round to scratch at the dog's face, its claws unsheathed, its mouth wide open, but the dog was hanging on tightly, his fangs exposed below his drawn back dewlaps.

The waiting clients were panic stricken, clutching their pets to them, lifting their feet to avoid the whirling dog. Mrs Parr, the owner of the cat, was screaming with terror. 'Get him off! Quick! Somebody! Get him off. Oh! Oh! Oh!'

But the dog was intent on his trophy and had no intention of giving it up.

The clients were behaving like a coop full of chickens

with a fox at their throats and Annette and Stephie were hysterical and no more use than a pair of mice.

Above the clamour Joy shouted, 'Who owns this dog?'

A small, agitated man spoke up. 'Bingo! Let go! Bingo! Let go!' He was sweating so much his glasses were steaming up. 'He hates cats.'

Mrs Parr shouted. 'Get 'im off! Oh hell!' and promptly fainted. Another client began to beat at the dog with a magazine, which only served to infuriate Bingo even further. He altered his grip on the cat, was now holding it even more firmly, and the cat had stopped struggling. Joy grabbed his collar, and instantly, Dan, appearing apparently from nowhere, took over from her, stood astride of Bingo and deftly manhandled the dog's head to the ground, keeping a firm grip with both hands on its head and neck and his knee on its flanks. Taken by surprise the dog released its hold on the cat and it crawled away, trembling, its fur bristling and its mouth open wide, spitting hoarsely.

Joy took charge.

'Right. Stephie! Ring for an ambulance for Mrs Parr. Annette! Capture the cat and put it in a cage in intensive care. Dan! Get that dog in the back and tie it up. Tight! I'll get a blanket for this lady.'

She came back into reception with a blanket and a pillow. A client with her own cat safe from harm in its basket, got up to give her a hand.

Mungo came out with his clients to find uproar. If Joy hadn't been so preoccupied she would have laughed at the astonished expression on his face. 'What on earth . . . ?'

Dan finally managed to drag Bingo out. Annette caught the petrified cat and carried it away to make it safe, and Stephie called out, 'The ambulance is on its way.'

'Thanks, Stephie!'

Dan came back and faced Bingo's shivering owner. 'He's yours?'

The man nodded.

'Why have you brought him in?'

'For his injections, it's time.'

'Yes?'

Realising that he was holding a very public discussion, Dan broke off and invited Bingo's owner into an empty consulting room.

The man shuffled after him, still sweating, still shivering.

'Sit down. Please.' Dan pulled the desk chair forward and waited for the man to sit, then leaned against the examination table and asked, 'Yes? Mr . . . ?'

'Tucker. Alan Tucker.' He pulled out a handkerchief and mopped his top lip. 'She should have had the cat in a basket or something. It wasn't Bingo's fault. Not at all, no. The cat spat at him and tried to scratch him. What else is a self-respecting dog supposed to do? I ask you.'

'Apparently you haven't got him under control or you could have stopped him.'

'Under control in circumstances like that? He's an angel at home. We've two children, little ones,' he gauged their height with his hand, 'this big and he's like putty in their hands. They can ride on him, sit on him, cover him up with a blanket as if he's baby, anything they like and he never murmurs. It's only cats he can't stand.'

Dan looked a little sceptical at this. 'So you say.'

Alan Tucker mopped his face with his handkerchief again. 'She should never have brought her cat in without a cage . . . it was her fault.'

'You have got a point there. But I can tell you this. Never once in all the years I've worked as a vet have I known of such an attack. All the animals are so overcome by the smells and the strangeness or have memories of having been here before for injections or treatment that they are usually very subdued. He was alarming.'

'I still say it was the cat's fault . . .'

'Well, Mr Tucker, quite what the owner of the cat will be thinking when she's come round I don't know. It has all been very distressing. You are a client of ours, are you?'

'First time. We've only just moved here, changed my job, you know. Dog's all upset, you know, children too. New vet, new house, new garden, different walks, it's all been too much for Bingo, and then, on top of all that, that bloody cat.'

'That's understandable. Now, I must see to the cat. But be aware, Mr Tucker, that he's nervous. Keep an eye on him when he's with the children. He's big, and could do a lot of damage. I'm serious, a special eye till he's calmed down. OK?'

Mr Tucker stood up. 'Thanks for getting him under control. I was too shocked to do anything. Never seen him like that.'

Dan opened the door. 'Take care, Mr Tucker. Bring him back when he's feeling happier. I'll get him for you and then I'll see to the cat.'

When Mr Tucker came back into reception holding Bingo tightly, the ambulance had just arrived and Mrs Parr was being taken out in a wheelchair. Mr Tucker said to her, 'I'm so sorry.'

Ashen-faced she replied, 'My cat. Where's my Muffin?'

Joy said, 'We'll take care of her, she'll have the best of attention. The vet's examining her now.'

'Thanks. I really don't need to go to hospital. I only fainted. I think I'll just go home.' She made to get out of the chair.

8

Joy gently pressed her back. 'Believe me, it's best to have a check-up just in case. And it will make me feel easier in my mind that you've been looked at. I'll ring tomorrow and let you know about Muffin, or if you feel up to it, you ring later today. I'm so sorry this has happened.'

After Mrs Parr had gone Stephie said, 'Why were you so insistent that she went to hospital? There was really nothing wrong with her.'

'You're a doctor, are you?'

'You know I'm not.'

'And neither am I. Best to make sure in case of legal proceedings.'

'But she's nice, we've known her for years.'

'She's never had her cat attacked before though, has she? She might feel she should be safe to bring her cat here, which is quite right, but today she wasn't . . . so . . . you never know.' Joy wagged her finger at Stephie and disappeared into the back to find Dan.

He had carried the cat into a consulting room and was gently examining her. She wasn't in the best of moods for a close examination and Dan was having to be very careful not to stress her more than necessary.

Dan glanced up at Joy as she watched his sensitive hands moving so sympathetically over the cat as he assessed her injuries. 'She's been punctured here, look, one of his fangs. She's in deep shock. We'll have to set up a drip, can't do anything until she stabilises. Nothing broken I think.'

'I'll set up the drip. The girls are all busy.'

'Are you sure?'

'Absolutely. If Mrs Parr had brought her in a cat carrier none of this would have happened.'

'Exactly. Mr Tucker says the dog's as soft as butter usually. Just cats he can't stand.'

With a wry smile Joy said, 'That's plainly obvious.'

'Even so, I've warned him to keep an eye on him. It really was a nasty attack.'

Mungo took a couple of minutes between clients to find out what was happening. 'No farm calls this morning?' he asked.

'None so far. Colin's out, but he only has three calls.'

'So what about the cat? How is she?'

'Shocked, Joy's setting up a drip. I've found a hole where his fang caught her, but she's too shocked for me to do anything about it.'

'New client, was he? Didn't recognise the owner.'

'Yes. Claims the dog can't abide cats. Otherwise no problem.'

Mungo shook his head. 'Rose not pupped yet then?'

Dan laughed. 'Not yet. You'd better not say that to her, she wouldn't find it funny at the moment.'

'Exciting times we live in, eh?' Mungo clapped Dan on the shoulder, added, 'Thanks for that just now. Got a client. Must go.'

Muffin the cat was an exceptionally beautiful Siamese, and one after another the staff came to see her. 'Isn't she gorgeous? Just gorgeous,' Stephie said, and Annette thought she was utterly beautiful too and very take-homeable. 'Hope she's going to be all right. The poor thing. I hate big dogs.'

'Muffin. It's a poor choice of name for such an elegant cat. Sounds like a name for an ordinary moggy, not an aristocrat.'

Rhodri came in at this point.

Stephie turned to greet him. 'Good morning, Rhodri, come to see our new patient?'

'Who organised this?'

'Dan did. You had a client and we had to do something quicko.'

'I see. Did no one think to consult me? I am the only small-animal vet on duty this morning.'

This outburst silenced the two girls because they honestly didn't know how to answer him.

Rhodri turned on his heel and went back to his consulting room.

Stephie looked at Annette and they both pulled a face.

'Honestly! He gets worse. It's always poor Dan he has his knife in.'

Halfway through the morning, Dan went home to Rose, promising Joy that if a farm call came in he would go. Rose was seated in her favourite chair by the French windows looking out on to the garden. Beside her on a small table was the book she'd put down the moment she heard him coming. 'Darling! What are you doing home at this time? How lovely.'

'It's one of those strange mornings when there are no calls for me. It can't last, I'm quite sure. You all right?'

'I'm fine. Absolutely fine. So you've had an idle morning then?'

'No, not really, just a bit of an upset at the morning clinic.'

'Dresden china I am not. Please tell me.'

'Sorry. Huge great dog attacked a cat in the waiting room. Total uproar.'

'Poor thing.'

'I had to tackle it to the floor and then drag it out and tie it up.'

'You didn't have to put it down?'

'It did occur to me that perhaps it would be for the best, but one can't just rush about putting dogs down; it's not on and it would give the Practice a bad name.'

Rose grinned up at him. 'It most certainly would. I shall have a dog or a cat sometime. I always wanted a pet but mother would never let me. Too messy, she said.'

'Then you shall. You can choose, so long as it's not a huge one like a St Bernard. This cottage isn't big enough.'

'Could you get me a glass of water, Danny, please? Save me having to heave myself out of this chair.'

'Of course. Nothing stronger?'

'Like orange juice?' Rose smiled at him. It was a smile he had missed those months while they'd been apart. He should never have walked out on her. But the blazing row he'd had with her mother over an entirely mythical 'woman' she swore he had hidden away, had hurt him beyond belief. There had never been anyone but Rose. He found a glass, turned on the cold tap and let it run to make sure it was cold. As he watched the torrent of water gushing out he remembered looking for Rose at that time and finding her climbing out of the pool after her daily dozen lengths. She had stood in front of him, water streaming from her, and said, 'You're still here, then? Just go away. I can't bear it. Go away.'

Dan hadn't been able to come to terms with the fact that she sided with her mother. 'You know there isn't anyone else. No one. On this earth. No one but you,' he'd told her.

He'd seen her hesitate, but a lifetime of agreeing with

her mother had overcome her natural inclination to believe him. Thankfully, she'd soon discovered the truth.

He turned off the tap, took the glass to her, and as he handed it over he bent to kiss the top of her head. 'Love you.'

Rose drank the glass right to the bottom before she said, 'I don't deserve you, my darling. I simply don't.'

'Clean slate, we said. You stay right there, and watch me mow the lawn. Got to do something. Can't sit about. I'll open the window. If you need anything, give me a shout.'

He glanced at her once or twice and saw she'd picked up her book again. Then the next time he checked, the book had slipped off her knee and she was asleep. Do her good. She didn't get much sleep at night now. It was just what she needed. He paused for a moment to admire her. Everywhere she went people stared. And no wonder. She really was beautiful. Halfway through cutting the lawn his mobile rang. It was a call to Tattersall's Cop. One of Callum's goats was ill, and he was worried. He didn't want to bring it in because his wife, Nuala, who was very ill, couldn't be left. Dan left the mower where it was, wrote a note and put it on the table beside Rose and left.

To get to Tattersall's Cop Dan had to cross the river in the centre of Barleybridge by the Weymouth Bridge and then take the left fork, called Cop Lane, in Wootton. He was struck once again as he approached Callum's farm by how smart it looked. Dan sometimes thought that Callum spent too much time keeping the premises in order. While that was commendable and something other farmers could do well to think about, keeping the farm immaculate didn't fill the coffers.

'Good morning, Callum. What's the problem?'

'It's little Sybil.'

Callum had bought the complete stock of a goat farmer who'd died, and amongst them were seven pygmy goats; perky, bright versions of full-sized goats, born with more than their fair share of curiosity. They'd been brought into a pen close to the house, and leaning on the gate alongside Callum, Dan paused to study them for a moment before going in. 'They all look fit. Which is Sybil, then?'

'The all-black one.' All seven of them were springing around the pen on a familiarisation tour. They were a mixture of black, white and fawn, and looked as though they'd all been in the washing machine that morning so fresh and smart did they look. What with their appealing looks and their cheeky antics, Dan couldn't help but smile at them.

'Settling down nicely, are they?'

'All of them are. Think they'd been getting a bit neglected towards the end. Nothing serious mind, but neglected.'

'What did you want them for, Callum?'

'Fancied a change and Nuala was keen.'

'How is she?'

Callum didn't reply for a moment and then he said, 'You'll see for yourself in a minute, she's coming out to see you. Wants to know about your wife.'

'I see. So why am I here? There doesn't seem much wrong with Sybil.'

'I reckon it's worms. Appetite like you wouldn't believe.'

Dan climbed over the gate and was immediately mobbed by all seven of the goats. Dan crouched to examine Sybil and found himself with pygmy goats endeavouring to raid his pockets, steal his mobile, climb on his back, and generally get in on the act by making their own diagnosis.

'How long have you been farming, Callum?'

'Fifteen years or thereabouts. Why?'

'Don't you know what happens when you put a billy in with nanny goats?'

Callum's eyebrows shot up when he'd absorbed what Dan had said. 'Oh God! You don't mean . . .'

'I do. Sybil's in kid.'

Callum rubbed his hands with glee. 'No! Never thought it might be that. Nuala'll be delighted. Delighted. Well, I never. That's great. Sure it is.' His tanned face almost split in two with delight.

'Not long to go, I shouldn't think.' He stood up, trying to escape the goats' attentions without knocking any of them down. 'In fact, this one looks as if . . .'

'That's Cassandra, she's Nuala's favourite.'

'. . . she might be too.'

Callum's Nuala came out of the house and walked slowly towards them, every delicate step an effort. Dan hoped his face didn't register the shock he felt when he saw her. She was emaciated beyond belief. It didn't seem possible that she was still able to stand upright.

Dan touched his cap. 'Good morning, Mrs Tattersall. I've just been giving Callum some good news.'

Callum interrupted. 'Let me tell her. Sybil's expecting!'

'Really!' Nuala's face burst into life and the small spark of what was left of her lit up her beautiful blue eyes. 'Well now, isn't that good news, for sure. When?'

'Within the week, I would have thought.'

'Within the week!'

Dan watched Callum hug her as though she were made of the finest glass. So tenderly.

'I might just see that. Yes, I might. They must look so sweet.'

'They do, Mrs Tattersall, nothing sweeter.' Dan noticed a grimace cross her face. Immediately Callum said, 'I'll take you in.' He picked her up as easily as he would a baby, and set off for the house, calling over his shoulder, 'I'll call you when she's in labour. Can't afford to take any risks.'

'Right. 'Bye, Mrs Tattersall.'

' 'Bye, Dan. My love to your Rose.' Her feeble voice just reached Dan and he was glad she couldn't see his face, because he felt so distressed. He looked at Sybil and said quietly, 'You'd better hurry up or she won't see that kid of yours. Do you hear me?' Sybil, however, had other things to think about as Callum had left the goats some titbits in the feed trough and she was concentrating on getting the major share.

Dan was almost home when he decided to ring the practice to see if there were any more calls for him, but found he must have left his mobile in the goat pen. One nil to the goats. He just hoped Rose hadn't been trying to ring him. He drove all the way back to Tattersall's Cop, parked his Land Rover, intending to knock at the farmhouse door, but saw a doctor from the medical practice in Barleybridge just going in. So he went quietly to the goat pen to find his mobile laid abandoned and unharmed in the long grass by the fencing.

It had a text message on it from Rose. 'Baby started.'

Chapter 2

It was eleven o'clock that night before things really got going with Rose, and it was half past one in the morning when the consultant decided a Caesarean section was advisable.

Dan was almost beside himself with anxiety, and even considered offering his services, after all he'd done plenty in his time, but arrived at the conclusion he'd probably pass out if he witnessed Rose having surgery and that he'd be better keeping her stepfather, Lloyd, company.

He was worse than Dan himself; taking sips from his hip flask, marching round the waiting room, tap tap tapping his fingernails on the table, asking questions to which Dan couldn't possibly have the answers, and generally behaving like someone on the brink of a breakdown.

'Have a cup of tea, Lloyd. I'll get one from the machine.'

'Tea? What good will that do. A glass of whisky, yes. Tea? No. I've nearly run out of whisky. Do they sell it here? No, of course not. Narrow pelvis they said. Big baby. God! If I'd known I'd've had you castrated.'

'Thank God you didn't. Rose wouldn't have wanted that.'

Lloyd gave Dan half a smile, which he smothered instantly by reminding himself that he should be ringing

17

Rose's mother. 'I should you know, she ought to know. She should be told. I'll ring her.'

Dan clamped his hand on Lloyd's mobile phone. 'Not here, it might interfere with the equipment. And . . . what's more, it's Rose's decision. She'll tell her if she wishes. Not you and not me.'

'You're damn right. Of course. God! I'm tired. What the hell are they doing all this time?' Lloyd stood up and began prowling again. 'I love that girl. Like she was my very own. She's a gem. Gutsy, you know. I've tried to shield her from her mother's more crass ideas, but . . . God! That woman's something. She's a hell of a woman to keep in check.'

Wryly Dan said, 'I know.'

Lloyd looked at him. 'Huh! You don't need me to tell you that. I could have killed her when I found out she'd driven you away.'

The door opened and the consultant came in smiling. Dan's heart felt fit to burst. 'All's fine! A wonderful baby boy, four kilos exactly. Mother's doing fine. Wonderful patient.'

He shook Dan's hand and offered his congratulations, and then Lloyd's. 'Mustn't leave out Grandad!' He pumped Lloyd's hand up and down vigorously.

Lloyd asked, 'What the hell's four kilos? What does it mean in America?'

Dan said, 'About eight and a half pounds. Wait here and you can see her after me.'

'But I . . .'

'After me.'

Dan and Lloyd were completely enraptured by the baby. Lloyd was convinced he looked exactly like himself, though how he worked that out Dan couldn't think. But everyone else said he was the spitting image of his father and he was. The same nose, and the same shaped face, but hair the colour of Rose's. He'd always imagined that all babies looked alike but this one was his and no doubt about it. Rose was bone weary but immensely happy, and kept saying, 'Isn't he wonderful? Aren't we clever? You and me?'

She came home three days later to find that Lloyd had been to the supermarket and bought up what appeared to be half its stock. He'd also bought another freezer to put in the garage and filled that too. 'Can't have you running out of anything at all. There's not a thing I haven't thought of. There won't be any need to shop for weeks. Now, let me have a hold of young Jonathan Daniel Franklin-Brown.'

Dan got out his wallet. 'Look! I must pay you for all that.'

'Nonsense. *He* is my reward and anyway money can't buy him.' He sat in a chair where the sun couldn't reach, holding Rose's son, in a world of his own.

Dan made coffee for the three of them, settled Rose in her favourite chair by the window, and gave her some post to open. She flung the junk mail on the floor, then voiced her anger when she recognised her mother's handwriting. 'She's written to me! She knows where I am.' Angry disappointment showed in her face. 'I know it won't be you, Danny. Is it you, Pa?'

Lloyd, absorbed in delicately smoothing his fingers over the baby's face and his tiny starlike fingers, time and time again, had to be asked twice before he answered. 'Mmm. I felt it only right. She is your mother.'

'She lost all her rights as a mother when she persuaded me that Dan was a no-good son-in-law. I shall regret right to my last breath being so influenced by her. You'd no right, Pa.' Tears poured down her face in rivers, unheeded. 'I feel awful. So miserable.'

Lloyd stood up and went to put Jonathan in Rose's arms. 'It's your hormones, I read about it in a book. Here, hold him, your mother can't take him away from you, he's yours and Dan's. I won't let her come between you and him, if I have to throttle her to do it.'

The phone rang. Dan went to answer it. 'Dan Brown here.'

It was Kate from the Practice. 'Sorry to disturb you when you're off limits so to speak,' she said, 'but you know Callum Tattersall, well, he's rung in to say Sybil is in labour and it's not going right. He wonders if you'd come out to see her. I told him you were off but he says he can't bring her in and you'll know why. Who's Sybil?'

'A pygmy goat. Yes, I do know why. I'll go. OK.'

'Thanks ever so much, Dan.'

Dan picked up his car keys from the hall table, and went back into the sitting room. 'Lloyd, you're not planning going somewhere, are you? Can I leave you to make lunch for Rose and yourself and be generally useful?'

'What the hell, you're not going out on a call?'

Rose interrupted. 'Pa! Don't interfere. What is it, darling?'

'Callum's goat having problems delivering. You know who I mean. I'll be two hours at most.'

'Of course. You go. I shall be fine. I guess Pa and me will cope. There's one thing for certain – we shan't starve to death. My love to Nuala.' She pursed her lips ready for him to kiss, so he bent to do as she asked and whispered his thanks.

When he arrived at Tattersall's Cop he found Sybil

ensconced on a makeshift bed in the kitchen with Callum seated on a chair keeping an eye on her, a glass of neat whisky in his hand.

'She's in a poor way.' There was a very slight slur in his speech, and it occurred to Dan that the bottle on the table had reached its present level that very day.

'Now, Sybil, what are you making such a fuss about?' After he'd examined her he asked how long she'd been in labour.

'I got up at half five to see to Nuala and decided to go check on Sybil while I was up. She was very restless then. Jesus! Don't let her die, it'll kill Nuala.' Once he'd said that Callum looked as though he wished he hadn't.

Dan ignored his mistake and continued to check Sybil. 'It's my opinion she can't deliver. Her pelvis is too narrow for such a big kid to get through. I'm going to have to operate.'

Callum shot upright, his face drip white and beads of sweat breaking out on his forehead. 'Operate! Oh God! No! I can't stand it. Not Sybil.' The remains of his whisky went down his gullet in a trice.

'If I don't, she and the kid will die a slow death. Pull yourself together, Callum. My Rose had a Caesarean only three days ago and she's home and doing well. So stop the blather and give me a hand.'

'I can't. I can't stand the sight of blood. Not Sybil's.' Tremblingly he refilled his glass, but Dan took it from him before he could drink it.

'When we've done you can celebrate with that.'

'But . . .'

'No buts.'

Dan did a businesslike job of the operation, aided and abetted by Callum who continually threatened to pass out.

When the tiny kid was pulled from his mother Callum was massively impressed. He ran excitedly into the hall shouting, 'It's a girl! All safe and sound!' Then rushed back in to eulogise over the kid all over again.

'Isn't it fantastic? Have you ever seen anything as wonderful as that? Why, it's astounding. Honest to God. A marvel!'

'Clean her up while . . .'

'It's a girl. That's what Nuala's always wanted, a little girl.'

'. . . I stitch up and finish off.'

Callum said decisively, 'Right. When we've done, we'll take her to Nuala to see. Her being so near the end I can do nothing but exactly as she asks. She just wants to hold her. To have a share in all this loveliness.' Callum concentrated on making the little kid as pretty as a picture for Nuala. 'Her hooves, look! Aren't they beautiful? So tiny, why, you can't believe she's real!'

'She is though and she won't be the last, by the looks of Cassandra.'

'Black with these white patches, you have to agree she's well marked.'

Dan finished closing up Sybil, and then suggested Callum took the kid for Nuala to see. He intended staying in the kitchen and getting washed before he left, but Callum insisted that Nuala would like to see him. 'She doesn't get much company, you know. People don't know what to say.'

So he followed Callum into the dining room now converted into a bedroom for Nuala. She lay in a big double bed, propped on snow-white pillows the colour of her face. If it were possible Nuala looked even more frail than the last time he'd seen her. There was no flesh on her face, it was quite simply skin stretched over bones. Once she had been pretty, he could see that. She was wearing a bedjacket so only her hands were visible on the counterpane and they too, like her face, were skin and bone. Nothing more. There was such a terrible stillness about her you could have thought she was already dead.

Callum, carrying the kid in a baby's blanket, laid it reverently on the bed beside Nuala just where she could reach to touch it. Her eyes glowed with delight. She whispered to Callum to put the kid in her arms, so he did, protesting that it was too heavy for her. She shook her head. Taking a big breath, which ran out before she'd finished speaking, Nuala said, 'I always wanted a little girl. Remember that time when . . .'

Callum nodded. 'What shall we call her?'

Breathing deeply she gasped, 'Carmel.'

'Sure, that's a great choice. Carmel it shall be. I'm going to take her back to Sybil now, she'll be missing her.'

The tiny kid made a sweet attempt at an anxious bleat, so Callum scooped her up in his arms and left. Dan said, 'Good morning, Mrs Tattersall. I'll be seeing you. Rose sends her love.'

Nuala looked at him and whispered, 'Thank you. God bless. Look after Callum for me. You know, when I'm . . .'

'Certainly, I most definitely will. 'Bye Nuala.' He smiled at her and raised his hand in a half salute, at a loss to know what else to say. Dan found Callum seated in the kitchen watching Sybil and Carmel getting to know each other.

'That's what we were going to call our baby that we never got to hold. Losing her broke Nuala's heart.'

Dan's answer to that was to squeeze Callum's shoulder in sympathy. 'Best be off.'

23

'There'll be no point in it all without her.'

'I'll call tomorrow perhaps, or better still, ring me if you need me. Right?'

'Right.'

Dan left Callum downing another whisky while he supervised Carmel having her first feed. He paused for a moment at the back door, thought about the cards life had dealt Callum, and remembered Jonathan Franklin-Brown and Rose and how happy he was by comparison.

'You say Dan's gone to Tattersall's Cop? That's good of him.' Joy looked over the top of her glasses at Kate but had to wait for her reply while Kate counted the money a client had given her for some budgie seed.

'That's right, exactly and there's your receipt. Thank you. 'Bye. Well, Callum rang to say his goat was in dire straits and he wanted Dan and Dan would understand, and so I rang him and Dan went.'

'Well, try not to ring him again, he needs this holiday, and with Rose . . .'

'I know but you see Callum's wife is . . . well she's dying and he can't leave her.'

'Ah! Right! I see. And your exams, Kate? How are they going?'

'Third paper on Tuesday.'

'Yes, I know but what about the two you've already done? Are you feeling happy about them?'

'Well, yes, I am, I seem to have aimed my revision in all the right areas so far, so fingers crossed. Thank you for giving me time off.'

'My pleasure. I don't know why I'm wanting you to do well though, because it means you won't be here after

September.' Joy laughed at her and all Kate could say was, 'Sorry,' with a smile on her face.

'You've done so well learning this job. Hardly a foot wrong all the time you've been here.'

'Well, not quite, I have had my moments.'

'Well, yes. There was that time when . . . and the other when . . .' They both collapsed with laughter.

'Seriously though, I shall be thrilled when you've passed and delighted for you to go. You've got just the right strain of common sense to make a good vet.' Joy picked up a stack of files from the counter and disappeared into the back to get on with some administration, leaving Kate on her own, as Stephie had had to go to the dentist for an urgent appointment. She wasn't by herself for long though because the afternoon clinic was beginning and the first booking was for a budgie to have its claws and beak trimmed.

The client came in carrying a cardboard box punched with dozens of holes to give the bird air. She was a strange person, this client, she believed quite adamantly that animals were far superior to human beings, yet could allow her rabbits' teeth to overgrow so much they couldn't eat, neglect her ponies' hooves so they could hardly walk, and her cats to have fleas to the extent they were completely overrun with them. Nevertheless, all of them at the Practice had a great affection for her and her eccentricities. Her appearance was out of the ordinary, to say the least. It appeared she'd used a builder's trowel to apply her make-up and her hair was blacker than black, if that were possible. Today she wore a full-length black skirt, which looked as though it had done the rounds of the Nearly New Sales for far too long, topped by a mustard yellow twinset covered in beaded embroidery, over which she wore a scarlet sequinned waistcoat. Miranda Costello was nothing if not colourful.

'Hello, Mrs Costello. Take a seat. Rhodri's almost ready for you.'

Mrs Costello wagged a finger at her. 'How many times have I told you, it's Miranda to all my friends.'

'Sorry. Habit, you know.'

'That's all right, dear. I do hope Rhodri won't be long, Beauty hates being shut in. Listen to him making such a fuss, he's usually so quiet when he can't see me.'

Mrs Costello sat herself down on a chair close to the counter and Kate made the foolish mistake of asking her how all her other animals were. The moment the words were out of her mouth she could have kicked herself. There followed a long monologue of how wonderfully intelligent her animals were and of the tricks they got up to and . . . with an indulgent smile, Miranda added, 'Listen to him talking to me. He's such a talker he is, aren't you, Beauty?' By then she had inched open the lid of her cardboad box to ensure that Beauty was in full working order and he'd swept out before she could stop him and perched in the top of the giant cheese plant in the far corner of reception.

'Oh! Beauty! Well, bless him, isn't he clever? Knowing just where to perch. Doesn't he look lovely all amongst the leaves? Come to Mummy, Beauty.' She held out her finger and made tweeting noises to Beauty, but he was listening to none of her enticements. Eventually she climbed on a chair and made a grab for him, and got him squawking and struggling in her hand. He nipped her hard on her fingers and made her squeal. She kissed him before she put him in the box, protesting and squawking, and fastened the lid back on. 'I told you he was clever and he is. Better company than people he is, and certainly more obedient.' Then Beauty went completely quiet. 'There you are, you see, he does know how to behave really.' She preened herself like a budgie might, and sat back to continue her monologue.

Kate listened with half an ear to her stories for a few minutes more, wishing all the time that Rhodri would hurry up with his lunch. Eventually he did open his consulting room door and call out, 'Beauty Costello, please. Good afternoon, Miranda, and how are you this afternoon?'

'Oh! I'm fine, Rhodri, and you?'

'Fine thanks. Claws again, is it? And beak I see.'

'That's right. Yes. His claws and his beak.'

While he looked for the right piece of equipment to do the job, Rhodri asked her how her menagerie was getting along. 'Oh! Fine, you know. Every one a treasure, the delight of my heart. Wouldn't know what to do if I didn't have animals to get up for in the morning. Dogs to walk, cats to feed, Beauty to clean out, stables to muck out, you know. Life's full of promise for me.'

'Good.' Rhodri slid the lid off the cardboard box cautiously; he wasn't in the mood for a bird flying round his consulting room resisting arrest. Without taking the lid off completely he slipped his hand in and felt about for Beauty. All he could find was an inert budgie. Laid on its back! Feet in the air! A sure sign of having gone to glory. Oh no! Not dead. He put a finger on Beauty's chest, but could feel nothing. In his very bones he knew it was all hopeless. He quickly replaced the lid, and said, 'I think maybe, Miranda, you'd better take a seat.' Rhodri, in a state of total panic, cleared his throat. This had happened to him once before and the client had threatened legal

27

action. He came over all cold and the stutter he'd thought he'd got rid of for ever came back. 'I-I think all is not w-w-well with B-B-Beauty.'

'What do you mean, "All is not well?"'

'He appears to have had a h-h-heart attack.'

'A heart attack! Well, get him out and do what they do.'

'I'm afraid it's t-t-too late for that.'

'Too late? Let me look.' She wrenched the lid off the box and saw Beauty feet up, laid motionless. 'You've killed him! You've killed him! My Beauty!' She picked him up and tried prising his beak open and breathing into his mouth but to no avail. Beauty was dead and gone.

'I'm so sorry, Miranda, so sorry. It must be the shock, you know, of being fastened up in the box when he's used to his freedom. A free-as-air budgie like B-B-Beauty, well . . .'

'Give him an injection, go on, something to bring him round.'

'Unfortunately there isn't anything I c-c-can . . .'

Mrs Costello clutched hold of the front of his white coat and begged and begged for Rhodri to resuscitate Beauty. 'Please. Please.' When she saw him shake his head she screamed and fell back onto the chair holding her handkerchief to her face, howling like a banshee. 'Beauty! Beauty! Beauty!'

At this point Kate, hearing the sounds of distress coming from Rhodri's consulting room, and noting that the level of conversation in the waiting room had been reduced to nil as the clients pricked up their ears, decided to go to his assistance. She gingerly opened the door in case Beauty was free again, but saw him laid on the examination table and recognised instantly what the problem was. 'Oh dear! It must have been the shock of it all.'

Grasping at straws Rhodri repeated, 'Shock of it all?'

'Well, he escaped in reception and Miranda had to recapture him from the top of the cheese plant. He was very upset, wasn't he, Miranda?'

The howling stopped while Miranda shrieked, 'Did I kill him then?'

'Not at all, it was no one's fault, was it, Rhodri?'

Rhodri shook his head. 'No one's. Budgies do this sometimes, stress and strain, different environment, travelling here, escaping, you know. It's all been too much for him.'

'Oh! My poor Beauty! What will his wife say? Oh! Beauty! I shall take him home and they can all come to his funeral. My poor Beauty. My little darling. My dearest Beauty.' She kissed him before she put him in the box. 'You are sure he's dead? Quite sure? I'd hate to bury him and then find . . .' Miranda looked hopefully at Rhodri.

Rhodri said reassuringly, 'Quite sure. Quite sure.'

Kate took her elbow and led her out into reception, still weeping.

Between sobs she said, 'I owe you, for the consultation.'

'There'll be no charge, Miranda.'

'Oh! Thanks.'

'You'll be all right getting home?'

'Oh yes, I've got the van.' She braced her shoulders.

'Are you sure?'

She nodded. Kate opened the door for her and saw her out to the car park.

'I shall miss him.'

'Of course you will, it's only natural. Drive carefully.'

Kate returned to have a private word with Rhodri. Closing the door behind her she said in a loud whisper, 'That was a close shave.'

'Too right. He was dead even before I put my hand in to get him out. I can't believe it, that's twice it's happened to me.' He completed his report of the consultation on his computer and said, 'You're a star, Kate. An absolute star.'

'Any time!'

'Don't tempt fate, I don't want that happening again. Who's next?'

Rhodri carried on with his afternoon clinic, with the niggling thought of Beauty's demise at the back of his mind all the time.

But he did have dinner at Megan's to look forward to, and tonight he would do his utmost to be polite to Megan's dad, Mr Idris Jones. About the only thing they had in common was home rule for Wales, after that their conversation was barely civil. The old man was the last of four generations of farmers and now he was crippled with arthritis and chronic asthma he had to rely on a daughter to carry on the farming tradition and with all that to bear he was bitter. Words could scarcely describe the extent of his bitterness. Made worse by the fact that his only son, Howard, had left home to become a barrister in London, unmarried and with no prospects of marriage, which meant there would be little chance of a successor to the family heritage.

But Rhodri was determined he wouldn't rise to the bait tonight, for Megan's sake, because she took the brunt of Mr Jones's unpleasantness every day of her life. When he thought of Megan his face broke into smiles. She was the loveliest, most beautiful, most delightful woman he'd ever met in his life, and he was determined, resolute even, that one day he and she would be married. He blessed the day there'd been all that confusion in reception, which had resolved itself by Megan coming to the Practice, pet sheep on a lead, to get veterinary help. To fall in love, on a bleak winter day with the wind blowing down from Beulah Bank Top fit to slice a man in two, was the last thing he'd ever expected, but it had happened. Gloriously, magically it had happened for her too.

At home, as he shaved for the second time that day, Rhodri promised himself that tonight he would broach the subject of marriage to Mr Jones, firmly and considerately. Though why he should have to ask his permission to marry Megan was beyond him; she was thirty-five and didn't need anyone's permission.

Showered, shaved and changed, Rhodri scooped up his pet ferret, Harry, from under a sofa cushion, shut him safely in his outdoor cage, and set off for Beulah Bank Farm singing his heart out with his favourite tenor solos from the *Messiah* as he drove, his spirits soaring the closer he got to Megan.

The climb up to the farm was spectacular. Mile after mile of wonderful hills piling one on the other with amazing views at every turn of the road. The farm itself stood tightly nestled into a hill, looking as though it had grown there rather than been built over two hundred years ago, and one didn't come upon it until the turn into the farm gateway. There it was, grey-stoned, solid, secretive almost, but inviting at the same time.

And there she was, Megan Angharad Jones, waiting in the kitchen doorway for him to arrive, arms outstretched, her whole face filled with a smile. Half the house was in shadow but the sun still shone on the back door, highlighting the glints of red in Megan's hair, the sparkle in her dark eyes, and he thought, not for the first time, of the wonders of the world and that surely it must be the eighth wonder that she loved him.

Rhodri went straight into her arms and kissed her hard and long. He stood back from her at arm's length and asked, 'How is it you always know when I'm about to arrive?'

'I'll let you into a secret. I look out of the kitchen window and as you drive over the humpbacked bridge I can just catch sight of you before you disappear into the trees and then I need to count to thirty-five and I know you'll be here.'

'And there was I thinking we were telepathic.'

'And a bit of that too!' They laughed at each other and, arms entwined, went to find her father. He was seated as usual in his winged chair, a rug over his knees, a pipe in his mouth, the *Daily Telegraph*, which he read from cover to cover every day, discarded in the wastepaper bin at his side.

'Good evening, Mr Jones.'

'It's you, is it? I'd forgotten.'

'Hasn't it been beautiful weather this last week? It's the sort of weather that makes you wish you were somewhere exotic under the palm trees with a soft breeze just beginning to take the heat out of the day. Isn't it now?'

'You wouldn't if you were me. This heat is stifling.'

'It must help the arthritis though.'

'Well, summer, I can't stand because the asthma always seems worse to me and, winter, I can't stand because of the arthritis. Gets me every which way.'

Rhodri didn't stop to think. 'You can't win, can you?'

Mr Jones rounded on him. 'Are you being impertinent on purpose?'

'I was trying to sympathise.'

'The only thing that saves your bacon is the fact that you're Welsh.'

'It's not the only thing that's good about me, Mr Jones. I love your Megan as you know. All we want to do is marry. Why can't you see your way to it?'

Mr Jones banged his fist surprisingly hard on the table beside him, making all the invalid paraphernalia on it jump and rattle and he shouted as best he could, 'I've said it and I'll say it again, she isn't marrying anyone. I need her. When I die, then she can marry.'

'But you've years of life in you yet, you know that. Years *we* could spend enjoying our life *together*.'

'Not while I'm alive. That sounds like Megan dishing up. Tell her I want wine tonight. Go on, tell her. Quick man, before it's too late.'

Rhodri moved his special table to one side so Mr Jones could lever himself up without any hindrance and said, 'I'll go *ask* her about the wine.'

'When I need my vocabulary correcting I'll let you know.'

They ate their meal at the dining table, Mr Jones at the head with Megan to his right, and Rhodri to his left. Rhodri wasn't well versed in the appreciation of furniture, but he could tell that the Jones family had dined off this very table for many, many years. The wood had a patina that only years of use and care could have produced. The chairs were the same, they invited you to sweep your hand across them for the sheer pleasure of touching the wood. In some ways it was a delight to dine in such splendour, in others an irritant because with the table came Mr Jones.

'Not enjoying your food? Young man like you, you should be wolfing it down.'

'I am enjoying it. Having to cook for myself makes me very appreciative of Megan's cooking. You're lucky, Mr Jones. Just wish I—'

'Rhodri!' Megan stopped him short of annoying her father again with one of his innocent remarks. 'It's Myfanwy. Her feet, she's limping. Can you take a look?'

Rhodri shook his head. 'I really shouldn't, I'm not a farm vet. They won't like it.'

Mr Jones snorted his disdain. 'Oh God! Professional etiquette rearing its ugly head, is it? You're a vet, aren't you? So get on with it.'

Rhodri addressed his reply to Megan. 'It puts me in a very awkward position. Can I get Dan to come? Is it urgent?'

'No. It's not urgent. Is he back at work then, after the baby?'

'Yes, he's back and full of being a father, though he says he hasn't had a full night's sleep since Rose got home.'

Megan smiled. 'Yes, of course. I imagine the baby will be just as beautiful as Rose.'

'God help it if it looks like Dan.'

Rather wistfully, Megan suggested that if the baby was half as beautiful as Rose he'd do all right. 'She's not just beautiful, there's a vibrancy about her . . . I wish . . .'

Her hand lay on the table while she spoke and Rhodri covered it with his. 'I agree Rose is beautiful and Dan's a lucky man, but you're just as beautiful and I'm just as lucky as Dan.'

'Hmm,' Mr Jones sneered, looking pointedly at Rhodri's hand holding Megan's. But Rhodri didn't remove it until he was good and ready and not before he'd taken her hand to his lips and kissed it reverently. The thought crossed Mr Jones's mind that Rhodri needed taking down a peg or two and that he was just the chap to do it. Matters were getting dangerously close to being taken out of his control and he wasn't having that.

Chapter 3

Rhodri was spending ten minutes he really couldn't afford at this time in the morning searching for Harry Ferret. He'd let him out for his early morning run around while he got ready and the little devil had disappeared. It was partly his own fault because he'd left the kitchen door open by mistake. Experience had taught him not to leave the house without getting Harry back inside his outdoor cage: left all day with the freedom of the house spelt total disaster, so he had to find him before he went to work and time was running out. Rhodri muttered to himself while he crept about in an attempt to sneak up on him unawares, but those bright brown ferret eyes and wickedly twitching whiskers were nowhere to be seen.

Ah! The bathroom! Yes! Got yer! Harry loved nothing better than a tussle with the loo paper and Rhodri found yards of it spilling all over the floor. 'You little devil, you!' Harry gleefully nibbled on Rhodri's ear and babbled his own brand of ferret talk to show his appreciation of Rhodri's tolerance.

With Harry safely fastened in his run in the garden, Rhodri checked his appearance in the mirror in the hall, made sure the house was secure and ambled out to his car. He sniffed the air and found it gentle and summery as it should be at this time of year. A hint of damp though, which might presage rain later in the day. Before putting on his shades he adjusted his rear-view mirror, winked at himself, and agreed with no one in particular that he was handsome in his dark Welsh way with his thick, jet-black hair, dark brown eyes and a sensuous mouth second to none. He shoved the car into reverse and backed out onto the road, jerked into first and set off to the Practice, arriving with only minutes to spare.

The car park was already filling up with clients' cars, so he was definitely much later than he liked to be. He raced in through the back door and into his consulting room, slapped his shades down on a high shelf along with his keys, took his freshly laundered white coat from the back of the consulting room door, buttoned it up, picked up the top file from the pile on his desk and saw his first client was Venus Costello, a cat. His heart sank. Not Miranda *again*.

When he put his head round the door into reception he saw it was filling up nicely with clients and Rhodri took on board the pleasurable buzz and excitement of a morning doing what he liked best. 'Good morning, everyone. Venus Costello, please!'

Mrs Costello stood up and bounced into his consulting room with a bright, 'Good morning, Rhodri. I was expecting it to be Graham . . .'

'Very heavy cold, poor chap, can't make it today.'

'Oh dear, I am sorry. I do hope it isn't anything serious, there's so much flu about.'

'Don't worry your head about him, he's tough. I've no doubt he'll be back tomorrow hale and hearty. Now, it's time for Venus's booster, is it?' He peered into the basket and saw Venus sitting with her back to him.

'Yes, it is. She's used to Graham, really. He's always seen to her. By the way, I've bought another budgie to replace Beauty, well, no, not replace, but you know what I mean. I've called him Toots. Beauty's wife, the shameless huzzy, has taken to him immediately. Had I better come back when Graham's better, they have such a rapport with each other?'

'Don't fret yourself, Miranda, I've done this thousands of times, there's nothing to it. She's used to coming here, isn't she? Now, I'll get myself organised and you get her out when I'm ready.' Rhodri checked Venus's card and prepared the syringe.

Though the door to her carrying basket was open, Venus didn't move, so Miranda put in her hands to lift her out. Venus gave an angry howl as she was placed on the examination table, shot Rhodri a belligerent glare as he approached with the syringe and took to her heels. She leapt from the table to the desk and hid behind the computer. 'Ah! Right. Miranda, you get her, I'll only panic her.' But Venus saw straight through his subterfuge and as Miranda, speaking in her softest, most caring voice, put her hand in behind the computer, Venus leapt out on to the top and began racing round the consulting room as if the Hound of the Baskervilles was on her tail. She hurtled about over every level surface she could find, from desk to chair, from chair to table, from table to shelf, to computer, to printer, to fridge, at such a speed she was almost a blur.

'Oh! Oh! Oh!' whispered Miranda, her earrings tinkling vigorously and her hands covering her mouth in horror and helplessness. 'What are we to do?'

Rhodri was at a loss for words. He couldn't face another crisis with Miranda, not so soon after the episode with Beauty. He dodged past Venus, as she shot from table to desk, to lock the door into reception, but as he did so

Venus sent his shades flying from the top shelf and he trod on them. Biting back an angry response, he raced to lock the door into the Staff Only section of the building. 'We mustn't panic! Stand quite still and so will I and she'll get tired. I've locked the doors so no one can come in by mistake; if she gets out of here we'll never catch her.' He put down the syringe and, dodging the flying figure of Venus, went to stand with his back to the wall and advised Miranda to do the same. 'Keep quite calm and don't speak. It's the only way.'

After a few minutes, with great relief, they noticed a definite slowing of Venus's mad race to avoid the needle and, when Rhodri saw her pause for a moment on top of the waste bin, he quickly stepped forward with an old towel he kept for securing cats who took pleasure in clawing a vet's hands to shreds, and flung it over her. 'There we are!' he whispered in triumph. Rapidly, he expertly wrapped Venus so that only her head was visible. She struggled but couldn't make her escape. Rhodri tucked her under his arm and gently stroked her head, speaking softly to her, so that gradually the fight in her dissipated, leaving her yowling in protest but not struggling.

Very, very quietly Rhodri said, 'Now, hold her like I'm doing, firm but not tight, no, no, don't take the towel off, that's it, firm but not tight. All I need to get at is her scruff. Gently does it, gently. Slowly.' Venus eyed him viciously, made to struggle free, admitted defeat, and allowed him to inject her. 'Well done, Miranda, well done. Put her in the basket.'

Mrs Costello was a shattered wreck by this time. 'Oh! Rhodri! Oh! What an experience. She's usually so amenable.' She tried to still her beating heart by fluttering her heavily ringed hands on her chest. 'I feel quite faint.'

Rhodri tossed the used syringe into the waste bin. 'I think next time you come we'd better make sure it's Graham who sees her. She obviously feels more relaxed with him.'

'I'm so sorry. So sorry to have caused such an upset. I'd no idea she would react like this.'

Rhodri patted her shoulder. 'Don't worry! No problem.'

'You're so kind. Has she scratched you?'

Rhodri shook his cuff down over his wrist to cover a nasty claw mark. 'She has not, no.' He turned to put the information into his computer. 'Are you all right, now?'

'I'm a little shaken, but I'll sit down in the waiting room for a while before I leave. Thank you, Mr Hughes, for being so kind.'

'All in a day's work. Good morning, Miranda.' He lifted Venus's basket from the examination table and handed it over.

In a caressingly sweet voice Miranda said, 'Come along, Venus, you naughty girl. What are you? A naughty girl. Yes, you are.'

With the door unlocked, Miranda left, Rhodri picked up the next file and got on with his morning's work.

Mrs Costello went to the reception desk to pay her account, and to her delight saw it was Kate on duty. 'Oh Kate, my dear . . .'

'Mrs Costello! You look quite flushed. Is everything all right?'

'Well, my dear, this naughty Venus of mine took a dislike to Mr Hughes and has been flying round the consulting room like a cat possessed.'

'Oh dear!'

'Exactly! Mr Hughes was so clever, he knew exactly what to do.'

'Has he managed to give her a booster?'

'Oh yes, eventually. We had to lock the doors to make sure no one opened them or else we'd never have caught her. He really is a wonderful vet, I feel so embarrassed that Venus was so ungrateful.' Miranda looked at Kate and thought yet again what a lovely looking girl she was, with her hair so nicely arranged, her fine dark eyes, and her lovely expression, so thoughtful and kindly. Just the kind of daughter she would have liked if only . . . 'Now, dear, tell me how much I owe.'

With her account settled Miranda asked if Kate minded if she sat in reception for a while till her heart stopped racing.

'Please, feel free.'

Once her heart had stopped beating so fast Miranda got into conversation with a client who had driven fifty miles for a consultation with Mungo Price. 'We never noticed there was anything wrong with him when we got him at eight weeks old, but as he's grown we can see there's a definite deformity in his hind legs. We've been recommended to come here, apparently he's very well-known in the veterinary world for his orthopaedic work.'

'I can assure you that if Mungo Price can't fix him, no one can.'

'Is that right?'

'Oh yes, they're all quite marvellous here. Quite marvellous. Rest assured, I'm certain Mr Price will be able to help. I must be off now. 'Bye, Kate!'

Kate waved her goodbye without speaking as she was on the phone taking a message from a client. 'Of course, of course. I'll check who's the nearest and let them know. Absolutely, yes, before lunch.'

Kate put down the receiver and groaned. They were already very shorthanded and could well do without any emergency calls this morning. She checked all the farm calls for the morning, then the map on the wall behind her. That, thought Kate, means ringing Dan, definitely not Colin, he's too far away to ask him to divert to the Chesham Chicken Farm. The manager had been well-nigh hysterical when she'd spoken to him, heaven alone knew what the matter was.

Dan protested. 'Can't Colin go? I'm not very *au fait* with chickens.'

'No, he's too far away.'

'Oh! Well. Never been there, could be interesting. I'll be half an hour though. If Bridge Farm ring, tell them I'll be there to do the TB testing in about an hour and a half.'

'That's fine, Dan, so long as you get to Crispy Chicken before lunch.'

'Right!'

When the manager opened the door to the second of the huge chicken sheds, Dan was stunned by the sheer number of birds inside. Hundreds upon hundreds of white-feathered birds scurrying about almost shoulder to shoulder, the ones nearest began scrabbling to escape him by climbing over the heads and shoulders of their compatriots. And the noise! He was deafened by it. They might claim they were free to roam, but . . . he guessed there was barely a square foot of space for each bird. They appeared to move collectively in great surges, as though they were all of the same mind. They looked perky enough though, from where he was standing. The shed was well ventilated, he had to admit to that. Huge extractors were stirring the air so that the smell, which would normally have been overpowering from so many birds, was just tolerable. The floor on which they stood was inches thick in wood shavings. Dan asked himself how on earth they managed to keep it so fresh looking. Good management, he supposed.

The manager said, 'What do you think?'

'About what?'

'About the way they're kept.'

'They're clean, they look healthy enough, bright, active, but at the same time I can't help but feel sorry for them.'

The manager studied Dan's face. He saw the strength in his features, the no-nonsense eyes, and the power of his personality. He'd be no easy pushover, this one. 'Haven't seen you before. Are you new?'

'Fairly new, we're very shorthanded, sickness, holidays et cetera today, so I've come instead of Colin. Name's Dan Brown.'

'I'm Bryan Buckland. I remember now, you're the one who upset Lord Askew! It was all round town.'

They shook hands.

'Quite right, but it's all been resolved.'

'So I heard. You've made quite a coup there I understand. Difficult beggar to get on with though.'

'Can be. But we've reached an agreement.' Dan laughed and Bryan Buckland laughed too, thinking Dan must be the first ever to know how to handle his lordship.

With no time for social niceties Dan got down to business. 'So, how many a day do you lose on average?'

'Ah! Well, that's the point. In a shed this size we usually find perhaps five a day absolute max. I can live with that, profit-wise, but these last few days it's gone from five to ten then fifteen then between twenty or thirty, and this morning it was forty-two. That's bad news.'

'Show me them.'

The poor pathetic remains were piled into a trailer standing outside the door, ready for taking away to an incinerator. 'Obviously it's in our best interests to destroy dead birds quickly. I've held these back for you to see.'

Dan didn't want to touch them with his bare hands, in case of passing any disease on elsewhere. With his ears still clamouring from the noise in the shed he poked them around with a stick. 'Can't tell from looking. They need equipment and expertise I haven't got. Post-mortem and such. You should seek advice from the state veterinary service. They're equipped to deal with situations like these.'

'If they start poking their noses in—'

'If they don't, you might find yourself losing the whole lot. In such close quarters, whatever they've got will pass round like wildfire, then where will your profit be?'

Bryan Buckland was obviously nervous. He bit his lip, looked at Dan, looked at the dead birds and asked, 'No idea what it is, then?'

'I'm not a poultry man and certainly not qualified to make decisions about such a large-scale operation like yours. You need an expert. But it's my opinion it could be Newcastle disease; it certainly can't be ruled out. However, you're probably more able to assess the problem than I am. You do realise it's a notifiable disease? If I'm proved right it would mean every bird slaughtered in this shed and the other two. Are they following the same pattern?'

Dan thought the manager looked sly. 'No, no, no. They're all right.'

43

'They soon won't be, if you're not careful. When will these be ready for dispatching?'

'Another six days.'

'Exactly?'

The manager nodded. 'It's all fine-tuned, this business. One day's feed too many and the profit margin starts on the slippery slope.' His right forefinger made a downward plunge. 'So you can't help me?'

'I'm afraid not. Wish I could.' Dan dug in his pocket and brought out a card with names and telephone numbers on it written in his flamboyant handwriting. 'This chap here, look, ask for him, I'll write the number down for you.'

'No need to bother, I have Mike Allport's number.'

'In that case then why have you called us?'

The manager gave Dan an apologetic stare. 'Didn't want to get officialdom involved if I could help it.'

'You must, absolutely must. I have to notify the authorities of my suspected diagnosis. I could be wrong, but I don't think I am. I'll call Mike Allport now. I can't leave until he's been to confirm.'

'There's no need.'

'There is. By tomorrow you could be in dead trouble. As chicken farms go you're doing a damn good job here. Don't ruin it for yourself, nor for these poor birds. I have to act *today*.'

Dan went back into the second chicken shed for another look. He walked up and down the passageway examining the mechanical feeders, looking for any chickens beginning to droop and lose interest in life, but found none. 'I'm ringing Mike Allport straight away.'

'Don't. Thanks all the same.'

Dan went to stand outside the shed to make his call. Bryan Buckland followed him. 'I said, don't call him.'

'I am not willing to sacrifice my professional integrity for some scheme of yours to avoid an informed diagnosis. It's more than my job's worth.' Dan dialled the number.

Bryan Buckland made to snatch the phone from him but Dan pushed him away.

'This is my livelihood. Don't do it to me.'

'I'm sorry. Am I speaking to Mike Allport?'

Bryan Buckland strode away, bitter resignation in every step. Shoulders bowed he headed for the office. Dan went to sit in his Land Rover to brood at the injustice of it all. But if he shut his eyes to it and took Bryan Buckland's attitude, his professional integrity would indeed be nil. He had to do it. Dan waited an hour and a half for the veterinary officer to arrive. An hour and a half he could have made good use of.

Those poor damn birds. Free to roam? It must be a nightmare living like that. Like being trapped in a concentration camp. Dan shuddered at the thought. But if they'd never known freedom in their short lives and they'd always been well fed . . . He rang Bridge Farm, his next call, to let them know he would be much later than he'd thought.

As soon as the veterinary officer arrived Dan leapt out and went to shake hands. 'Dan Brown, Barleybridge Farm Veterinary Practice.'

'Gerard Hookham. Newcastle disease you say?'

'I'm almost one hundred per cent sure. Check for yourself. Second shed. He's kept the dead ones for you to see.'

Dan stood aside and watched Buckland and Hookham greet each other. He felt there was a camaraderie between the two, which didn't sit well with someone who had impartial decisions to make. He could be wrong though.

When the two of them came outside again Gerard Hookham was shaking his head. 'I'm not convinced. In fact I'm sure it isn't.'

'Are you certain?'

'I have probably got more experience than you with poultry and I'm telling you it isn't Newcastle disease.'

'I see. And that's your considered opinion, is it?'

Gerard nodded and stepped back a little, suddenly aware Dan was someone to be reckoned with. 'Yes. It is.'

'Well, I'm certain I'm right. What are you going to say if next week they're dying like flies?'

'They won't be. Forty-two today is a fluke.'

'What is it then?'

'Just one of the hazards of having so many birds together.'

'If I'm proved to be right . . .'

Gerard smiled.

Dan grew angry. 'What about spreading the disease? You go onto dozens of farms, you could spread it. Have you no conscience, man?'

'I've told you it isn't what you think.'

'On your head be it.'

Dan turned on his heel and went to leave. Before he did so he poured some powerful disinfectant into his welling-ton boot bowl and washed down his boots and his car tyres. He made a rather ostentatious performance of it for Gerard's benefit and left for Bridge Farm.

On his way he tried to remember if they kept poultry. He had a suspicion they did, and so instead of driving into the farmyard, which he normally would have done, he left his Land Rover out in the lane as a precaution. He put on his disinfected boots and walked into the yard where there was some furious clucking and squawking going on from some Welsummer chickens. Fine, upstanding pedigree birds they were, and Dan was glad he'd taken precautions.

By two o'clock he was back at the Practice ready for lunch. The staff had always known right from the day Dan began working there that, for some reason, he and Rhodri Hughes didn't hit it off. Nothing specific, but there was always that sense of touchiness between them and for why no one could make out. They were both first-rate vets, versatile, agreeable, pleasant with clients, skilful, but somehow they . . . and this lunchtime was no exception.

'Hey boyo! That's my mug.'

Dan examined the mug he was drinking from. 'I thought this was mine.'

'Yours is like that but the printing's red on yours. That's green so it's mine.'

'Does it matter? Here, you have this – I've only taken a sip.' He handed the mug across the table.

Rhodri shook his head. 'No, thanks, not when you've been drinking from it. But remember in future.'

Dan looked up at Rhodri, his face humourless. 'Trouble is with bachelors, they get set in their ways.'

Rhodri's swarthy skin flushed and he remained silent. Dan wasn't to know that last night he'd proposed another wedding date to Megan and been refused. To save himself from being taunted, Rhodri walked out of the staff room taking his lunch with him and left Dan to eat alone.

He decided to eat his lunch outside on the old bench by the back door. Damn that blasted man. Why did he let him get under his skin? Why couldn't he just ignore him? Rhodri sank his teeth into a smoked salmon sandwich Kate had been out to buy for him, and brooded on his bachelor state, beginning by damning the domineering old man who kept such a tight rein on his unmarried daughter and ruined her life. Twice they'd named the day and twice her father had had a bad asthmatic attack, been rushed to hospital and hovered at death's door for days. Rhodri had convinced himself that the old man brought on the attacks himself. Could you do that with asthma? In his mind he trawled through friends and relatives for a doctor in the know, but realised he knew none.

Rhodri had suggested that they married secretly and told her father afterwards when the deed was done, but Megan, being a straightforward, honest character, refused. She wanted her father to give her away. When she'd said this Rhodri had replied, 'But that's archaic. You've been your own person for years, you don't need anyone to give you away.' But Megan had stuck to her guns. 'I want him to do just that, please, I know it's only right. I'm sorry.'

Maybe she didn't want to marry him. Could it be her way of escaping life's challenges? Rhodri kicked some loose gravel away from under his feet, opened the plastic casing of his slice of apple pie and began to eat it, but couldn't taste it. He looked up at the hills beyond the Practice car park and deep in his heart longed for the bleakness of the Welsh mountains. It was all too mild hereabouts, even the air he breathed wasn't bracing enough, nor the landscape, nor the people.

The back door opened and out came Kate. 'Your extraction's arrived, Rhodri. Sorry.'

'OK. Just finishing my coffee. Ask Sarah One to get him ready.' Teeth extraction. Diseased teeth, all because the owner didn't take enough care. Six out. No wonder the poor dog's breath smelt. He crumpled up the sandwich wrapping, placed it neatly in the plastic casing that had held his apple pie, gulped down the last drop of coffee, examined his mug and questioned why he had made such a fuss of Dan using it. He'd have to apologise, no, he damn well wouldn't. He wouldn't give it another thought. Instead he'd think about Megan and going out with her for a meal tonight.

Six extractions, four spays and a castration later Rhodri left for home. He'd take Harry Ferret out for a walk first, then have his shower, then call early for Megan.

The moment he heard Rhodri's voice, Harry unrolled himself from a deep sleep, and came to the front of his cage, stretching luxuriously. 'Oh yes! Here I am slaving away earning money to support you and what are you doing? Sleeping the day away. What a life! Time you went out to work and earned your keep.' Harry appreciated the nuzzling he got from Rhodri when he lifted him out of his cage. He slipped inside Rhodri's jacket and snuggled down while his red harness was found and the front doormat was checked for post. Then, holding the lead, Rhodri set off for a walk, out of the garden down the footpath that ran alongside their fence and out into the field behind the house.

Harry scurried along, keeping pace. No time for dawdling until Rhodri had worked the tensions of the day from his stocky frame and was able to wander carefree. Well, almost carefree, apart from the long, nagging loneliness of not being able to be with Megan all the time. Rhodri shaded his eyes and watched a kestrel hovering, but it didn't dive and he lost interest. He'd known for certain that Megan was his kind of person when she'd taken so readily to Harry. Seemed a daft criteria for a life partner but it mattered and she knew it did. She also loved

Welsh male voice choirs, and adored hearing his wonderful tenor voice singing the old Welsh songs. Megan swore he could have been a soloist on the concert stage had he not wanted to be a vet. He'd give her six more months and then . . . and then? What? Her da couldn't be left to live on his own. Megan wouldn't do that anyway. No, whichever way he looked at it, he'd have to live with them on the farm, but the thought of eating every meal with the old man made his spirits drop even lower.

Without warning a huge cloud covered the sun and a chill wind began to blow. Rhodri decided to head for home. Lengthening his stride Rhodri turned back, still with no solution to his lovelife. He just wished Dan had no reason to say that he was set in his bachelor ways. Dan had everything Rhodri wanted, a home with a beautiful wife in it and a newborn son.

Chapter 4

Rose took Jonathan to see everyone at the Practice when he was just two weeks old. She went in their lunch hour and immediately found herself surrounded by admiring faces.

'Why, he's beautiful, Rose, absolutely beautiful. Can I hold him?' This was Joy, eager to join Jonathan's admiration society. 'Well, there's no doubting who his father is. He's just like Dan, isn't he? So like him it's almost comical.'

'I guess he is. There's no mistaking, is there? Danny's as proud as punch.'

'Of course he is. He's a changed man since you came back, you know.'

'Is he?'

'Oh yes. He was very difficult to get on with, but he's soft as butter now.'

Everyone wanted a turn at holding the baby, including Letty, Colin's wife, who had come in especially to see him. 'Here, give him to me.' She sat herself down on Joy's chair and held out her arms. Joy handed him over and Letty rather awkwardly took him from her. 'Am I getting it right?'

Rose laughed. 'Yes, of course you are. Actually, you're not looking quite well, Letty.'

'No, just some bug I've picked up.'

'Are you actually sick?'

'Not really, no. You're very lucky. Maybe I'd better give him back to you or I'll be tempted to take him home.'

Before they knew it Sarah One and Sarah Two with Bunty came in to join Jonathan's admiration society followed by Stephie and Kate.

'He's gorgeous. Absolutely gorgeous.' Kate gave Jonathan her finger to clutch and he did with a surprising strength. 'He's so strong and he's got his father's looks.'

Rose had to laugh. 'Everyone says that. I feel quite jealous.'

'Don't worry. Have a girl next and she'll be like you.' This from Letty who was still captivated by him.

'Have a heart, Letty.'

'No, it's best. Close together and then they all grow up at the same time. No good having too big an age gap.'

Stephie muttered to Kate, 'Little she knows about it, anyone would think she'd had a whole tribe of children.'

'Sssh! She'll hear you.'

'Can't quite see Colin . . .' Stephie nudged Kate and winked. 'You know.'

'Are you going to have some more children?' Letty asked Rose.

'Hopefully, but not yet awhile.'

'You should. People like you should have babies.' Without warning, Letty burst into tears and left Joy's office.

She left behind an embarrassed silence. To fill it, Rose said, 'I'll just go show him to the clients.'

'You do that.' Joy stood to one side to let Rose out. 'They'll love him – they've been asking when they'd see him. Back to work all of you. I'll just go find Letty, see she's all right.'

Joy found Letty sitting in her car crying as if her heart was breaking. She opened the driver's door and said, 'Letty! Please don't cry.'

But Letty couldn't stop.

She fumbled in her handbag for a tissue and dabbed her cheeks, but still the tears rolled down. 'It's this blessed sickness, I never feel quite right. What a fool you must think me.'

'Not at all, babies get you like that. Well, they get me like that.' She went round to the front passenger door, opened it and got in beside Letty. 'Shall I get Colin?'

'No, no. He has enough on. I'm just being a fool.'

'No, you're not. It just goes to demonstrate that you're human. Come back in, have a cup of tea or something.'

Letty stopped crying and turned her blotchy wet face to Joy. 'No, I won't. I don't want to see the baby again.' She stared straight ahead and after a moment commented, 'I've not been very kind, have I? In the past?'

'Well . . .'

'No, be honest. No beating about the bush.'

'It's not for me to say.'

'Please, Joy, be honest with me, even if it's going to hurt. We've known each other long enough for you to be totally frank.'

Joy was completely thrown by this touchy-feely Letty. It was a Letty she had never known. 'If you want the truth, I'll give it to you, but it won't be nice. So I've warned you, right?' She thought for a moment. 'You've been a miserable, unkind, edgy, frosty, nit-picking person and very difficult to like. Thought yourself right about everything, you know, and you weren't always. And as for the way you've treated Colin in the past! Though you have changed for the better of late, I must admit.'

Letty flinched as though she'd been hit. 'I see.' She stared through the windscreen. 'I see. Not just Colin though. What about Dan?'

'Especially about Dan. He's a thoroughly decent chap, you know. He speaks his mind, I'll give you that. But . . . he is rock-strong, fair-minded, and straightforward, and he's done this Practice a lot of good, hasn't he? And I've grown to like him.' Joy half turned to smile at Letty. But Letty ignored her. Instead she started up the car and put it into gear. 'Hold on, Letty, let me get out.' Joy struggled to open the door and Letty reached across to open it for her. Joy got out, but before she closed the door, she said, 'Letty! I don't like the idea of you driving when you're like this. Come in, just to talk, eh?'

Letty shrugged her shoulders and the car began to move, so Joy had no alternative but to shut the door and let her drive away. She watched Letty disappear into the main road thinking that she'd never seen her so emotional since she'd known her. Actually asking for people's impressions of her! Unheard of. Perhaps she shouldn't have been so blunt. All that emotion right there at the surface. There was something definitely wrong with Letty.

As Joy passed the accounts office Kate called out, 'Oh, there you are. We've been looking for you. Rose is just going.'

'Oh, right.'

Rose asked Joy if she'd done something wrong. 'Did I say something I shouldn't? It's not like Letty, is it? Is she still here?'

'She's gone. For some reason she's very upset and she won't tell me what it is. So don't worry. I'm going to catch up with Colin and have a quiet word. Lovely to see you, Rose, pop in any time. You'll be most welcome.'

'Should I go see her? Would she mind? Apologise or something?'

'Well, I expect she'd prefer to be alone right now, because she asked me what people thought about her, and I told her. I wish I hadn't, but she insisted.' Not for the world would she tell Rose it was the baby who had upset Letty.

'Perhaps I'll send her a card, yes, I'll send her a card.' At this point Jonathan began to cry, a pitiful, heartfelt cry that couldn't be ignored. 'That's his I-Am-Hungry cry so I'd better go.' Rose left in a flurry of goodbyes and good wishes.

Joy saw her to the car. 'You've got a lovely baby there, Rose, you must be very happy.'

'Oh, we are, Danny and I, very happy.'

'I'm glad, so glad. Be seeing you.'

After Rose had left, Joy rang Colin and told him of the afternoon's episode and how worried she was. Colin didn't reply for a moment and then said, 'I'm worried too. She's not a bit like herself. I've only one more call, I'll go straight home from there.'

'Good, she might need a large dose of TLC.'

'Of what?'

'TLC. Tender Loving Care.'

'Ah! Right. I'll see she gets it.'

So Joy went home that afternoon feeling uneasy about Letty. Duncan had started another contract and with him being withdrawn, his mind on solving his computer problems, she guessed she wouldn't be on the receiving end of some TLC. In fact she'd be lucky to get a word from him all evening.

But the moment she opened the front door she could smell . . . what was it? Beef casserole? Chicken? So she was to get some loving care after all.

She found him in the kitchen putting a dessert in the fridge. 'Duncan! How wonderful you've started the meal. What's in the oven?'

'That rooster who kept waking you up and driving you mad.'

'Not the Duke of Wellington?'

Duncan laughed. 'The very same. The dish is called Joy's Revenge.'

Joy put down her bag on the table and pulled out a chair. 'I don't know if I can eat him. I got very fond of him latterly.'

'Well, you'd better, there's nothing else. We need to stock up.' Duncan kissed her and asked, 'How's it been?'

'Rose brought the baby in. He is gorgeous, very fair skin like Rose, but dark-haired and so like Dan it's laughable. And Rose of course, as slender as ever, looking perfectly lovely. I do envy her. She's one of those people who, if you called at the house on the off chance, and she was wearing torn jeans and an old sweater and her hair was all over the place and she was painting the ceiling, would still look beautiful. It simply isn't fair.' She smiled ruefully at Duncan.

'You look beautiful always. No matter what you wear. You never give yourself enough credit.' Duncan had his back to her so she couldn't see if he was sincere or simply teasing.

'Duncan?'

Duncan turned to face her. 'I've put a bottle of your favourite wine in the fridge so all we need to do now is sit down with a drink and wait. I've done the dessert too.'

'Duncan?'

But he'd gone into the sitting room and was at the drinks cupboard getting her a vodka and tonic.

'Duncan? Look at me.'

When Joy saw his face she almost choked. He was looking at her as though he couldn't get enough of her, as though his immense love for her was almost too much for him to bear. His eyes were shining with love for her, for *her*.

'Darling! Oh darling! I'm never fair to you, am I? I don't know why you keep on loving me as you do.' She held her arms wide, but he shook his head. 'Please.'

'No. Mungo's still there between us. You will not let him go, will you?'

'I do try, but then it all comes back again as bad as ever.'

'I could kill him, if I didn't like him as much as I do.'

'Duncan. Don't.'

'Both of us, with unrequited love. Ironic, isn't it? You know at bottom that he'll never leave Miriam. Doesn't that hurt?'

'He doesn't know how I feel. I never give him a clue. Never.' There was something in Duncan's face she couldn't interpret. 'Why are you looking at me like that? What are you thinking?'

'He knows, my love, and has done for a while.'

Joy shot to her feet, horrified by the thought. 'I've never told him how I feel. It must be Miriam who told him. I can't believe it of her.'

It was Duncan's turn to be shocked. '*Miriam* knows?'

Joy sat down again, her legs having gone weak with shock. 'She's known right from the first day she met me. She told me the other week.'

Duncan stared at her trying to take in what she'd said,

then he threw his whisky down his throat and poured himself another before he answered her. 'Well, it wasn't Miriam who told her husband you loved him.'

'No one else knows.'

'Are you sure about that?'

Did they all know then? Joy felt . . . Well, she didn't know what she felt . . . Did they all whisper behind her back? She'd never noticed if they did. Never. If Miriam didn't tell Mungo, who did? An awful suspicion dawned on her.

Ice cold with anger, Joy looked Duncan full in the face. 'Was it you?'

Despite her anger she noticed Duncan didn't even have the grace to look ashamed. 'Yes.'

'Yes? How could you? How could you?' This time she leapt to her feet and faced him, her fists hammering on his chest, to emphasise her anger. 'How could you? My deepest secret and you've told him. Why? Why?'

Duncan gripped her wrists tightly and forced them away from him. 'Can you believe I'm capable of jealousy? Me? Laid-back Duncan? Self-absorbed Duncan? That Duncan who lets his life slide by year after year, patiently waiting? Doing his computer programmes, salting money away for that wonderful day when his *wife* finally gets round to loving him and they can travel the world on a gargantuan honeymoon? Imagine that! Funny, isn't it?' He released his grip, drank his whisky and walked away from her into the kitchen.

But Joy couldn't let what he'd said go without knowing exactly how long Mungo had known. She followed Duncan into the kitchen and asked him point-blank. 'When did you tell him?'

He was lifting Joy's Revenge from the oven. When

he'd placed the dish on the worktop he said, 'That night they came for a drink and we'd just got Tiger and she paddled in her water bowl. Don't ask me why I did but the demon jealousy was sitting on my shoulder that night, and that good-looking-I-own-the-world sod walked in and I couldn't resist. It gets to sound more like a Whitehall farce every day. You didn't know he knew, I didn't know Miriam knew, but you knew she knew because she told you, but you didn't tell me she knew. He didn't know you loved him, he told me never ever to tell Miriam you loved him, now I've found out she's always known, so I needn't have bothered to keep my lip buttoned.' Duncan spooned the sauce over the chicken, tasted it and added another spoonful of wine. 'Ten minutes more, and Joy's Revenge will be ready.'

Unexpectedly the thought exploded in her head that the whole situation really had become a farce, like Duncan had said. Joy felt ridiculous. Completely ridiculous. She had become a laughing stock, particularly if everyone at the Practice had guessed how she felt about Mungo. She only had to think his name and the feelings she had for him surfaced, but had they become like beloved old shoes that fitted beautifully, comfortingly, but now it was time to bin them? Well, she'd brace herself to eat Joy's Revenge and then see how she felt on a full stomach. Good food always helped to gear up her thought processes and that night was no exception.

But the happy atmosphere usually engendered by fine wine and good food didn't happen. Duncan rapidly became morose and abrupt. No amount of telling him the news of the day from the Practice could cheer him.

'I'm sorry. Duncan?'

He raised his face from looking at his dinner plate and

she saw the pain there. The skein of his hair, which always fell across his forehead despite his efforts, was brushed impatiently back from his face and he said, 'One day, you know, all hope will be gone for us.'

'Hope?'

'All hope that one day it will be me you love.'

'But I do.'

'No, Joy, you don't. You cling helplessly to your feelings for Mungo, uselessly really, as well you know. Why can't you see that?'

'I can. But I can't help it. And I do love you.'

'Not like I want it. Rather more like you'd love a devoted spaniel. Not with fire.' Duncan clenched his fist and held it up and shook it to demonstrate the strength of his feelings. 'Not with deep desire. Not with overwhelming desire for *me*.' He thumped his clenched fist against his chest. 'Your love isn't even a comforting, all-embracing, cuddling kind of love. That might be tolerable. What we have isn't even that.'

Joy remained silent, well aware of the truth of what he said. If only she could love him like he wanted. But she couldn't. 'I do try.'

Duncan's face registered such disappointment at the word 'try' that Joy felt as though she'd been whipped. 'Joy! I was fool enough to believe when we married that your love for me would grow, and all it would need was patience on my part. But I've worked to fan the flames. Recently I've come to realise there isn't even one small jet of flame to fan. And still the years roll on. I believe you when you say you try, but you shouldn't have to *try*! Now . . . now, I'm reaching a point where I don't care a damn whether you do or not.'

'You've given up on me? Is that it?'

Duncan nodded. 'You could say that. I've waited and I've just run out of time and patience.'

'But what shall I do? What can I do?'

'Abandon Mungo. Love me instead.'

'But look at the times you've ignored me for weeks on end. When it's been like living with the walking dead? Work! Work! Work! That's all it's been for weeks on end. What about those times? Eh?'

'It's never been as bad as that.'

'But it has. It has, from where I'm standing.'

'I can't help it if my work drives me and drives me till I hardly know I exist as a person. It's the only way I have of earning a living, even though I know I get right to the wire with it, time after time. But then it gets better when I've resolved the problems.'

'Oh yes. It gets better, but not better enough. You're still withdrawn, still an odd bod. At the Practice they know what you're like – don't want to go anywhere, don't want to socialise. They've asked you times without number to go out for a drink to celebrate something or another, but Duncan go? Oh no! You're so arrogant, so self-obssessed, you don't care what people think of you. Not one jot. And for you to tell Mungo I love him, that . . . that, I cannot forgive. I bet you enjoyed the telling, didn't you? Mmm? Relished it. I bet you did. Not caring how much you upset him. Not thinking about how he'd cope, how *he'd* feel. Oh no!'

'Why *ever* should *I* give Mungo's feelings even a moment of consideration, when he's stolen my marriage from me? Tell me one reason why I should? Come to think of it though, there wasn't anything to steal, it wasn't a real marriage in the first place, was it? You loved him even then. It's all been a complete lie. It leaves a very bitter taste. Why should I have to feel *grateful* if I rouse the smallest response from you when we make love? Make love? Huh! That's a misnomer if ever there was one. *Love.* Huh!'

Joy couldn't find an answer and wondered how on earth she had arrived at this desolate bleakness of soul. Duncan stood for a moment, looking down at her, then he left the table and went to stand outside in the garden, looking at the lights of Barleybridge far below, hunched up, feeling crucified.

Joy cleared the meal away, Joy found washing that needed putting in the machine, Joy needed to take a bath to relax her, and Joy was asleep in bed before he came up. When she awoke next morning Duncan had gone. A note said: '*Gone walkabout. Yours for always, Duncan.*' It sounded so final. She was used to him leaving to walk alone to clear his thinking processes, but he'd never written '*Yours for always.*' Never, ever. When he said 'walkabout' he meant walking for the day, and sometimes he rang her and asked her to pick him up from somewhere and he'd be refreshed and more like himself. It always did him good, to walk alone for mile upon mile. So perhaps he'd ring her tonight.

Occasionally he would mean longer than a day, but he had his present contract to fulfil so he'd have to be back. She sighed with relief. Obviously he did mean just for the day. Of course, just for the day. All the same Joy checked his sock drawer and found he'd taken several pairs of his walking socks, changes of underwear, sweaters. So he was going for a while. Something akin to a pain filled her chest.

A phone call as soon as she arrived at the Practice that

morning put all thoughts of Mungo and Duncan out of her head. She raced out of her office calling, 'Anyone seen Dan? Has he gone?'

Colin answered her. 'He's here, sorting his post in the staff room.'

Joy found him reading a letter from the laboratory, punching the air with delight.

'I knew I was right! I knew it! This letter proves it.' Dan looked up and raised an eyebrow at Joy. 'Yes?'

'Crispy Chickens?'

'Yes. Why?'

'Bridge Farm are protesting because the State Veterinary Service intend culling all their flock.'

'Why?'

'Because I've just had a call to say that as Crispy Chickens have now got Newcastle disease and all their flock are about to be slaughtered, there's a strong chance you might have carried the disease to Bridge Farm.'

'I knew I was right. The idiots. Anyway, I disinfected myself before I went to Bridge Farm.'

'They say it's because of you going straight there, you could have carried it.'

'I'll ring Bridge Farm straight away. There's absolutely no need for that flock to be slaughtered. I'll tell them I'm standing up for them. It's wholesale murder it is.'

Before Joy could stop him, Dan had phoned Bridge Farm and told them his position. He followed that with a call to Bryan Buckland and another to the Veterinary Service. By the time he came off the phone he was boiling with temper. 'It is sheer blind stupidity. Sheer stupidity. I don't know when I've been more angry. Think of all the people who've visited, all the lorries that have delivered to Crispy Chickens in the week since I was there. They've all to be traced. It's criminal. Absolutely criminal. There could be an epidemic. What's the point of reporting a notifiable disease if they can't recognise it when they see it?'

Joy tried to calm him down. 'Dan! Dan!' By now he was pacing the staff room like a caged lion, planning terrible revenge.

'There's one thing for certain — they're not culling all those chickens at Bridge Farm on my account. I'm not having it. Definitely not.'

'I don't see how you can stop it.'

'Neither do I at the moment, but something must be done.' Muttering threats of drawing and quartering Mike Allport and hanging Bryan Buckland from his extractor fans Dan stormed out to start his calls.

'Dan! Don't do anything stupid, will you? Speak to Mungo first. Right?'

She heard him call out, 'I will.' And hoped to heaven he wouldn't do anything too damaging. Joy followed him out into the car park. 'Look here. Mungo will decide on the right course of action when he's had a chance to talk things through with you. Don't whatever you do go to Crispy Chickens, will you?'

'No, because I might murder Buckland. A whole week! God!'

'Exactly. So . . . leave it with me. Right? I mean it!' She began to return indoors but turned back to say, 'And whatever you do, don't go to Bridge Farm either. Do you hear me? Mungo will know what action to take. OK?'

'Of course, you're right. But it's dammed urgent if we're going to stop them. First, I'm going to see Phil Parsons's new bull.'

Dan went off with his list of calls, in no mood to suffer

fools gladly. As he turned onto the track that led to the Parsons' Applegate Farm he determinedly pushed his anger to the back of his mind. He parked in his usual place, on the track and not in the yard, and changed into his boots before he got out. The farm was just as muddy and chaotic as it had always been but there was Phil leaning on the gate waiting for him, grinning cheerfully. 'Wait till you see this one, Dan! He's a beauty.'

Phil's cat came running to greet him, and Dan bent down to stroke her. 'Morning, Scott. Morning, Phil. Well, lead me to this magnificent beast.' Phil led him across the filthy yard into the byre he'd renovated with such loving care for his old bull, Sunny Boy. The byre was still immaculate, a fitting setting for a prize bull. The new bull graced it equally as well as its previous occupant. He was young but already showing the signs of a perfectly splendid adult. There was a sheen to his black coat, which only good breeding and good food could have brought about. He was restless, moving about and stamping his feet with a kind of pent-up vigour that was a pleasure to witness.

Dan leant on the wall and admired him in silence.

Anxious for an opinion to corroborate his own, Phil asked, 'Well, what do you think?'

'I think he's a prime specimen. Indeed. Yes. A prime specimen. Where the devil did you pick him up, Phil?'

'At an auction. Farmer packing up, selling everything, including the farmhouse, fed up to the back teeth not making money at the job, and I went along.' He tapped the side of his nose, well, more accurately tapped his balaclava in the area of where his nose would be if one could see it. 'Heard a rumour, you know how it is, glad to be shut of the lot and everything might be going cheap. So

Blossom and me went along and there he was, one of the last lots. Blossom nudged me and I nudged her and told her not to look too enthusiastic but you know Blossom, anyways, things went according to plan, and I got him for a song. What do you reckon?'

'I reckon you've got a gem. An absolute gem. What have you called him?'

'Blossom's named him Star. What do you think?'

'Spot on. Oh yes. Spot on. Star! I like that.'

'Well, he is, isn't he? A star.'

'He certainly is. Is he friendly?'

'Hamish is training him.'

'How is Hamish?'

Phil looked at Dan as though pondering what to say. 'He's OK. Got over Sunny Boy goring him, but the youth still isn't up to scratch in here.' Phil banged his chest.

'Not talking yet, then?'

Phil shook his head. 'Not yet, but Blossom keeps hoping. The youth's been through something terrible that's for sure, what, we don't know, and we can't ask the authorities for any help else they'll be for taking him away and that wouldn't do. He's happy and that's what matters after all. One day it'll come when he's been loved enough.' Phil fell silent after his final perceptive statement and the two of them leant companionably on the wall watching Star.

Dan heard the rapid tap tap tap of Blossom's high-heeled shoes and she appeared carrying a tray with three glasses on it. She and Paul were so totally mismatched. Dan found it hard to believe that this peroxided, heavily made-up, dazzlingly dressed, twiglike person could possibly be the wife of stout, rotund, good-natured, shambling old Phil. She held out the tray. 'Here we are, take one. A whisky to toast our new bull. Isn't he brilliant, Dan?'

'He most certainly is, Mrs Parsons. I reckon Phil's got an eye for a good bull. He doesn't get taken in by a lot of show, but recognises stamina and good breeding when he sees it, and that counts.' Dan raised his glass. 'To Star. Long may he reign!'

'To a perfect physical specimen!' Blossom clinked Dan's glass with hers and by the twinkle in her eyes when she winked at him, it wasn't only the bull she was toasting. Time he went, Dan thought.

'How's your son and heir, Dan? Doing well? And Rose? We'd love to meet them both.'

'Well, perhaps sometime when I'm calling I'll pick them up and bring them along. I'm sure Rose would like to meet you, too. Must go. Other calls.' His visit with Star had cheered him considerably but at the back of his mind was the problem at Bridge Farm.

After Dan had left, Joy sat pondering the situation with Newcastle disease and what it would mean at Bridge Farm. It would be a terrible shame if their chickens had to be slaughtered, after all they weren't any old chickens but a pedigree flock. It would have to be dealt with very delicately. Thinking of delicate problems reminded her of Duncan. She wondered how he was. Striding out over the hills in his steady, relentless pace.

Joy took the photographs she had picked up in her lunch hour out of her bag. There was a particularly striking one of Duncan leaning on a fence looking ahead, apparently oblivious to the camera. She'd caught him in profile and focused on him so that the camera was looking slightly upwards at him. Anyone else would have admired the drama of that shot, and briefly so too did she. He really was eyecatching. Almost handsome, with his high cheek-bones and . . . Help! She wouldn't tell anyone he'd gone. They'd never notice. They all knew how withdrawn he was. She hastily put away the photographs and went to see if Mungo was free for five minutes to talk about Bridge Farm and its problems, not knowing that Dan was already on his way there.

He deliberately pulled up in the lane and didn't drive into the farmyard, which he would normally have done. The farmhouse was on the roadside with a short path between lawns and flowerbeds leading to the house. There wasn't a single sound of chickens. His heart sank. Surely they hadn't already been to slaughter them? He got out of his car and stood listening. A voice shouted from the farmhouse window. 'Dan!'

He raised an arm in salute. 'I've come to see how things are progressing.'

'Thought you were them coming. Come in.'

It was only when he moved nearer that he saw Mr Bridges had a gun pointing at him. Dan walked towards the house door, realising as he did so that there was another gun trained on him from an upstairs window.

He went in the house without knocking because the door had mysteriously been opened for him as he approached. In the kitchen with Mr Bridges were three of his sons, all armed with shotguns. 'Mrs Bridges has made a big pot of coffee. Want one?'

'Yes, please. I'm not too late, am I? They haven't already been?'

Dan felt like a dwarf. Mr Bridges himself and all three of his sons were well over six feet tall and big with it. Mrs Bridges was a tiny person shaped like a cottage loaf and looking incapable of producing boys of their great size. He heard big boots coming clattering down the stairs and yet another of the Bridges boys appeared, shotgun in hand. 'Did I hear coffee's on the go?' His voice was so like his father's it was uncanny.

'No, you're not too late. We've shut 'em all away 'cos they're bloody well not killing 'em. They'll get killed first. Get yer coffee, Gab, and up the stairs quicko.'

'I am on your side, but I didn't think things would get this far. Thank you, Mrs Bridges.' Dan's coffee was in a pint mug and he wondered how on earth he'd manage to down that lot and not give offence by leaving half of it. All of them had pint mugs, except Mrs Bridges who was sipping her coffee from a delicate china cup and saucer. She might have been a tiny woman but there was authority in her voice when she spoke. 'Sit down, Dan. Gab's watching out. That lovely wife of yours keeping well? And your little son?'

'She is, thank you, I didn't know you knew her.'

'Not much goes on in Barleybridge that we don't know about. It may be a sleepy old place but it doesn't mean we're deaf, dumb *and* blind. Lovely girl, she is. You haven't got any more where she came from, have you? These great lummoxes of mine won't get from under my feet. Gab's the eldest, so you can find someone for him a.s.a.p. They all need women like your Rose.' There were groans of heartfelt approval of Rose from them all and the red-haired one said with a good-natured grin, 'Shut up, Mum.'

'You're too good to them all, Mrs Bridges.' Dan raised his pint pot to her and sipped his coffee. It was steaming hot, rich with cream and a distinct hint of rum. 'This is excellent.'

Things became convivial, shotguns were laid aside and lots of leg-pulling and camaraderie ensued. The atmosphere became quite party-like until the laughter was abruptly halted by Gab shouting from upstairs, 'They're here!'

Instantly the boys left the kitchen, went to other downstairs rooms with windows facing the garden and when their father shouted, 'Fire!' they all let off their shotguns into the air. This brought the Veterinary Service's vehicles to a grinding halt. A great roar of delight went up from the Bridges family. In the midst of it all Mrs Bridges quietly and calmly began kneading a great mound of dough on her kitchen table, her small, floured hands working it with furious energy.

Dan said hesitantly. 'I say, you wouldn't actually . . . you know, fire at them? Properly, would you?'

'Try me,' came the grim reply from Mr Bridges.

Matters intensified when Mike Allport gingerly got out of his car, stepped onto the garden path and shouted, 'Now, Mr Bridges, you know it has to be done. Put the guns away and let us get on with it.'

'One step nearer . . .' Everyone heard the cocking of his trigger.

Mike Allport shouted, 'Don't let me have to get the police in.'

'Get who the hell you like, you're not slaughtering my flock. Get off my premises, you're trespassing. Fire!' Mr Bridges fired another shot into the air, which prompted the other four guns to go off, and Mike Allport to get back into his car. The noise was stunning and served its purpose in warning Mike they meant business.

Give him his due, thought Dan, Mike Allport isn't backing off. But he was phoning someone on his mobile.

He was getting the police no doubt. It occurred to Dan that this put him in an awkward position. Aiding and abetting? Or innocent bystander held at gunpoint? 'Shall I go out and have a word? See what I can do?'

Mr Bridges turned the gun on him. 'Don't move, unless you want a barrel load from this in your backside. You're here and here you stay.'

The kneading stopped and a quiet voice said, 'Steady, Billy, Dan's not the enemy.'

Mrs Bridges's moderate tones cooled the hot atmosphere a little but Mr Bridges kept the gun trained on Dan. 'I mean it. They are not ruining years of careful breeding all because they think they have a right. Not one of my birds has died, and, if they were going to, they would have done so by now. So you keep right out of it.'

'Can I phone the Practice? They'll be wondering where I am. I've calls to make.'

'Very well.'

Dan went by the window to get a better signal and dialled in. It was Kate who answered his call. 'Hello, Kate. Dan here. I can't do my calls for the forseeable future today. Can Colin or Zoe do them for me?'

'Are you ill?'

'No, I'm at Bridges Farm and we're under siege.' As casually as he could, he whispered, 'Guns, you know.'

'Oh! my God! Guns! You mean you're being held hostage?'

'Well, not quite, but I can't get out and I think Mike Allport has sent for the police.'

'I thought your voice sounded funny. Right. We'll reorganise things. Let us know as soon as the situation frees up. Take care, Dan. Shall I tell Rose?'

'Under no circumstances. She mustn't be worried. Do you hear?'

'Right. We won't phone her. Take care, Dan. 'Bye.'

The situation didn't free up as Kate put it, in fact it became worse because the police arrived and Dan pointed out to Mr Bridges the penalty of threatening a police officer with a firearm.

'To hell with that. This is bureaucracy gone mad, and someone has to take a stand.'

'Where are the chickens?'

'Shut in the big barn at the back with Ben and Gideon on guard. Crack shots they are, like all my boys. Fire!' The salvo of five guns firing at once was deafening.

Mrs Bridges placing baking trays and loaf tins in the Aga said, 'Heed what he says. Don't loose your head, Billy.'

'Better that than dying of shame.' He opened the window further and shouted out to a uniformed inspector, 'These guns will be put away when those so-and-so's leave my farm. Tell them to leave.'

'They have a duty to do.'

'The murdering beggars have no duty to do here. My chickens are not infected. Full stop. I'm a reasonable man as you know, but I defend my right as an Englishman to guard my property as I see fit.'

'Now, now, Billy. Let's have some sense here.'

'Say that to that Mike Allport. He's the one who needs to see sense. One step out of that car of his and he'll get both barrels.'

'That's threatening language, that is.'

'I know it is. Don't think I don't mean it. I'm a man of my word.'

Tugging at Mr Bridges's jacket sleeve, Mrs Bridges said softly, 'Don't back yourself into a corner, Billy.'

Dan tried again to ask for a chance to negotiate, but found himself on the business end of Mr Bridges's gun. 'No negotiation until he's left the premises.'

'Tell them that.'

Mr Bridges shouted through the window. 'I'll talk to a police officer, but not to one of *them*. Tell them to leave.'

They all watched while a conference took place out in the lane. Mike Allport backed up and disappeared round the bend in the road. Mr Bridges put down his gun and told his boys to do the same. Josh came clattering down the stairs again and, leaning his gun against the table, slouched onto a chair. 'You're not giving in, Dad. Understand?'

'I know, I know.'

The police inspector came in. 'Good morning, Mrs Bridges. Nice smell of baking bread.'

'There'll be a loaf for your Tina, if you behave like a gentleman.'

'Now, now, no bribes.' He laughed, took off his cap and placed it upside down on the table, smoothed his hair where his cap had ruffled it, and said, 'I've to remain impartial, I have. Yes, indeed, impartial. Hard for me though, my dad being a farmer, my sympathies are all with you, Billy.'

Dan spoke up. 'May I speak in support of Billy's actions?'

'You're . . . ?'

'Dan Brown, vet at Barleybridge Veterinary Hospital. I informed the Veterinary Service that I considered that Crispy Chicken had Newcastle disease, which as you are aware is notifiable. They came out, examined the birds and in front of me and Bryan Buckland said no way was I right. Over a week later they declared I was right after all, so his birds were slaughtered. Then they began tracing to find out where the disease could have been carried to in the interim. I'd come straight from Crispy Chicken to here, having disinfected my boots and my car before I left, which they watched me doing.' Dan tapped the table to emphasise his point. 'There is no sign of the disease in this flock, I have Mr Bridges's assurance on that. So if after two or three more days there is still no sign I would say he is completely free. If he can have some days' grace it is my opinion that slaughtering the birds on this farm is entirely and completely unnecessary. In fact it would amount to a crime.'

'Coffee, Richie?' Mrs Bridges handed the inspector a mug of her special brew of steaming coffee. 'I've put extra sugar in just how you like.' She turned her back to the policeman and winked at Dan.

Richie forgot about being impartial when he tasted the coffee. 'Just how I like it, Mrs Bridges.'

She smiled and went to get some bread rolls out from the Aga as calmly as if shot guns and police in her kitchen were an everyday occurrence. The rolls were placed to cool on a wire rack at Richie's end of the table and they noticed him sniff appreciatively. The atmosphere in the kitchen had become relaxed and homely and the inspector stretched out his legs and sipped his coffee, seemingly enjoying the hospitality.

They all chatted about farming news, and the latest gossip in Barleybridge and the inspector got teased about his Tina, who appeared to be well-known amongst the Bridges sons, and just as they were thinking they were getting their own way without any serious threat to life and limb, Mike Allport drove back and parked in the lane outside the house. Mr Bridges stood up, dashed to the open window and prepared to fire a broadside, but Mrs Bridges knocked his elbow purposely, he missed his target and the shot spattered viciously against the front door of Dan's Land Rover.

When Joy heard that Dan had disobeyed her orders and, as a result, his Land Rover was peppered with shot, she went ballistic. 'Wait till Mungo hears about this.'

But all Mungo could do was laugh, and he made her furious. She could have hit him she was so angry.

Chapter 5

It was impossible to resist going out to take a look at the Land Rover. Joy point-blank refused, so she and Rhodri were the only members of the staff who hadn't seen the holes by teatime that same day.

Dan said, 'I can't think why Joy is so wild with me. We got the result we wanted. They're giving Mr Bridges three more days' grace so long as no one leaves the farm or visits it.'

Mungo, still amused by the whole incident, laughed some more. 'Joy's angry with me too, because when she told me what had happened I roared with laughter and she can't forgive me for it.'

'She did say I shouldn't go until we'd got some advice from you, but it was urgent, desperately urgent. However, I suppose there's a first for everything, I've never had a loaded gun pointed at me before.'

Mungo clapped a firm hand on Dan's shoulder. 'Well, it's certainly made you the hero of the day; just glad you weren't sitting in it when he fired. However, I'm not paying to have the door replaced, it's not worth it. The blessed thing's almost ready for the scrap heap, anyway. Do you mind?'

'Not at all. I don't care what I drive, so long as it gets me from A to B.'

Neither had realised that Rhodri was standing behind them listening to their conversation.

'I've come to see the hero, I have.'

Mungo moved aside so Rhodri could see the holes in the door and, with a broad grin on his face, said, 'He'll never live it down, will he?'

Rhodri instantly realised the kudos Dan would have driving to the farms. Every owner would have heard the story of the siege and no doubt embellished it with excessively heroic deeds by Dan.

'Bit childish, if you ask me.'

Dan, deflated, said angrily, 'What, exactly, do you mean by that?'

'Always wanting to be the centre of attention, you are. If it isn't wrestling mad dogs to the ground and dealing with the injured cat, when you're farm animal and not small, you're seeking media attention with all your heroics. At gun point, my eye. Old Bridges wouldn't hurt a fly.'

'You were there, were you?'

'No, but I've heard the story a dozen times this afternoon. The whole of Barleybridge will have heard by now and any minute the press will be sniffing around. Everyone in Barleybridge knows you were instrumental in getting Lord Askew back on our books. "Magic he is with horses," they all say. Magic! Huh!' Rhodri stared at the holes, ignoring Mungo, who looked angry and as though he was about to intervene. ''Spect you'll have Rose hanging on every word, typical American making a sensation of the smallest thing.'

'For your information Rose is English with an English passport, and has her feet firmly on the ground. I don't know what I've done to deserve this backlash from you,

Rhodri, but I wish you'd stop it. It's turning into a bloody vendetta, and none of it is my fault.' Dan spun on his heel and went back inside. He stormed into the staff room, boiled the kettle, made himself a mug of tea and too late realised he'd picked up Rhodri's mug. So what? he thought.

Joy was leaving to go home when she paused at the back door and saw Mungo having a go at Rhodri. She only heard the gist of the conversation, but it sounded as though Rhodri was being told not to be so childish, to pull himself together and get his life sorted out. Rhodri stumped over to his car and drove away. Mungo came back in, his face ugly with temper and in no mood for Joy to say, 'He didn't deserve that. It should be Dan getting told off for disobeying *me*, and I bet you haven't said a word about that.'

'And you, Joy, need to remind yourself who is in charge here. You may be Practice Manager but you're not managing *me*. Dan's done nothing to cause Rhodri to be so unpleasant and if there isn't an improvement in his attitude I shall be having something serious to say about it. Right?'

'Oh! That's how things are, is it?'

'Yes.' Mungo raised an eyebrow at her. 'Do you have a problem with that?'

Joy looked away. She was so furious with him she knew she'd say something she'd regret, so she reined in her temper and answered, 'No problem at all. See you tomorrow.'

Joy rushed home, hoping Duncan would have returned but he hadn't and her bad mood sat badly on her all evening and kept her awake till the early hours.

★

Rhodri, however, couldn't rein in his temper. He drove home like a madman, rushing red lights, mounting the kerb on corners, going over zebra crossings when he shouldn't and in general behaving like a driver from hell. He screeched to a halt outside his house, dropped his door key onto the gravel and unwittingly kicked it under the car as he got out. He went in the shed to get a garden hoe to reach under the car and hook it out, trapped his fingers in the shed door and eventually arrived on his doorstep in despair.

Not even Harry could disperse Rhodri's gloomy mood. Still, Megan would be here for dinner tonight. He was doing soup followed by a gutsy salad, some toffee ice-cream, which they both adored, and then coffee, though no, it would be tea because Megan preferred it.

Having a shower, changing his clothes and organising the meal went a long way towards assuaging his distress. By the time he was setting the table he was singing 'Bread of Heaven' and feeling more like himself. How he longed to have Megan for his own. To have Megan to come home to, Megan to go shopping with, Megan to sit watching TV with, to love and to cherish. This terrible need he had was what had driven him to say what he'd said this afternoon. Dan seemed to have just about everything. A star of the Practice and a star at home, because it was obvious that Rose adored him. You only had to see her face when she looked at him; there was passionate hunger there, and a look on her beautiful face that came close to reverence. And a son, Dan had a son. He, Rhodri, didn't mind what he got, boy or girl, so long as it was his and Megan's.

No, he wouldn't wander down that path, no, not today. It was ridiculous that in this day and age he and Megan had never slept together. If Dan knew that, he'd be so scornful.

He heard her car pulling up outside and because of his thoughts he was suddenly shy of meeting her. He wiped his sweating palms on his trouser legs and listened for her voice. 'Hi Rhodri! It's me.'

Rhodri stood beside the dining table, awkward, speechless almost, all his problems about her foremost in his mind.

The door from the little hall flew open and there she stood, glowing with health and vitality. What a lucky man he was! She swept into his arms and kissed him heartily.

'Darling!'

Rhodri showered her with kisses instead of speaking, gripping hold of her.

'Darling! Let me go!'

'Sorry.'

'That's all right.'

'Food's almost ready, come in the kitchen with me while I serve.'

'Right, Rhodri bach.' Megan teased him by tidying his hair. She knew he didn't like her to do that, but something had to happen to break his dour mood. He relaxed against her, making strange moaning noises as though his feelings were getting the better of him.

'Rhodri! I smell burning.'

They both rushed into the kitchen to find the soup just beginning to catch on the bottom of the pan.

'Hell!'

Megan found a fresh saucepan and tipped the soup into it. She took a clean spoon and dipped it in the soup and tasted it. 'Salt! It needs a speck of salt and it'll be fine.'

Rhodri watched her at his cooker, in his kitchen,

looking as though she lived there. Watched her hands, those hands she kept looking so fineboned and almost poetic in their movements despite the hard farm work she did; Megan should have been an artist or a musician with those hands. He stopped her switching on the gas under the soup by taking her hand to his mouth and kissing it. He turned it over and examined each of her slim fingers in turn, feeling their softness, luxuriating in the pressure of her hand on his as he caressed the scoop of her flesh at the base of her thumb.

He cleared his throat. 'Think we'd better eat.'

'It's that strict nonconformist upbringing you had that holds you back, isn't it?'

'Holds me back?'

'From doing what we both want. I'm almost panting here, waiting for you to make the first move!'

'My da would kill me if he knew I was in danger of being seduced by someone I wasn't married to.' His voice trembled a little.

'Your da wouldn't understand the pressures we're under. We're both quite old enough to do exactly what we want.'

'But should we? And there's your da too. And he's not two hundred miles away.'

'Rhodri, my darling . . .'

'I need you tonight more than ever.' They stood looking out of the window across the valley, side by side, arms around each other's waists, squeezed tight.

To break the deadlock Megan turned on the cold tap and flicked water at him. 'Better cool you down, then.'

'And you!' Rhodri splashed water at her. Megan released him and, cupping both hands to collect the water, threw it at him. Rhodri picked up a glass from the draining board, filled it and made to throw it at her, Megan twisted out of the way too late, and the water caught her full on her face.

'Right! This is full-scale war!' She took a plastic jug, began filling it with water, while Rhodri desperately tried to force her away from the tap. But he hadn't bargained for how tough she was. She half filled the jug and as he set off out of the kitchen bent on escape, she aimed and caught him on the neck and shoulders.

'You've wet my best jumper!' Rhodri turned back, pinioned her arms behind her, leant her against the edge of the sink and kissed her. 'You're right, Megan, we are old enough.'

'This making love business has made me disgustingly hungry.' Megan spooned her soup in as fast as she could. 'It was your first time?'

Rhodri flushed bright red. 'No. But my first real time and it meant more to me than I could ever find the words to say.' He was managing to look at her by the time he added, 'Thank you.'

'Less of the thank you, Rhodri bach. We're equal partners in this enterprise.' Her dark eyes viewed him from above the rim of her spoon. 'In fact, after I've eaten, I could be prevailed on for an encore.'

Rhodri emptied his soup bowl. 'It's the risk.'

His word of caution stopped her in her tracks.

'I know.'

'It is a risk. What would your da say if . . .'

'Damn and blast him! He ruins my life at every turn. I should have been born a boy.' Megan burst into tears. Even hugging his arms around her did no good.

'Stop it! Stop it! You'll have me crying next. Please,

Megan. Stop crying. I'm very glad you're not a boy. I really wouldn't fancy you if you were.'

Megan had to laugh. 'I've a good mind to make love again just to spite him.'

Rhodri let go of her, saying, 'Can you go on the pill? Or something. Or I'll do something, shall I?'

'I shall, from tomorrow. See the doctor, then we can do what we like. Yes. Definitely. Yes. I will. But tonight, I'm finishing my meal, that salad looks too good to forgo, and after that I shall make love to you like there's no tomorrow.'

'Toffee ice-cream to finish?'

'We'll eat that in bed.' Though slightly shocked by her unsuspected decadence, Rhodri agreed and decided this newly released Megan was a revelation in his sheltered life.

'It looks to me as if the cat has been at the cream, Rhodri. You're looking in fine fettle, this morning.' Dan took a closer look. 'I even think you might have . . .'

'Dan! Here's your list.' Kate handed it to him with a slight shake of her head. She knew exactly what he meant. Rhodri had got a spring in his step and half a smile on his lips this morning, but she didn't want him upset because she had to work with him all day. 'First call Tattersall's. If you could remind him he owes us, three months now.'

'Do my best. What does he want me for?'

'He rang last night and left a message on the answerphone asking you to call this morning. Didn't say why.'

'Oh, I see. That's odd of him. Not got your results yet? No? Right, I'll be off, then.' Dan gave a thumbs up and a wink to Rhodri but got no response. Tattersall's. Poor Nuala. He hadn't thought about her since he'd delivered Sybil's little kid that day. He checked his list while he waited at the traffic lights, but it didn't say what he was called out for.

Tattersall's Cop was as smart as ever. Grass well clipped. Bedding plants flourishing, buildings as trim as usual, nothing to warn him of what he would have to face when he did find Callum. He wasn't around the farm buildings, which were oddly silent. Almost unnervingly silent. Not even Callum's two dogs there to give him their rapturous greetings. So Dan went to the farmhouse door, knocked and opened it. 'Hello, it's Dan here. Where are you, Callum?'

Tentatively he opened the kitchen door but Callum wasn't there. Whistling loudly to make sure people knew someone was in the house, he began to wander about the downstairs of the house calling upstairs, 'Callum! It's Dan. You asked me to come.' Finally he braced himself to knock and then open the door of the room where Callum had laid Sybil's kid on the bed beside Nuala and she'd named her Carmel. He pushed it open slowly saying, 'It's me. Dan. Callum! Are you there?'

His heart juddered.

Then raced.

Throat tightened.

Breathing stopped.

He swiftly closed the door behind him and stood against it, his heart pounding as though he'd climbed a mountain at reckless speed.

He drew breath with a sound like a shriek.

She couldn't be, could she? And him laid there?

Holding her.

When his pounding heart had slowed and he'd calmed his spinning mind, he slowly opened the door again.

There was the smell of sickness in the air. Such stillness

too. Surely she was dead. Very cautiously he walked towards the bed.

'Callum? Callum?'

Nuala's eyes were wide open, but she was dead to this world.

And Callum? He was laid on his side, facing Nuala, an arm under her shoulders holding her close.

Dan touched his shoulder and shook it slightly. 'Callum?' No response. 'Callum?' He pressed his fingers to just below Callum's jawline and felt for a pulse. And there was none. Vomit began rising in his throat and Dan fled, overwhelmed with horror.

When he'd finished heaving up his breakfast in the drain outside the back door, Dan wiped his mouth and stood, ashen-faced, deciding what to do. Doctor? Police? Doctor. He'd know what to do. He had the Health Centre's number on his mobile because of Rose and Jonathan so he rang and explained and they promised a doctor immediately. To still his bursting heart Dan decided to do something positive and went to feed the animals. He found the two rescue ponies had gone, as well as the lame donkey they'd taken in from the sanctuary, the three cows, two dogs, and the half a dozen chickens Nuala had kept for the house. So he'd planned it all, except she had died before he'd found a home for the pygmy goats. He could hear them tap tapping about in their stable.

He opened up the top half of the door to see how they all were. There was an instant clamour and all except one were on their hind legs, pawing at the door. The one that wasn't was laid at the back of the stable, quite still. In the gloom he thought it might be Cassandra, Nuala's favourite. When Dan had finally prised the door open without letting any of them escape he found that Cassandra had died while attempting to give birth.

He lifted her dead body out onto the cobbles, put feed in the trough to keep the others going, filled their water bucket and then firmly shut the lower half of the door behind him, clipping back the top half to let in air and light.

When the doctor came Dan explained the circumstances and left him to go in by himself. Dan stood in the kitchen looking out of the window, waiting . . . knowing what he was waiting for.

The doctor came in and went to the sink to wash his hands. 'Both dead. A blessing for Nuala, there was nothing left of her but a beating heart. As for Callum . . . He's left a note for Dan. That's you, isn't it?'

From his pocket he took an envelope and then busied himself at the kitchen table filling in forms. Dan had assumed it would be a few brief words but no, Callum had written a letter, and with it a long list of who to get in touch with, who to inform, where the furniture had to go and the addresses and telephone numbers of relatives who needed to know. Directions, also, about their joint funeral, which church, which hymns.

The letter was almost his undoing. It read:

Dear Dan,

We shall both be together in heaven when you read this. My darling Nuala fell asleep for ever in my arms at teatime today. That strong dear heart of hers could fight no longer and she had already lost the will to suffer any more. I'm writing this at the kitchen table where she and I planned our useless money-making schemes. Without her, I have no fight left in me.

We may not have had success in business but where it really matters we did. She and I were childhood sweethearts, married at seventeen and never had a bad day ever after. Nuala could see the funny side of anything at all and we spent more time laughing, even when she was so ill, than any other couple in Christendom.

If you want to tell anyone what happiness is, think of us. We had it in spades.

Thanks for all you've done for us, and your kindness in not flinching when you talked to Nuala, she valued that. Thank Rose, too, for bringing the baby. He gave Nuala such joy.

Yours sincerely,
Callum and Nuala Tattersall

Dan folded the letter. Before he read his instructions he asked the doctor how Callum had died.

'Overdose of Nuala's painkillers, I suspect. There's hardly any left in the bottle. He certainly meant business. I gave him a prescription only yesterday. I'll have to inform the police, you understand.'

The phone rang so Dan went to answer it. 'Tattersall's.'

'Phil Parsons here. That isn't Callum, is it?'

'No. It's Dan Brown.'

'Something wrong?'

'Yes, well . . . bad news I'm afraid. I've just found both Nuala and Callum. They're both . . . dead.'

There was a long silence from the other end of the phone. 'But I spoke to him only yesterday, afternoon, it was. What the blazes has happened?'

'Can I tell you some other time?'

'What a sad business. Nuala, yes, but Callum . . . I was ringing to say I'm coming to collect his pygmy goats. He's sold the others to a goat farm but they didn't want the pygmy ones 'cos commercially they're not much good, so I said I'd have them for Blossom and Hamish. I paid him a few days ago, but we've been getting the shelter ready for 'em. Hamish and me, shall we come?'

'Right now, you mean?'

'Yes. Straight away.'

'Yes, I've got to wait for the police, so come, yes.'

'If you'd rather I didn't . . .'

'Well, Phil, someone has them to feed, so why not and if you've paid for them . . .'

'Right. We're on our way.'

Phil must have disconnected because Dan was left standing looking at his receiver. Still severely distressed by the morning's events, thoughts tumbled through his head with frantic rapidity. Rose, here with Jonathan? Phil taking on the goats. Callum killing himself for love. Rose had never said she'd been. Suicide. He'd miss Callum. Poor Nuala. I wonder why Rose came?

She told him at lunchtime. It was his half day and he'd gone home, glad his ghastly working day was at an end.

'Here, hold your son and heir and get up his wind while I make lunch. I can see you're upset. Tell me.' Rose carefully handed Jonathan to him, and waited.

'You didn't tell me you'd been to see Nuala.'

'Ah! Yes. I met Callum in the supermarket and we talked, so I went. Is it Nuala?'

'Yes. Rose, she's died. But so too has Callum.'

Rose drew in a long breath. 'But how? He wasn't ill. He didn't . . . kill himself?'

'I'm afraid he did and I found them when I went in

response to a message he'd left on the answerphone last night.'

Rose flung her arms about Dan and he drew such comfort from her sympathy. 'Oh darling, how dreadful.'

'Once I'd got over the shock, they looked so peaceful, together. The ultimate in happiness. You'd never met Callum, how did he know it was you?'

'Took a look at Jonathan and realised he must be yours, and then he asked me if I was your wife, just to make sure.'

Dan peered at the baby's face in amazement. 'My God!'

'So I went.'

'He thanked you for that in his suicide note. Said it gave Nuala great joy to see the baby. I'll have to spend the afternoon ringing all the people on Callum's list. Not exactly a pleasant occupation. But it's the least I can do. He never got on well with the other farmers round here. They all thought him feckless. One scheme after another, but a great chap.' Dan sighed, adjusted his hold of Jonathan while he wiped his mouth of milk. 'Part of life's rich pattern. Must put it all behind us.'

Rose gripped his shoulder and smiled to herself. Knowing he couldn't put it all behind him as easily as that and understanding he was taking this attitude because of his concern for her, she answered, 'Of course. Yes. Life goes on. Actually, tomorrow I'm having tea with Letty.'

'Letty? Colin's Letty?'

'Who else? She's not at all well. I think I'm going to persuade her to go to the doctor, she can't go on like she is. And I upset her the last time I saw her and she cried, so I feel guilty.'

'She's difficult to get on with.'

'I know. That's the challenge.'

Chapter 6

Rose arrived at exactly two forty-five, the time Letty had specified. Jonathan wasn't exactly full of joy, and she had hoped the drive in the car would put him to sleep. Which it did, but the moment she tried to lift him out he woke, miserable and weepy.

Letty and Colin lived in a dream cottage. Roses around the door, thatch on the roof, lovely old red-brick walls with timbers exposed here and there. To Rose, with her American heritage, it seemed utterly, utterly splendid. Before she could knock on the door it had been opened by Letty and she was standing beaming from ear to ear welcoming the two of them in.

'Oh Letty! What a wonderful house! It's like a picture book. I've always longed for a house with roses around the door. You are so lucky.'

'Come in, Rose! It was derelict when we bought it and it took hours of work with damp proof courses and septic tanks and new floorboards and things. It must have been two years before it was really habitable.'

'Well, it was well worth it. If it's not asking too much, can I look round before I leave? You know what we Americans are like about old houses.'

Letty visibly gathered herself before she agreed whole-heartedly that Rose could look round. It almost seemed to

Rose that Letty found her request intrusive, so she thought to leave it for the moment.

'Can I put Jonathan down here? You haven't got a dog or a cat, have you?'

'No. We haven't and yes, of course you can. Isn't he beautiful?' Letty bent to stroke Jonathan's head. 'So like Dan. I didn't like Dan when he first came you know, in fact I insisted he was dismissed.'

'I'm sorry. I didn't know. Do you like him now?'

'Oh yes. He's been a real asset to the Practice. He's like me you see, speaks straight from the shoulder, no messing, and like doesn't always get on with like, does it?'

'No, I suppose not. When you know Danny like I do, you know he's pure gold.'

Letty looked Rose up and down. 'I like your dress. You've an instinct for what suits, haven't you?'

'I guess I could lose some more weight though, I can only just get into this dress. Specially round the top.'

'Sit down. You still look lovely. You always do. I'm envious of that.'

'Hey! This isn't a Rose Franklin-Brown admiration day. I want to know how *you* are. Last time we met I thought you weren't looking too well.'

'Kettle's boiled, I won't be a minute.'

Letty rushed to the kitchen and Rose could hear her organising cups and opening the fridge and pouring milk. In a moment she was back carrying a tray and placing it exactly in the middle of the coffee table. Jonathan began to grizzle again. 'Sorry, this isn't one of his best days. Here, darling, have your comforter.' Rose popped his dummy into his mouth and Jonathan sucked loudly on it.

'You approve of dummies, then?'

'Oh yes. If he's unhappy, why not?'

'Lots of people don't.'

'Well, that's up to them. I've read all the books and then some and I'm determined to do as I think fit. No milk for me, thanks.' Rose accepted her cup and sipped it gratefully. 'This is lovely tea.' She stretched out her long elegant legs under the coffee table, wriggled her shoulders to get more comfortable and asked again how Letty was.

'Well, I'm no better. Can I confide in you?'

Rose nodded. 'Confide away.' She gave Letty an encouraging smile.

'I mean really confide, I'm not really into confiding in women friends, but then I haven't got any. I'm not very good at women's chat, you know, all girls together.'

'Neither am I, but I'm a good listener.' She gave Letty a beautiful smile, the sort of smile that made Dan's heart do head over heels, and Letty began to relax. She drained her cup of tea in one go, dabbed her lips, laid down her napkin, placed her teacup and saucer on the coffee table exactly lined up with the tiles on the top, cleared her throat, fidgeted for her handkerchief, straightened her skirt and then said so softly Rose could hardly hear, 'I'm so afraid.'

Cautiously, fearing what she might be told, Rose asked, 'You are? What of?'

'Either I've got something wrong with me or I'm going quietly crackers.'

'You are?'

'I think I might be pregnant. I haven't told Colin, he won't like the idea, you know.'

'Won't like the idea! Of course he will. How can he not like it, a lovely man like Colin? He'll be thrilled.'

'But I can't be pregnant though, can I? I mean, after all these years. So I must be ill. *Cancer* or something.'

'Have you seen the doctor?'

'No. I daren't.'

'But you must.' Rose hesitated, thinking about how to phrase her next question. 'Why do you think you're not pregnant and that it must be cancer?'

Letty flushed with embarrassment. 'I've missed . . . you know . . . four times now and I'm always so sick. Sometimes actually sick, but mostly feeling sick. Sometimes I retch and retch and nothing happens. It leaves me exhausted. I can't keep food down, and I could swear my stomach has swollen.'

'That sounds remarkably like being pregnant. But it's no good not knowing. What makes you say Colin will be angry? You've got to find out one way or the other. If you're not pregnant and it is something serious . . . they work wonders nowadays. It's no longer the death sentence it was, you know.' Then Rose remembered Nuala and could have bitten her tongue out. 'I'll go with you, to the doctor; either way you need a friend.'

Letty got out her handkerchief and blew her nose. 'You see, Colin doesn't want children.'

'How do you know that?'

'He told me once. He said, "I do not want children. Our lives are perfectly satisfactory without children all over the place." So he means it. How do you bring up a child when its father doesn't want it?' Letty looked up at Rose and almost pleaded for understanding.

'With difficulty I should imagine. Dan and I . . . well, I know it sounds intensely coy and mushy, but we want to make babies together. Our babies, you know. Men are immensely proud when they've proved themselves to be male in every aspect. I honestly don't think you need worry about Colin. He may need time to become accustomed to the idea, but believe me, when he holds in his arms a child born of his flesh, the whole picture will change. He's such a caring man. Well, that's how he always seems to me.'

Letty didn't answer.

Rose tried to catch her eye. 'Yes?'

'But if it's cancer . . . I've still got to tell him.'

'I guess that he'd rather hear about a baby than cancer. Which do you think would be the worst?'

Letty began to smile.

'I'd come with you to see the doctor.'

'Would you? Would you really? I could be brave if you were with me.'

'Make an appointment, let me know and I'll come. Honest to God. I'll come.'

'I feel better already. It could be a week at least, you know what it's like getting a doctor's appointment these days. Unless you're actually dying . . .' Letty gave a single, painful sob, got things under control, then said, 'I do appreciate you offering to come. I don't deserve it, really.'

'Of course you do, what the heck. I'll gladly go with you. In fact, ring right now.'

'No. I won't do that. I'll ring when you've gone.'

'No time like the present. Here.' Rose got her mobile out of her bag and pressing the appropriate keys had the phone ringing out sooner than it takes to tell.

'I can't. I can't.'

'Then shall I?'

Letty nodded.

'Hi! This is Rose Franklin-Brown speaking on behalf of Mrs Letty Walker who is a patient of . . . ?'

'Dr Mason.'

'Dr Mason. She urgently needs an appointment, but a

proper one, none of this emergency business, two minutes and you're out with a scrip in your paw. This is a serious matter and needs instant medical appraisal. Next Friday? You mean Friday of this week? Oh! Friday of next week? It won't do.' Rose felt Letty pulling at her sleeve. 'Just a moment.'

'Don't worry. Next Friday will do.'

Rose ignored Letty's plea. 'If she were a dog I'm sure a vet would see her tomorrow, most likely today. I wonder if it would be better if she went to the vet instead? She'd at least get immediate attention.' There was a pause while Rose listened. 'I'm not surprised, I don't find it funny either, believe me. *And I'm still waiting.*'

Rose sat listening to the muffled altercation going on at the other end of the line.

'Yes, it is urgent.' Rose listened and then said, 'Her symptoms?' Rose's voice was full of apology. 'I'm so sorry, I'd no idea I was speaking to a doctor. I do beg your pardon. Oh! You're not a doctor, then to whom am I speaking?' Rose winked at Letty. There was a pause while Rose listened and then Letty heard her say, 'As you're not a qualified medical practioner I fail to see what telling you her symptoms will achieve. So *we're still waiting for an appointment*. Absolutely. Yes. Twenty minutes. Yes. Thank you.'

Full of dread, Letty looked at Rose.

'If we go now you can be seen straight away and I guess that's what we should do. I'll drive. No, Letty, I know what you're going to say, but it's better to get it over with.' She scooped up Jonathan, now fast asleep, gave Letty's arm a squeeze and said, 'I know I'm inclined to hassle, but it's for the best, isn't it?'

Reluctantly Letty nodded. She would never have allowed Colin to take over like she'd just allowed Rose.

'Purse, Letty.'

'Oh! Yes. I should have a bath or a shower or something before I go.'

'No time. I'm quite sure you're the cleanest possible person, so don't fret.' Rose gave Letty a reassuring grin and gently pushed her out of the door. 'Keys?'

'Oh. Yes.'

Five minutes from the surgery Letty said, 'I'm sure I'm troubling them for nothing. Let's go home. It's the menopause come early or something.'

'If it is, then at least you'll know for sure. But being sick all the time doesn't sound like it to me.' She stopped speaking while she negotiated a notoriously difficult roundabout and then swung with practised ease into a parking space right outside the surgery. 'Right. Here we are. Wait while I get Jonathan out, it takes a minute.'

Letty, glad of any excuse to delay facing the truth, stood by the car twisting her hands in agitation, trying to think up good reasons why she shouldn't go in. Rose, sensing how very distressed she was and thinking she'd be just the same if it was her, heaved the baby carrier onto her arm and putting on her encouraging face despite her dread, took hold of Letty's free arm and led her into the surgery. She whispered, 'Sit down, make yourself look even more ghastly than you feel.'

At reception Rose said, 'I've brought Mrs Letty Walker for her appointment with Dr Mason.' The receptionist referred to the screen on the desk and with a condescending look on her face said, 'I'm afraid you must have got the wrong day, there's no appointment down for her. I've just come on and no message was left for me to that effect.'

'She has an appointment, because I have just made one over the phone. We were told to come straight in and we have done.'

'Well, I'm sorry, but he hasn't any free appointments until next Friday. Can I make one for then?'

'No, you may not, because we already have one. So, get checking.'

Luckily at that moment Dr Mason came out of his consulting room, couldn't miss seeing Rose and almost rushed to greet her. 'Mrs Franklin-Brown! How wonderful to see you! How are you and the little babe?'

'Absolutely fine, thank you, Dr Mason.'

He held out his hand to shake Rose's as though she were a long lost friend. 'And what can I do for you?'

Pointing at Letty, Rose answered. 'My friend here, Letty Walker, is your next appointment.'

The receptionist sprang to life. 'I beg your pardon, she is not . . .' Then she shrank back in her chair, intimidated by the threatening look Rose had given her.

The welcoming smile slid from Dr Mason's face. 'Ah! Right. I don't think I have a free . . .'

Rose smiled sweetly at him, one of those dazzling smiles of hers that no one could resist, and he succumbed to her charms. 'But perhaps I can fit her in. This way, Mrs Walker.'

Patiently Rose waited for Letty to emerge from the consulting room. She occupied herself looking round the room at the motley collection of people waiting their turns, categorising them and wondering what their complaints were. They all looked remarkably fit and she came to the conclusion that half of them at least had minor ailments they could have treated at home. No wonder they said Letty couldn't have an appointment until the end of next week, the place was cluttered with malingerers.

Letty came into the waiting room, eyes red from weeping and grim-faced. It wasn't until they were back in the car that she spoke. 'Rose.'

Head down in the back of the car busy securing Jonathan's safety seat, Rose replied, 'Mmm?'

'Rose. I've a card here to go for a scan . . . right now.'

The alarm bells began ringing in Rose's brain. For a moment she went quite still and then carefully closed the back door and swallowed hard. 'You have?' Hoping it sounded much more casual than she felt.

'I'm supposed to go right now. But I think I'll leave it till tomorrow. There isn't time.'

That urgent? Hell! Rose thought. 'Well, then we shall. If he's arranged it for you for today we'd better go. Scan appointments are as rare as hen's teeth. They must have had a cancellation. You direct me.' She patted Letty's knee and then leaned across to give her a reassuring kiss.

'Turn right out of here, then first left turn and then the left fork, no, no, right fork and we're there.'

'So, we did right then, getting a quick appointment.'

Letty was obviously preoccupied and didn't answer, so Rose paid attention to her driving instead. She pulled up in the first available space in the hospital car park, switched off the ignition and took hold of Letty's hand. 'Best get it over with. Eh?'

'Oh Rose! I never thought for one minute I'd have to go for a scan. I'm absolutely bowled over with it.'

'Well, the only way to tackle it is head on. Straight in for the big punch, no messing.'

'Oh yes. I may be a while though. What about Jonathan?'

'Don't worry about him. If he needs feeding I shall feed him, I've no fine sensitivities about the matter. Come on.'

So Rose did feed Jonathan because he began his I-Am-Starving routine the moment she sat down to wait for Letty. It seemed an age, worrying about what Letty was to learn. At least they hadn't let the grass grow under their feet. Full marks for that. No, siree. But that meant it was urgent, didn't it? Poor Letty. Poor Colin. They'd both need all the support possible.

Eventually just as Jonathan had fallen fast asleep with his stomach so full he was fit to burst, Letty returned. A transformed Letty. A bouyant, bouncing Letty. A shining Letty who bent to kiss her cheek and kiss the baby too.

'Oh Rose! Oh Rose! Come on, let's go.'

She picked up Rose's bag and hastened her out of the hospital. 'Oh Rose!'

Scurrying along behind her Rose said breathlessly, 'You've got the all clear then. It isn't cancer?'

Letty nodded her head.

'Oh!' With the baby firmly strapped in, Rose got into the driving seat. 'Thank heavens for that. What is it then?'

Letty said. 'I must be the biggest fool under the sun.'

'Oh, I don't know about that, you'd have to go a long way to beat me.'

Looking out of the side window to avoid Rose's eyes Letty said, 'I can't believe it but, they say, they say,' Letty took a deep breath, 'I'm about four months pregnant. I feel such a fool. At forty-seven, it's not a joke, is it?'

Shocked, Rose took in a great gulp of breath, then huge relief made her blurt out, 'It is not funny!' But Rose began to laugh, in fact she roared with laughter, until she complained of a stitch in her side. 'Oh Letty! All this worry. All these weeks. A baby! Oh my God! No wonder you thought you had a lump. Some lump!' She went off into peals of laughter again, leaving no pause for Letty to speak. In the end it was catching and Letty began to laugh too. Then relief and thankfulness became two emotions too many for Letty and streams of tears began running down her cheeks and yet she was laughing at the same time.

Rose got out a tissue from Jonathan's bag of necessities and gave it to her. 'I can't believe you didn't think it could be a baby.'

'I'd given up all hope years ago and . . . at forty-seven I didn't dare think it, for one moment. I knew I felt differently, more sentimental and such, and I caught myself drooling over some kittens at the Practice one day, and there was that day when I cried when you brought Jonathan in and I couldn't bear the sight of him. I was so desperate thinking that it was all much too late for me and Colin. Life didn't seem very fair that day. But I never thought . . . would you have done?'

'If I'd never been pregnant then I suppose perhaps I wouldn't. Jeez! Colin's going to get a shock. Catch your breath and then ring him. Go on, use my phone.'

'No, no, I'll wait till I get home. Thanks.'

'I insist. Think how pleased he'll be. What's his mobile number? Here, it's ringing.'

Colin had just come in from a full day of calls and was standing by the reception desk talking to Kate. They were discussing her options if her chemistry grade wasn't an A. 'But it will be!' said Colin. 'It's bound to be.'

'It isn't bound to be. I got a D last time and it's a big jump up to an A. Sometimes I think I've done all right, others I'm totally convinced I've done really badly, like last time.'

'It is not the end of your life if you don't get in. It might feel like it, but it isn't. There are other avenues for you.'

Colin's mobile began ringing and he hadn't appeared to notice. Kate said, 'That's your phone, Colin.'

'So it is.' Colin took it from the clip at his waist and switched it on. 'Oh hello! It's you. Something wrong?'

Kate watched him as he listened, saw his face go pale. 'The hospital. For a what? The line's breaking up. Say it again. A scan? Whatever for? Are you ill? I didn't know you had an appointment. Yes. Yes. What? I thought you said . . . You did. Hell's bells! How did that happen? Yes, yes, OK. I'll be home as soon as I can. Jeepers creepers!' Colin switched off his phone and stood gazing at it.

Kate asked, 'Everything all right, is it, Colin?'

Colin looked at Kate. 'She's getting a lift home from the hospital.'

'Letty?'

Colin nodded, eyes fixed again on his mobile, preoccupied and silent.

'Are you all right? I mean, is it bad news?'

Dazed might have been the best word to describe Colin's appearance, he moved like a man in a trance. Finally as he reached the main door and opened it he said, 'Kate! You won't believe this, but I think Letty said she was pregnant. She can't be, can she?'

Kate grinned. 'No good asking me, how could I know?'

'Mmm. No. Of course you don't. I can't understand it,' Colin said and left, shaking his head in disbelief.

But when he got home Colin was finally convinced because Letty showed him the printout of the scan and there for all to see was a baby. A baby he'd fathered, a child Letty had conceived, a child, which, after nearly sixteen years of marriage, was nothing short of a miracle. A total, definite, absolute, downright, without any doubt at all, *miracle*.

'I thought I had cancer.'

'Why didn't you say?'

'I was too frightened.'

'Letty!'

'Rose made me go. You know what she's like for being so sweet and kind, somehow I just came out with it and said how terrified I was, so she made an appointment for me at the doctor's and took me. She was dreadfully rude to them, but it meant I got an appointment straight away. I've been such a fool! I daren't believe that I might be pregnant.'

Colin studied the printout again. 'It is true, isn't it?'

'Oh yes! But they don't tell you if they can see it's a boy or a girl, unless you ask.'

'Did you ask?'

Letty shook her head. 'I was in shock. It never occurred to me. I couldn't believe what was happening. I told Dr Mason he was wrong. I refused to believe him, in fact. I said I'd got cancer. I told him I couldn't possibly be pregnant, not after years of giving up all hope. But it's true. Isn't it? I mean, look.' She showed him the printout again.

'When we wake up in the morning and it's still true then I shall really believe it. I can't take it in right now.'

'I thought you . . . you said . . . you said ages ago you didn't want children. I was so disappointed when you said that, it took me weeks to get over it. You see, I thought I was a disappointment to you, I know they said we were both OK, keep trying, but I honestly felt it must be me.'

Colin put an arm around Letty's shoulders and kissed her temple. 'I remember saying that, I only said it so you wouldn't feel too badly about not having children. Thought it would help.'

'So you are pleased then?'

'Of course I am.' He squeezed her shoulder again, his eyes on the scan. 'I can't believe it.'

'Neither can I. It feels like a dream. I've been so disappointed so many times. All that yearning and longing. Maybe that was why I bullied you so much.'

Colin opened his mouth to protest that she hadn't.

Letty laid a gentle finger on his mouth. 'Hush! *I know I did.* Don't try to be kind. I did, Colin, and I'm ashamed of myself. Rose says Dan is pure gold, and I could say the same about you. Pure gold. And I'm sorry I've been so unpleasant all these years.' She stretched out her hand to straighten his tie for him. 'It was you sent me those flowers and the complimentary card from that beauty shop and the weekend in Paris. You organised that, didn't you?'

Colin nodded.

'I never guessed, you know, not till just now. Pure gold, I said, and pure gold you are. Thank you for that. It was just what I needed. It made such a difference to me. It made me a new person, lighter hearted, kind of. But it did the trick, didn't it?' Letty laughed up at him and was rewarded with another kiss. 'We'll light the stove, I've laid it, it just needs a match, and to celebrate we'll have a pre-dinner sherry before we eat and talk about babies and what we'll need. Dinner won't take five minutes to put together.'

Colin looked at her with a solemn expression on his face. 'Mothers-to-be shouldn't drink alcohol.'

Letty's hand flew to her mouth. 'Ohhhh! Of course not. I never thought! That's the loveliest thing anyone has said to me, ever.' A younger, fresher, more vibrant Letty kissed him on his mouth and then said, 'I've always loved you, Colin, but it kind of got lost under layer upon layer of resentment and anger. But that's sloughed away like a snake shedding its skin and it happened all in a moment.'

The news was all round the Practice by first thing the next morning. The reaction to the news went from sheer hysteria at the amazingly unexpected announcement, to wholehearted delight. Colin had to take huge amounts of leg-pulling from the male members of the staff, someone suggested with a wink that it must have been the trip to Paris which had done the trick, others said how pleased they were for Letty and for him, and Dan mentioned the sleepless nights and the upheaval a small baby can make in a household, but shook his hand with vigour as he congratulated him.

Colin took it all in good part but found Rhodri's response difficult to understand. He didn't say the right words and the expression in his voice was all wrong. 'Lucky man, you are, Colin, bach. Very lucky. Bit of a surprise for us all, let alone you and Letty. Still, congratulations are in order.' And he'd shaken Colin's hand with less enthusiasm than if he'd been congratulating him on winning the father's race at a school sports day.

But Colin wasn't to know how despairing Rhodri was. He'd had as much as he could take from Megan's father the previous night. Megan had asked him to go for a meal and take a look at their farm cats while he was there. She'd managed to capture them all in the tack room close to the house when she fed them that afternoon.

'They're mostly feral cats who appear and disappear at will. These two black ones are ours, we brought them with us when we moved, the rest we kind of inherited. I don't know much about it but I wondered if they had cat flu. Some of them are very low in spirits and three of them have sticky eyes. What do you think, Rhodri?'

Rhodri counted ten cats altogether. 'You feed all these every day?'

'Well, our own two come in the house and are fed morning and night, but the others I feed out here every afternoon, and our two turn up in the hope of stealing food but they never do, they're too soft to put up a fight.'

'I suppose you never handle these others.'

'They won't let me.'

'See the grey and white, I'm pretty sure that has flu. Its eyes are all bunged up and I saw it sneeze just then. Appears listless too, disinterested kind of. Those two ginger ones might be going the same way. Are yours vaccinated? I expect they are.'

'Yes, definitely. They won't catch it, will they?'

'They shouldn't. The only way is for me to prescribe antibiotics and you put it in their food every day, and hope for the best.'

'Is that all we can do?'

In the dim light in the tack room, Rhodri looked at her, the wholesomeness of her refreshing his spirits after his hard day. 'Give me a kiss.' She did with her familiar gusto, arms wrapped round his neck, hair tickling his face, and in his nostrils the lovely fresh smell of her he so loved.

'Must go in, Rhodri, the vegetables will be boiling dry. You always smell so nice, of tweed and disinfectant.'

'Oh! Thanks. I did shower before I came out.'

'Doesn't matter, it's always there, but it's the nicest possible disinfectant. My favourite, but that's only because it's you. Come on, see Da.'

Rhodri's heart sank. The price he had to pay for

Megan's company felt too high tonight. Old Man Jones was sitting scrunched up in his favourite chair, all the trappings of an invalid scattered on the usual table. Tonight, despite the warmth of the August evening, he had a rug over his knees.

'Good evening, Mr Jones. How's things?'

'Much the same. Grateful for the slightest easing of the pain. What about the cats? Megan says she's asked you to take a look.'

'That's right. I'm fairly certain they've got flu. Well, some of them have, but the thought of taking blood samples from that wild lot! So I've decided a general intake of antibiotics will possibly do the trick, and we'll have to keep our fingers crossed.'

Mr Jones almost snarled, 'I've told her not to bother with the wild ones. They're a waste of her time. As if she doesn't have enough to do. Damned idiotic of her.'

Rhodri sat himself down on the sofa. 'It's her kind heart, she can't help but adopt them.'

'You should know.'

Rhodri looked at him and raised a questioning eyebrow. Mr Jones said with a sarcastic lilt to his voice, 'Well, she's adopted you.'

'Are you putting me on the same level as a feral cat? Am I no more than that?'

Mr Jones shrugged his shoulders. 'Take it how you like. That's how I see you. You're also a waste of her time.'

Rhodri, angry because he'd used the same words about him as he had about the cats, answered angrily, 'That's insulting to me and to Megan. We love each other, a fact you appear well able to ignore. Do you know what she said to me the other night?'

'How could I?'

'She said she wished she'd been born a boy.'

'She's right, I wish she had.'

'Don't you feel that's terribly sad?'

'Not at all.'

'Well, you should, you should be ashamed to have made her feel like that. Ashamed.'

Mr Jones painfully levered himself out of his chair, and standing as upright as he could he shouted, 'You are a guest in my house, how dare you speak to me in that way.'

Rhodri rose to his feet expecting Mr Jones would topple over any minute but he didn't, he didn't even search for his stick.

Rhodri shouted equally as loudly, 'Because what I've said is true. She sticks by you, managing your farm, taking orders like a lackey when she'd prefer to be taking part in real life instead of being locked up here with you. You're a tyrant. A bully. A selfish, mean-minded bully. But you're her da so she takes it, but watch out because one day the worm might turn.' He sat down again, more angry than he could remember.

'She'd *never* leave *me*. And if you think for one minute that she'd leave me to marry you, I can tell you now she *never* will. So you might as well stop sniffing after her like a randy dog. Just disappear and get a job somewhere else. You're not welcome here. Now, help me into the dining room, she must have got the meal ready by now. Come on, where's my stick? Jump to it.'

Rhodri was so full of anger that he decided to leave Mr Jones to find his own stick and stagger into the dining room alone, but Megan came in and asked him to help her father. 'I've put the food out. Would you like wine tonight, Da?'

Mr Jones shook his head. 'No. Ale will do instead.'

'Oh! I thought we'd have wine with Rhodri being here. I'll get a bottle.'

'Did you hear me? I said no wine.'

Megan blushed with embarrassment. 'Would you like wine, Rhodri?'

'As it would appear we are going against your father's wishes, then I suppose we both have to say no, him being the grown-up.' He put such an edge of sarcasm in the tone of his voice that Megan quaked.

Mr Jones's colourless eyes focused on Rhodri. 'Insolence will get you nowhere. You're a boy, a fresh-faced youth, you are. I don't know why Megan bothers with you.'

Megan leapt to Rhodri's defence. 'Da! Rhodri is my guest. Please! Make an effort to be polite.'

'In my own house I shall behave as I wish. Seeing as we all feel able to speak our minds tonight, we may as well have it out here and now. I shall not under any circumstances permit you to marry. Not under any circumstances. Let that be an end to it.'

Rhodri, normally intimidated by Mr Jones, answered with firm determination. 'Has it occurred to you that we could be married by the weekend? All completely lawfully because both Megan and I are above the age of consent. It's only her affection for you which prevents us.'

For the second time that night, Mr Jones got to his feet without assistance. 'If you dare do such a thing I shall disinherit her. Mark my words I shall.' He wagged a finger at them both. 'Do you hear me?'

'I hear all right. I might remind you that I earn a perfectly adequate salary, ample to support the two of us, and I own my house so we'd have a roof over our heads. We don't care where your money would go. We don't need it. We shall marry, whether you give your consent or not. I will not give up that happiness for anyone. Not even you. We'll find a way, believe me.' He said it in such a matter-of-fact way that it was a moment before Mr Jones fully comprehended what he'd said. Rhodri started to eat his dinner though the fish tasted like chalk and the potatoes like cotton wool. As for the peas and carrots, they resembled the Plasticine ones he used to make in his childhood in the Manse.

Megan sat with her hands on her lap, head down, suffering.

Mr Jones abruptly sat down again. White-faced and breathing heavily. Lost for words. He reached for his stick and raising it high he whipped it down, aiming to hit Rhodri with it, but Rhodri dodged and the stick crashed onto the table, breaking his plate, scattering the food and smashing his glass of water. A deep silence fell. For a moment no one moved.

Appalled, Megan broke the spell by shouting, 'Da!'

Rhodri hastily pushed back in his chair to prevent the water running onto his trousers.

Mr Jones sounded as though he was being strangled. Every breath he took scored its way into his lungs as though each would be his last. He fumbled to loosen his collar and began gesticulating with his hand. Megan rushed for his inhaler, when she gave it to him he inhaled deeply several times and gradually his breathing relaxed and became more normal. Even so it was loud and rusty. Much to Rhodri's relief, as he didn't fancy having to do mouth to mouth with Mr Jones. In fact he doubted if he would bother to, anyway. The nasty, conniving old man that he was.

'Now Da! What a to-do! Let me help you back to your

chair. I'll keep your dinner warm, no problem.' She helped him up and holding him by the arm she guided him away from the dining table, but Rhodri couldn't help notice the vicious glance Mr Jones gave him as he passed his chair. No, it wasn't vicious; it was triumphant. So that's how the cookie crumbles, thought Rhodri. He *is* a conniving old man. All he wants is to make sure that Megan stays with him to make his meals and do his washing and look after him when he's ill. Without her he'd have to go into a home. Uncharitably Rhodri decided that would be the best place for him too.

The remains of Rhodri's dinner had spread from his plate onto the tablecloth, soaked to a sloshy mess by the water from his glass. With Megan distraught and Mr Jones's rasping breath dominating the house, the evening was in ruins and Rhodri decided it was time to leave.

Heavy with disappointment he declared, 'I'll go, Megan.'

'Come in the kitchen.'

He followed her in and closed the door behind him.

'Rhodri, you should never have answered him back. He'll be ill all day tomorrow now.'

He took her hand to his lips and kissed it. 'Megan, you are a slave to that man. No father has the right to keep you tied like this. Hand and foot, you are. Hand and foot. It simply isn't fair.' He brushed away her hair from her face. 'When are you going to claim back your life?'

'What can I do? What can I do about it?'

'Stand up to him. That's what. Get help to look after him, let him see he can exist without you at his beck and call.'

'He won't have anyone but me.'

Rhodri gave a great sigh of despair. 'Exactly. Exactly. I love you so.'

'I love you.'

'Then we've got to plan.'

'What though?'

'Don't know yet. Goodnight, love.'

'Here, take your pudding, it's sticky toffee.' Megan placed a portion in a lidded bowl and handed it to him. 'It's best you go, give me a chance to calm him down. I'm so sorry about what he did, so sorry. Got to get back to him. Goodnight.'

Rhodri went out into the night, desolate.

So when he heard Colin and Letty's wonderful news, he found it genuinely hard to be happy for them. They were getting all he dreamed about and the events of last night seemed to have pushed the dream even further away. What had possessed him to stand up to the fellow? He must have been out of his mind. Getting Mr Jones to like him had been his aim from the start but all that patient work had gone in a single flash of temper. Daring to attempt to hit me though! Rhodri wished he'd snapped his stick in half, though he'd have looked a fool trying to do that, it was an almighty thick stick. He went to bed, thoroughly depressed and full of anguish, and seeing no way out of his situation.

Chapter 7

Kate went to bed that same night also full of anguish and dreading the morning. Fortunately for her the post always came early and she hoped that tomorrow would be no exception. Exam results! Oh God! What a fool she'd been to think she could get a good grade just doing tutorials with Miss Beaumont, a chemistry teacher from school. She should have had more sense. She flung off the duvet and lay under the sheet, hot and uncomfortable.

She and Mia, her stepmother, had been in their new flat three months now, and though she liked it Kate still hankered for the old house where she'd grown up. For the familiar sounds, the friendly smell of the place, the garden; though she'd hated working in it, she'd always been able to leave it to Mia because she loved gardening. Here they had communal gardens kept strictly regimented with none of the casual charm that a garden of Mia's was capable of. Park benches to sit on and architectural features rather than the mad medley of Mia's country-type garden. Still, moving had triggered Mia into going back to her painting, which was a blessing for her, and at least the frantic activity that her dad's death had set off in Mia had abated and the relaxed, sweet-natured person Kate had always known had returned.

Would she get an A, or would she get a B, or worse still a D, like she'd got first time round? Kate decided that if that were the case then she'd do Zoology or something instead, because although she loved working at the Practice, doing reception work did not tax her brain nearly enough.

I'll let you know, Dad, what I get. I know you'll be pleased whatever it is. Just wish you were here to crack the bottle of champagne you'd been keeping for the Big Day, as you called it. Tears slid quietly down her face and she wiped them away with a corner of the sheet.

Kate tossed and turned and eventually fell asleep but kept waking because of the heat and her own agitated state of mind. About three o'clock she was fully awake and went to make herself a drink of tea. A terrible sickening feeling had come over her. *Failure*. It was staring her in the face. But as Mia would say, she could only do her very best. As she sipped her tea from a mug she'd had since she first went to secondary school and only used when she needed mountains of emotional support, Kate realised that it was all too late anyway. The die had been cast. Whatever would be would be, no matter how much soul-searching she did, no matter how many times she went over her answers, no matter how many times she saw the question paper in her mind's eye, it was all over and done with. Finished. Decided.

Well, she had done her best and if she wasn't good enough to get in to veterinary college then so be it. It wasn't for her. But she remembered the time she'd helped Scott of blessed memory deliver the calf, and when she and Dan had been chilled to the bone during lambing at Tad Porter's, and the warmth of Connie's kitchen and the frail young lamb she'd fed. All the wonderful kindness so peculiar to a farming community. Then she started laughing about when she hosed Scott down after he'd fallen in Phil Parson's slurry pit, and a large tear came in her eye which she angrily brushed away. Scott couldn't stand commitment, which was why he ran away from her, back home to Australia. But it was for the best. She'd never have qualified if anything had come of their affair.

The kitchen clock, once holding pride of place in a schoolroom and rescued by her dad when the school was being pulled down, chimed out four o'clock. Kate went to bed and her last thought as she slipped into a dreamless sleep was, whatever happened tomorrow she'd still be Kate Howard, and the sun would still shine and the clock still chime. She comforted herself with 'Time and the hour run through the roughest day.'

The first she knew about the morning was the sound of Mia placing a breakfast tray on her bedside table and pulling back the curtains. 'Post's come.'

'Oh no!'

'It's here. The letter. Can I stay while you open it?'

Kate shot upright, eyes wide open. 'Yes, of course. Give me it.'

She tore the envelope open, pulled the sheet of paper out, and in one swift movement sprang up to stand on the bed shouting, 'Yes! Yes! Yes!' with a clenched fist punching the air. 'I've done it! Mia! I've done it. I have! I have! Look!'

Mia studied the paper and read the magic 'Grade A'. 'Oh Kate! Oh Kate! That's wonderful! You clever girl, you! I'm so proud. Vet college, here she comes!'

Kate leapt off the bed and flung her arms around Mia, so tightly she could hardly breathe, but Mia didn't mind. This was the day of days. 'What a pity you have to go into work.'

'Oh! It isn't a pity at all. I'm so looking forward to telling everyone! Can you believe it? I'm so excited. I'll ring Miss Beaumont and tell her. She'll be so pleased for me. Last night I convinced myself I'd failed and was thinking up some alternatives, but I haven't failed, have I? Oh Mia! I feel quite sick. Help! I do really.'

'Calm down. Here, have a cup of tea, it might settle your stomach. You can't be ill on a day such as this. You can't.' Mia poured a cup of tea for her, and made her sit in bed with her pillow to rest against. 'Steady, steady, sip it.'

Kate looked up at her. 'Mia! Wouldn't Dad have been delighted?'

'Delighted! There isn't a word in the English language big enough to describe his pride. He'd have been like a dog with two tails. Maybe he knows. Somehow, in that great big yonder wherever he is. I like to think he does.'

'So do I. Oh Mia! It's like a great weight has lifted from my shoulders. They'll all be so pleased for me at the Practice. I'll ring the minute I've eaten my breakfast. Have you eaten?'

Mia shook her head. 'Too excited.'

'Well, go get something and share my teapot. You can sit here while we let it sink in.' Kate patted the bed, and moved her legs to make more room. 'Look, just here. Please.'

When Mia came back Kate was looking concerned. 'What's the matter, Kate?'

'I've just realised I'm so excited I haven't given a thought to you.'

'Why should you? I'm excited too.'

'I know but—'

'But nothing. Now's the time for me to get a job. I shall

only have myself to look after and getting a job after all these years will be the best thing for me.'

'Are you sure?'

'Absolutely.'

'They'll be needing someone to replace me. The money isn't much but it would be a start.'

'Oh! I don't know about that. They wouldn't want me.'

'Why not?'

'No. No.'

'Nonsense, you'd be lovely with the clients and you love animals.'

'No, Kate. It won't do at all. Think of my asthma. I'd spend all my time with watering eyes and striving to breathe.'

'Of course, I never thought. But what are you going to do?'

'Paint. And possibly work in the art shop in the High Street.'

'Have they a vacancy?'

'I don't know but I can always ask. Mrs Boulder is thinking of retiring, and not before time. They've given her the nudge a few times but she won't take the hint. She's immovable.'

'Boulder by name and Boulder by nature!' The two of them collapsed in a fit of giggling, which lightened the atmosphere and made them both feel light-hearted.

'Oh Mia! Isn't it wonderful? I know I'm not in till one but I'm going to phone and tell Joy. She'll be so pleased.' Kate flung back the sheet, got out of bed and charged into the hall, leaving Mia in the bedroom alone.

Mia looked up at the ceiling deep in thought. After a while she said, 'Well, Gerry, you've got what you wanted.

Your darling daughter at vet college. Aren't you pleased? She's done it, exactly what she wanted. I can't begin to tell you how pleased I am.'

Kate was back in the bedroom before Mia realised. 'Mia, who were you talking to?'

'Your dad. I often do, especially when it's something about you.'

Kate swallowed hard. 'I never realised.'

Mia patted her arm. 'What did Joy say?'

'She's thrilled and they're cracking a bottle of champagne at lunchtime specially for me.'

'Good. You enjoy yourself, you deserve to, all the work you've put in this year. Don't worry about me, when you go to college I shall be busy making a life for myself. And there'll always be you home in the vacations. Won't there?'

'Of course.'

Mia looked around the bedroom and said, 'I'm glad we've moved to this flat. I'd never have coped in that house. Too many memories, you know.' She got out her handkerchief and blew her nose. 'What am I doing crying on a day like this? Get up, you lazy girl, and get some ringing round done! Miss Beaumont for a start.' Mia busied herself collecting together their breakfast things. 'Go on, into the bathroom, quick smart.'

On the stroke of one o'clock Graham opened the bottle of champagne they'd been keeping for Kate's Big Day. Valentine filled the glasses standing on Miriam's silver tray and Zoe served them all where they stood in reception. When everyone had a charged glass in their hand they raised them to Kate and wished her all the best. She came in for a lot of kissing and masses of good wishes.

Joy hugged and kissed her, putting both their glasses in jeopardy. 'What a wonderful day. Absolutely wonderful.'

Mungo pecked her cheek and clapped a hand on her shoulder. 'Brilliant. You'll have a whale of a time. Don't forget us, will you?'

Dan, Valentine, Stephie and Annette all wished her well. Clients began to arrive for early afternoon appointments and a second bottle of champagne was opened so they could join in the celebrations. By the time the two bottles had been emptied the atmosphere was convivial to say the least.

Joy clapped her hands. 'Sorry! Everyone back to work. I'll clear the glasses. Let's make a start.'

Dan called out, 'Speech! Speech! Silence for Kate's speech.'

Kate's face was flushed from the champagne and she was in no mood for thinking clearly. 'I can't. Sorry.'

But a chant begun by Dan and supported by everyone else started up. 'Speech! Speech! Speech!'

Kate said, 'All right then. I'm no good at speeches, but thank you for all your good wishes and for this.' She held up her glass. 'Thank you for being so kind to me, and making me one of the team and I'll do my best to bring you credit when I'm at college.'

Mungo shouted, 'Three cheers for Kate. Our clever Kate!'

The cheers bounced off the walls, making Kate want to hide in her accounts office. Eventually things got back to normal, Stephie behind the reception desk, Kate to accounts, Joy to sorting her paperwork, Bunty and Sarah Two to assist Mungo with a tricky operation, and the clients to discussing their pets' symptoms.

Stephie brought Kate a mug of tea during the afternoon. She put down the mug on Kate's desk and said, 'I shall miss you when you've gone.'

'I'll miss you. I'll miss everyone. Everyone's been so kind.' Kate invited Stephie to sit in what she called her consultation chair. It was a rackety old thing, which Joy kept saying she would take to the tip, but somehow never remembered to do so.

Stephie sat down in it, adjusting her position to avoid slipping off it onto the floor. 'Do you miss Scott?'

'Not any more.'

'What about Adam?'

'Certainly not Adam, though I do wonder what he gets up to nowadays since he struck out on his own.'

Stephie looked uncomfortable.

When she didn't reply Kate asked her if she had something to tell her.

'Yes. I have.'

'Well then?'

'You know Adam?'

Kate nodded.

'Well, we . . . we've . . . been going out a bit.'

Kate's eyes were large with surprise. 'You and *Adam*?'

Stephie nodded. 'Yes. Not till after the day he arrived with the bouquet to say sorry to you. But, yes, we have. He's altogether different now. In a few short months he's changed completely. He even does things spontaneously.'

'Wow! And his mother?'

Stephie had to laugh. 'I told her off good and proper. She's eating out of my hand now.'

'I don't believe this, she was always so . . . clinging with Adam.'

'She isn't any more. I told her if she didn't lighten up I'd make sure she never saw Adam again.'

Kate was appalled and at the same time full of admiration for Stephie. 'You didn't!'

'I did. That soon sorted her out. Told her to get a life of her own, and leave Adam to live his.'

'Well!'

'So . . . we're thinking of getting engaged. Is it all right, I mean with you, you haven't still got the hots for him, have you?'

'No. Why didn't you tell me sooner?'

'Because, Kate, I felt embarrassed about it. I saw him at a club, soon after he brought you the bouquet. He was there with his new flatmates and I knew one of them and it went from there.'

'But, his mother wanted to live with Adam and me, is she . . . ?'

'No, she isn't. I straightened her out on that score too. She can be quite pleasant . . . that is if you stand no nonsense from her.'

'Well, good luck to you, Steph.'

'So it's OK, then?'

'Fine. Absolutely fine.' Kate handed Stephie her empty mug. 'I hope you'll be very happy. I'm just so amazed. I never thought.'

After Stephie had gone Kate shuddered. Adam and Stephie? She shuddered again; remembered the night he went wild with temper and she'd escaped into Sainsbury's and rung her dad for help. And his ridiculous bowling outfit, which he thought so groovy. His obsession with doing the same thing week after week. Tuesday, bowling. Friday, cinema. Sunday, lunch at the usual pub. Nothing could be allowed to disrupt his routine. She shuddered again when she thought about him kissing her. Stephie was welcome to him. But maybe he had changed. She hoped he had for Stephie's sake.

Kate's next visitor was Rhodri. He just about managed to put a small degree of enthusiasm in his voice when he congratulated her but she knew his heart wasn't in it.

'Just sorry, Kate, that I wasn't here for the champagne. Called out to a whelping. Sorry, then.'

'That's fine, Rhodri. Successful, were you?'

'Successful?'

'With the whelping.'

'Oh yes. But they shouldn't breed from her. Bulldog. Very narrow pelvis. Saved three. Wanted to bring her in for a Caesarean but they wouldn't have it. "Using a knife on her? We can't allow it. Oh no!" They didn't give a thought to the agony she was going through. I've told them, this is the last time.' He slumped down on the chair Stephie had just vacated and sipped his tea.

Kate waited for him to say something but he didn't, so she made a pretence of getting on with the accounts. Eventually she asked, 'Are you all right?'

Rhodri looked up at her, preoccupied and distant. 'Right as I shall ever be.' He stood up, leaving his mug on her desk and went off, meeting Dan going out through the back door to the car park.

'Good news about Kate, isn't it, Rhodri?'

'Of course. I'm glad for her. Though why anyone should want to be a vet I can't imagine at this moment.'

'There's worse jobs. Like working in a call centre. I'd go mad, completely mad, working in one of those.'

Being the same height their eyes were on a level and Rhodri looked straight into Dan's and said, 'You're mad already.'

Dan, startled by Rhodri's obvious enmity, drew in a deep breath and said, 'Me? Mad? What do you mean by that?'

'You just are.'

'I most certainly am not.'

'Mad for money, mad for forging ahead, mad to succeed at any price.'

'I don't take kindly to remarks like that. I think you should have a good think about what you've said.'

'I've never liked you since the first day. Arrogant. That's what you are. A big dose of humility would not go amiss.'

'Just a minute . . .' Dan stood back and looked at Rhodri, seeing not an angry man but a sad misfit. 'Look, I don't want to pick a quarrel with anyone, least of all a colleague.'

But Rhodri was apparently determined to pick a fight and squared up to Dan. 'Is that so?'

Kate couldn't help overhearing the quarrel and went out into the corridor hoping to calm things down. Rhodri saw her and said, 'Here comes another one full of herself.'

'There's no need to speak about Kate in that way. She's a right to be full of herself today. She's succeeded, which apparently you've not or you wouldn't be like this. None of us want an argument with you . . .'

'Well, you're getting one. You haven't been in the place five minutes and you've got a partnership.'

Dan opened his mouth to justify himself but decided against it. 'Hmm. I've work to do, even if you haven't.' He endeavoured to get past him to get on with his calls but Rhodri wasn't having it.

'I haven't finished yet.'

'Well, I have.'

Kate intervened. 'Please, Rhodri, let him leave. He's got calls to make, and you've got clients waiting, I know for a fact.'

The fight went out of Rhodri when he heard Kate's calming voice. Neither Dan nor Kate missed the bitter tones in his voice though when he answered, 'Mustn't have them all waiting for me, must I?' He turned and headed towards his consulting room.

Dan raised his eyebrows at Kate. 'What the devil was all that about?'

'Don't know, but something's not right.'

'It'll be that Welsh maiden of his that he's so keen on. Turned him down . . . again.' Dan began to laugh.

'It's not funny, Dan. He loves her to bits and she has a father she can't leave.'

'Sorry. Sorry! Got to go. But I didn't start it, remember, it was him.'

Rhodri greeted his first client as warmly as he was able in the circumstances. It was Miranda Costello, dressed head to toe in dark brown shaded velvet, with a strange brown velvet turban inexpertly wound round her head and not quite covering her dyed hair. She pointed to her cat basket. 'Rhodri, it's this young man.'

'A new cat?'

'Oh, you don't know. No, he's my new dog. I took him on from a friend who isn't able to walk him any more and I said I'd take him but I'm beginning to regret it.'

'Why is that?'

Miranda looked round the consulting room to make sure there was only her and Rhodri present and said softly, 'I don't like to say it in front of him because I don't want to embarrass him, but he's,' she mouthed the word, 'incontinent'. All over the place. Both, you know. I don't want the others to begin copying him. I thought it was because he's upset at being moved but he's been with me three weeks and it doesn't get any better. I know I've a lot of animals and it takes me all my time, walking them and attending them and I know I'm a bit happy-go-lucky about fleas and things, but I won't allow that. Absolutely not.'

'What breed is he? He must be small to get him in your cat basket.'

'Oh he is! Look!'

Rhodri peered into the wire front of the basket and saw the smallest, fully grown Yorkshire Terrier he'd ever come across. 'Never have I seen such a tiny dog! Why, he's minute.'

'You wouldn't think so if you were cleaning up after him.'

'Is he friendly?'

'Oh yes. No trouble.'

'Did the previous owner say why she couldn't cope with him?'

'Just that she couldn't take him out any more. Rheumatism, she said. I fell for him straight away. He's a little beauty, isn't he?'

'He is. Get him out. What's his name?'

Miranda began to laugh uproariously, but controlled herself for just long enough to blurt out, 'Goliath.'

For the first time for a while Rhodri laughed too. 'Goliath! Are you pulling my leg?'

'As if I would. It's true, that's what she called him, and I can't change it, can I?'

'Of course not.'

Goliath, out on the examination table, looked as though butter wouldn't melt in his mouth. He was neat and smart, and a tough looking little chap with bright, alert eyes under a mop of unruly black and tan fur, and an engaging personality which made you smile when you looked at him. He wagged his stump of a tail and looked up at Rhodri, panting, with his tiny pink tongue lolling from the corner of his mouth. A little gem, thought Rhodri as he examined him.

'Have the other animals accepted him?'

'Without a murmur. In fact he's boss dog.'

Surprised, Rhodri said, 'He is?'

'Oh yes. It took him three days but he made it. One growl from him and the cats, and the dogs, were putty in his paws. He sleeps in whichever one of their beds he chooses, and it's a different one every night. When I feed them he chooses whose dinner he eats. He's a rascal.'

'I think you have a dominant dog problem here. Before you know where you are he'll be dictating to you. But . . . to be a successful dog owner, you, Miranda, have to be the leader of the pack, like it is in the wild, where the leader stands no nonsense.'

'But I am.'

'Not according to this little chap. He's mastered the animals and you'll be the next. That's what this messing all over the place is, a way of dominating you. Next he'll be biting you if you don't please him, just as the leader of a pack of dogs would do, and you don't want that.'

'You think so? But look at him, he's so sweet.'

'And he knows it. He might be a toy dog on the outside, but in his head he thinks he's Hitler.'

'What shall I do?' Miranda looked at Rhodri as though he were the high priest of dog psychology.

'You've a battle on your hands. A long one too. But in everything, you must have the upper hand. What you say he must do, he must, whether or not he likes it. If you say "Come", don't let him off if he defies you, even though he looks so sweet. Which he does.' Rhodri was scratching him behind his ears and Goliath was loving it. 'Try doing dog training with him, at a class if you're not sure what to do. You've got to get the upper hand. I've examined him and short of taking an X-ray, I can't find anything the matter with him. Try my plan. If you're not succeeding in the least little bit, bring him in and we'll have another look. But I'm almost certain, from what you've told me, it's a psychological and not a physical problem.'

'Thank you. Well, I'll have to work at it, won't I?'

Rhodri invitingly opened the wire front of the basket and patted the blanket inside. He tried out his command voice. 'Come along, Goliath, in your basket.'

Goliath eyed Rhodri eyeball to eyeball as though weighing him up, made the decision that it suited him to allow Rhodri the upper hand and meekly trotted into the basket and sat down.

'Oh! Look at that. He knows you've rumbled him. Bless. Isn't he sweet?'

'He won't be if you don't master him. It's all for his own good in the end. He'll be a much nicer dog for you to live with.'

Miranda gazed at Rhodri, full of admiration. 'You're so wonderfully wise. What I would do without you I don't know. Thank you.'

Her appreciation of his skills went some way to salve Rhodri's wounds, but not entirely, for the wounds were deep. He really rather felt as though everyone in the world was successful in anything they attemped. Look at Kate. Missed out on Vet college and here she was with a place ready and waiting. Dan, *Dan*, damn and blast him, gets his wife back, plus a baby, and not only that but Colin, stick-in-the-mud–wife–battered Colin finds himself about to become a father. What had he got? A house and a ferret. Much as he loved Harry Ferret he had gone lower down in his priorities than Rhodri had ever imagined possible. As for Old Man Jones . . . if he died tomorrow, he Rhodri Hughes, would be more than capable of dancing on his grave. As he finished completing Goliath Costello's record, Rhodri decided that action had to be taken. He'd work out a plan and ring first thing tomorrow. She wouldn't be able to refuse.

Chapter 8

Rhodri rang Megan when he knew she'd be having breakfast in that vast farmhouse kitchen of hers. She answered after the second ring, her voice weary and resigned.

'Beulah Bank Farm.'

Eager to tell her his plans and full of love for her he said brightly, 'It's me, my darling. Good morning.'

'It's you. I'm so tired. I've had a terrible time with Da. Up and down all night.'

'I'm so sorry, sweetheart, so sorry.'

'It does no good to answer him back, you know. I've learned that over the years.'

'I'm sorry.'

'I think it best if we don't see each other, for a week or two, till it all blows over.'

Rhodri met this reply with complete silence, unable to believe what he'd heard.

'Are you still there, Rhodri?'

'Yes.'

'It's for the best.' He heard a break in her voice as she spoke. 'I'm sorry, Rhodri, but I can't take any more.'

'But I was just going to say that—'

'No, my love . . . we'll just play it cool for a while. OK?'

'Cool? For how long?'

'As long as it takes.'

'Please, Megan, you need—'

'I need time for Da. That's all. Just for a while.'

But there was a finality in her voice that angered Rhodri. 'You're not meaning to throw away everything we have, are you?'

Megan hesitated. 'No.'

'I love you. You love me.'

'We can't have everything in this life. I'm going to put down the phone, that's Da calling.'

'He can wait a moment. Look! I've got a plan—'

''Bye, Rhodri.'

He knew from the tone of her voice that she was starting to cry. Damn that bloody old man. How dare he ruin Megan's life because he wanted to be looked after. How dare he? What human being had the right? Mr Jones apparently. Rhodri was burning up inside with love for Megan. He wanted so desperately to give her a life but after all his resolutions of the night before about taking action, *fait accompli* and all that, he was exactly where he was, and always would be, for the rest of his life.

Rhodri recalled Mr Jones trying to strike him. He'd only missed because his own reactions had been sharpened by learning to move quick sharp when he was treating animals who didn't take kindly to even the slightest degree of interference. A bitterness formed in Rhodri's soul, a hard core of bitterness and what was worse, anger at Megan. How could she reject him? He thought about that night they'd made love. The supreme joy he'd felt bounding through him as they'd laid in each other's arms afterwards. She'd reached his innermost soul that night.

Didn't it mean anything to her now? Who was it who had made loving a sin?

That triumphant old man.

Rhodri arrived at the Practice that morning nothing like the person who, only a few short days ago, had been so full of happiness and with a spring in his step. He felt desolate and even considered giving in his notice. Small animal practices were always looking for staff. He'd have no problem getting another job. No, he would not. He opened his consulting room door and called out the name of his first client.

Kate called out, 'They've not arrived yet, Rhodri. You can relax.'

Rhodri nodded and went back into his room thinking he'd open his post while he waited. But Kate came in. 'In fact the first two of your appointments are going to be late.'

On the spur of the moment Rhodri said, 'Doing anything imperative at lunchtime?'

'Not specially.'

'Come out for lunch with me?'

'OK. That will be nice. Thanks. Where shall we go?'

'Not much time, can't get as far as the precinct, so shall we say the new snack bar down the road? Food's good I'm told.'

'That's lovely. See you at one in reception. Fingers crossed I don't get held up.'

Kate told Joy about her lunch invitation and Joy said, 'Good idea. That's nice of you. He does seem down in the dumps, it'll do him good.'

'I think it's Megan. Her father still won't agree to them getting married.'

'Frightened I expect.'

Kate looked at Joy and asked her what he had to be frightened about.

'See it from his point of view. Megan marries, they want a home of their own, children perhaps, who looks after him I ask?'

'Ah! Yes, of course. I see what you mean.'

But Kate got a different view of Mr Jones when she talked to Rhodri over lunch.

Kate sat back in amazement. 'Hit you? Whatever for?'

'Because I stood up to him and told him there was nothing on earth to stop Megan and me getting married except him. I told him good and proper how selfish he was.' Rhodri peered glumly into his vegetable broth as though searching for something reprehensible in it. He tore another lump of bread from his roll, smeared a small splodge of butter on it and devoured it as though it were his last bite.

He briefly related the events of that terrible evening and Kate, realising his desperation, said as kindly as she could, 'My advice is to let it cool off for a few days like she said. It must be exhausting getting up time and again during the night, she's bound to feel defeated this morning. See it from her point of view. She can't walk out on him, can she? Be honest.'

Rhodri envisaged those gnarled hands of his, with their stiff knobbly joints and twisted fingers, struggling to prepare a meal and in that gentle, sentimental, Welsh heart of his he had to admit, Kate was right.

'Well, then. You've to win him over, haven't you? Megan you've already got in the palm of your hand, but him ... you've really gone and done it as far as he's concerned.'

Rhodri looked up to find himself staring straight at Dan's back. 'Oh blast! Not him. Don't look round.'

'Who is it?'

'Wonder boy Dan.'

Kate whispered, 'Rhodri! We can't pretend we don't know he's here, in a place this size.'

She glanced over her shoulder, caught Dan's eye and beckoned to him, patting the table invitingly and smiling at him. He came across with his tray and noticed they'd all chosen the same thing from the menu. 'Great minds think alike! Is it good, then?'

Kate nodded. 'It is. Very nice. Best thing on the menu.'

'That's what I thought. Do you mind if I join you, Rhodri?'

Rhodri looked up, 'There's nowhere else at this time of day. Sit down.' He felt cheated; Kate was a good listener and he'd just got into his stride, and now the opportunity was lost.

Dan began on his soup. Kate continued with hers. Rhodri watched Dan spooning in the soup as fast as he could. 'Hungry then, are you?'

'Been up at Tad Porter's, it might be summer but by heck was it cold. And windy. Rain spitting in the wind, you know. They'd even had a slight frost last night. It puts an edge on one's appetite, believe me. ''Spect it must be the same at Beulah Bank Farm, isn't it, Rhodri?'

Rhodri didn't reply. So Kate said, 'In more ways than one!' Meaning the atmosphere *in* the house as well as out. Rhodri gave her a warning glance, which Dan intercepted. 'You're not flavour of the month then with Old Man Jones?'

Still Rhodri didn't reply. Kate said, 'You could say so.'

'I was up there the other day, he's a sick man.'

Rhodri grunted. 'Less sick than he makes out.'

'Come on, Rhod, he *is* a sick man, only a fool would say he wasn't.'

Rhodri rose to his feet, his face like thunder, 'I know what I'm talking about. He puts it on to keep Megan chained to his side. When he chooses he can get out of his chair just like that,' Rhodri snapped his fingers, 'but he insists that Megan or I, when I'm there, help him up. He's a malevolent, embittered old fraud.' Rhodri picked up his mug of coffee, downed the whole lot and stormed out.

Dan half rose from his chair but changed his mind. 'I've stepped on his toes and not half. Sorry. Didn't know things were so bad.'

'He stood up to him the other night and they had a frightful row.'

'That's not the way to go about it.'

'It's difficult when you're in love like he is. What riles Rhodri is that her father orders Megan about as though she were his slave. I feel sorry for her.'

'Mmm. I'm up there on Thursday for routine TB testing. Perhaps I'll see what I can do.'

'For heaven's sake, don't make things any worse. He worships Megan.'

Dan thought for a while. 'It is a problem, isn't it? Three people locked in without a solution. But I don't like to see people, especially thoroughly good people, letting the years pass by when they could be so much happier than they are.'

'You do rub him up the wrong way.'

Dan turned to look at her. 'What have I said just now that could possibly have annoyed him?' He raised his eyebrows to emphasise his point.

'Pointing out how sick Mr Jones is. Crikey! Look at the

time. Joy will be giving me the sack.' She began putting on her cardigan.

'I doubt it. Finish your coffee and we'll saunter in together. I'll make your excuses.'

'What makes you think you can win Joy over about anything? She's really annoyed with you about going to Bridge Farm, when she said you shouldn't.'

They did, however, saunter back to the Practice and wandered in without any trouble because Joy was in Mungo's office talking about Rhodri.

'Joy! I heard him being quite abrupt with a client yesterday. It won't do. They don't come here to be chastised.'

'Sometimes they blinking well need it.'

'They may do. Heaven alone knows I've had a few of those myself over the years, but from their point of view they are willing to pay for advice and treatment, but not, and I repeat, *not*, to be told off.'

'What do we do then? Bop Old Man Jones over the head and get an immediate solution?'

Mungo grinned. 'Well, if it has to be done I'll gladly—'

'Seriously, Mungo.'

'I don't know. We've all had ups and downs in our private lives, but it shouldn't be allowed to interfere with one's professional life.'

Joy got to her feet. 'I agree. I'll have a word.' As she came out of Mungo's office she caught sight of Dan talking to Kate. She pointedly looked at her watch and said, 'Could you be gracious enough, Dan, to get back to work or is that asking too much?'

'On my way, Joy, on my way.' Dan gave her a cheerful wave and headed for the car park.

To Kate she said, 'You set off with Rhodri and came back with Dan?'

'Rhodri lost his temper with us and walked out.'

'I see. Right. That's it.' Joy marched off towards Rhodri's consulting room, the light of battle in her eye. But he wasn't there. Eventually she found him sitting in his car. She opened the front passenger door and got in. She seemed to be doing a lot of counselling just recently sitting in cars.

'This won't do.'

Rhodri glanced at her and gave her such a fright; he looked as though he was in hell. Joy cleared her throat while she decided what to say next. After a moment's pause she said softly, 'No problem is unsolvable, you know. There must be an answer somewhere.'

'Tell me. If I stand up to him, he has an attack and makes Megan ill with worry and attending to him. If, in his eyes I behave myself, then he claims a victory. He'd treat a dog better than he treats me.'

'He's frightened.'

Wryly Rhodri answered, 'Is he? I don't think so.'

'Oh he is! Frightened of losing his place in the world and sinking into a kind of wheelchair mentality. Are you not going up there at the moment?'

Rhodri shook his head. 'No. Megan asked me not to.'

'I think, despite your better judgement, you'd better grovel. Really grovel to him, just to get yourself back in his good books, so you can at least see Megan.'

'Mmm.'

'You see, Mungo heard you being a bit brutal with a client the other day and as he rightly says they don't pay to get told off. It's not like you, Rhodri. What were his exact words? Oh yes. You mustn't let your private life interfere with your professional one.'

'Right.'

'Which you are doing now. Sitting here brooding, when you should be in your consulting room ready for the off.' Joy patted his leg. 'Now come on. Inside. Please. With a smile on your face. You love your job really, you know.'

Rhodri made to get out, changed his mind and then changed it again, and finally stood out on the tarmac. He waited until Joy had got out, then locked up the car and marched towards the back door. Joy caught up with him and as she drew level he said, 'Have you ever been hopelessly . . . in love with someone and can't see a way out?'

'Oh yes. It's very painful.'

Rhodri looked at her and said, 'Of course, I'd forgotten. Sorry.' He pushed open the back door and let her through first. Her cheeks burned with embarrassment because it was the first time ever she'd had confirmation that the staff knew about her love for Mungo. How humiliating! It was enough to destroy her love for him instantly. The pain in her chest that had come when she'd realised Duncan had gone serious walkabout grew worse by the day. Mungo had never spoken a truer word than when he'd mentioned the ups and downs of one's private life. Well, so far so good, she hadn't let it slip that Duncan was missing, so she wasn't letting it affect *her* professional life. She went to her office, leaving the door open so she could hear Rhodri calling the name of his first patient. Ah! There it was. 'Paddy Tattersall.' New client, thought Joy. Thumping great dog, thought Rhodri.

Paddy was a gigantic Irish wolfhound. A vast, grizzled,

grey creature with the softest, kindest, most appealing eyes any dog could hope to have. Rhodri didn't think he'd ever seen such a huge dog. In fact he would be better described as a pony. He was so tall he could rest his chin on the examination table and when he wagged his tail the papers on the desk were swept to the floor. His diminutive owner said firmly, 'Paddy! Sit!' So Paddy sat. 'Open your mouth!' So Paddy did. 'Bad tooth, I think. Look, down there. At the back, this side.' Mr Tattersall poked a finger down inside the cavern which was Paddy's mouth. 'Broke a piece off chewing on a stone a while back and sure there he is with a bad tooth.'

Rhodri peered inside and saw how bad the tooth was. He even put his own finger down inside. The centre of the very back tooth was rotting away and the outer edges were beginning to crumble. 'He seems very relaxed.'

'Oh he is! Not a bad thought in him. No indeed. Not a bad thought.'

'How old is he?'

'About four. I think.'

'Beautiful dog. Nice nature.'

'Can you pull it out?'

'Well, not this minute, he'll need an anaesthetic.'

'No. Just give him something in his gum to numb it as if he were a person, like at the dentist, and he'll let you do it.'

Appalled by the prospect, Rhodri considered for a moment and then shook his head. 'No way. Unnecessary suffering and all that. It's too big a risk. What if the tooth breaks up when I start pulling, which it well might seeing the condition it's in. I might hurt him. No, I'm sorry, he'll have to be put out. There's no way I can tackle it without . . .'

'And I'm telling you he'll be OK. Soft as butter he is. Soft as butter.'

Rhodri pretended to be assessing the pros and cons of doing as suggested, but had already made up his mind. 'No, it's too big a risk. Can you bring him in tomorrow afternoon, one thirty?'

The diminutive owner looked disappointed. 'Very well, then. One thirty it is.'

'You're not any relation of Callum Tattersall, are you?'

'I'm a cousin. Declan Tattersall. That's me. I've inherited the farm. They've let me live in it till the papers are all sorted. Then it's legally mine. Wonderful for all the children, living there. So much space.'

'How many have you got, then?'

'Six, ah! No. Seven. That's right, seven. We've certainly livened up the old place.'

'I can imagine. I saw Callum a time or two with his dogs, great chap, so sad about him and his wife, lovely lady. She'd have been thrilled to bits to have your children running about the farm.' Both Declan and Rhodri were silent for a moment while they both thought of Nuala's joy, and then Rhodri said, 'Right then, one thirty tomorrow. He'll be ready to take home by about half past four.'

Paddy rose to his feet and filled all the available space between the door and the examination table. His tail wagged cheerfully and whisked Rhodri's pen and calculator from his desk, then he ambled out with Declan who, Rhodri swore, could have ridden on his back, and his feet would have been dangling.

When Paddy came back the following afternoon Sarah One and Sarah Two had prepared an operating room by moving the table over to one side and leaving a wide floor space for Paddy to lie down on, and laying the operation cloths on the floor instead of the operating table. Declan insisted on coming into the operating room with him and instructed Paddy to lie down. 'Roll over, Paddy.' So Paddy rolled over onto his side. He lifted his head for a moment to give Declan a baleful glance as though saying to him, 'Now what have you let me in for?' and then laid it down again and closed his eyes. 'There we are! Ready and waiting. I swear he could speak if he could.'

'I'm sure you're right,' Sarah One said, trying to get her mind round how they would move him to get on with the next operation, after the tooth had been pulled out.

Declan surreptitiously drew a handkerchief from his pocket and wiped his eyes. 'I'll be back. Four you said.'

'About four, half past might be better.' Sarah One opened the door for him and Declan crept from the operating room mopping his tears as he went. 'He's a close friend you understand.'

'Of course. He's a lovely dog. So gentle.'

But Declan, overcome with emotion, was unable to agree and simply nodded his head.

Later that afternoon those waiting in reception for their appointments thought they'd been invaded by an entire children's home. The main door flew open and a hoard of children ran in followed by a man no bigger than the oldest boy. Bubbling with excitement they went to the desk and proclaimed in varying degrees of lucidity that they'd come to collect Paddy and was he all right and could they take the tooth home like they did when they went to the dentist?

Declan was carrying the smallest girl, who was shriek-ing, 'Paddy' at the top of her voice. So when they stayed still long enough to be counted, the clients found there were five girls and two boys. All clean as new pins and well dressed.

'My God!' said one client. 'Thank heavens they're not all mine.'

The man sitting next to her said, 'Same 'ere. Who'd want that lot?'

Joy said, 'I'll go make sure Paddy's ready. We've taken the tooth out and—'

'Have you saved it? We want to take it home.' This from a tiny girl who didn't look old enough to speak.

Joy peeped over the desk at her and said, 'We've saved it in a special box.'

'Ohhhhh! Lovely. Can I go to get Paddy?'

Before Joy could reply the whole tribe of children followed by Declan had invaded the rear premises. Joy hurried after them but was too late as they were opening each door as they came to it calling, 'Paddy! Paddy!' as they went.

Rhodri came into the corridor and shouted, as though addressing a ship's crew in a hurricane, 'Quiet!' They stopped instantly, much to Rhodri's surprise. 'Paddy hasn't come round properly from the anaesthetic, so you need to be quiet and gentle. Can you do that?' He put his finger to his lips and said, 'Shhh. On tiptoe.'

They squeezed into the operating room and gathered round Paddy. He struggled to his feet and tried to wag his tail, but it would only wag in fits and starts and his legs clearly weren't his own. Declan's elder son took hold of his leash and, very softly, they all tiptoed out and then crept down the corridor with Paddy, who was trying desperately to keep on his feet on the slippery floor.

Declan took a fistful of notes from his back pocket, laid them on the reception counter and said, 'Take what you need.'

Kate counted out what was needed to pay the bill and handed the rest back to him. They all left one after the other with Declan leaving last. 'Your receipt. I haven't given you your . . .' But Kate was too late, they'd all flooded out into the car park. 'I'll post it,' she shouted.

'I'll say this for them, they're well behaved,' said a client holding a glass tank with a particularly evil-looking snake in it, which was writhing about.

'There's some could learn a lesson from them,' said another client, looking daggers at a small boy who would keep poking his fingers into the hamster cage she was holding.

Rhodri relived his moment of triumph when he'd asked the children to be quiet for Paddy's sake. Such moments added satisfaction to his job. Yes, he had to admit he loved it, and tonight he was going to grovel to Mr Jones like he'd never done before to anyone. A performance to rank with Richard Burton, or possibly Anthony Hopkins. He would rehearse his speech on the way there.

Rhodri drove to Beulah Bank Farm that same evening as he'd promised himself he would. He didn't ring first, because that would have given Megan the opportunity to tell him not to come, but he had popped into the precinct and bought a big box of Mr Jones's favourite chocolates. They were handmade Belgian, totally gorgeous, and utterly too expensive for words. For Megan he had a bottle of perfume, which after much sniffing and discussion he'd bought because he thought it suited her personality and in any case he loved the smell of it and fancied Megan smelling of it.

As he crossed the humpbacked bridge, he remembered Megan telling him that, when she knew he was coming, she watched from the kitchen window to see him crossing it and then counted to thirty-five. He felt sad she wouldn't be doing that tonight.

He arrived in the farmyard as quietly as possible, wishing to keep his presence secret. There was no Megan to greet him, and suddenly, though he knew she didn't know he was coming so there was no reason to feel disappointed, an ominous feeling spread over him and he decided it was one of the worst ideas he'd ever had. But he was there and he was going through with it.

He decided to knock and open the door, and called out, 'Megan! It's me, Rhodri!' His joyful greeting was met with complete silence. He laid his gifts on the kitchen table and went into the hall. He opened the sitting room door and put his head round. Mr Jones was sitting in his usual chair, reading. 'Hello, Mr Jones. Hope you don't mind me coming in like this. I called out but there was no answer.'

Mr Jones looked over the top of his reading glasses at him and said, 'Surprised you've the gall to come again after what you said the last time you were here.' He closed his book and took his glasses off, placing them on his table amongst his sick man's clutter.

Rhodri went further into the room and stood before Mr Jones, hands behind his back, contrite. 'That's what I've come about. To apologise. I had no right, no right whatsoever to speak to you as I did. Under no circumstances should I have allowed myself to behave in that manner and I would be grateful if you would accept my apologies for behaving in such an unseemly and totally disgraceful way. Quite inexcusable.' Too late he remembered the chocolates but immediately decided that maybe to hand them over straight away would be too gushing for words. Rhodri waited for a reply.

Old Man Jones studied him from under his eyebrows, his eyes unfathomable. 'Apology accepted, but it makes no difference to the marriage question. Megan is not marrying you. Not while I'm alive.'

'I can understand that. You being in need of care. I can see why.' He took a deep breath. 'But we must be allowed to go on seeing each other.'

'I don't think so. There's no point.'

It was on the tip of Rhodri's tongue to question that last statement but just in time he changed it to: 'Is Megan out this evening?'

'She's asleep in bed. Tired out.'

'I see. I've been into the precinct and bought you a box of those chocolates you like. I'll go get them. Part of my apology, you know.'

He returned to the kitchen and picked up the chocolates and crossed the hall to give them to Mr Jones. 'Thank you, Rhodri. I'll open them now and you can have one with me.' But the intricate ribbon bows, tied time and again to seal the box, defeated his gnarled hands and he had to humiliate himself by handing the box back to Rhodri and asking him to open it.

'You choose first.'

Rhodri chose a liqueur, and held the box while Mr

Jones picked one for himself. 'Marzipan, I'll have that one.'

They were silent for a moment while they each enjoyed the delicious flavours of their chocolates. Then Mr Jones beckoned him to hand back the box, pushed the lid back on and said, 'Makes no difference you know, these.' He pointed to the box. 'No difference at all. Megan's needed here, for the farm and for me. I'm her da and she owes me.'

Rhodri agreed. 'You need her, I know.'

'You've got the message then?'

'I've got the message all right.'

'Good. Well, you might as well go, there's no point in wasting my time with useless chit-chat.' He put his reading glasses back on and picked up his book. Removing his bookmark he began to read.

Rhodri stood fidgeting like a small schoolboy in the headmaster's room. The self-centred, miserable, mean old codger. Then he saw the twisted fingers clumsily trying to turn a page, and he wondered how he would feel if he were as handicapped as this old man.

'Goodnight, Mr Jones. I've a present for Megan. I've left it on the kitchen table.'

'Very well. Goodnight.'

Rhodri got into his car and started up the engine. He didn't move off, but sat full of gloom at the disappointing outcome of his evening. Then he thought he heard Megan's voice. He looked out and there she was waving to him from an upstairs window.

He got out and went to stand below her window. 'Megan!' All the passion he felt for her welled up inside him. She might have just woken up, but she looked so beautiful. Almost ethereal.

'Rhodri! I'm coming down.'

The house door opened and there she was crumpled, but comely. She ran into his arms and held him tight to her. 'I'm so sorry I said don't see me, but I was so tired, and so worried. I'm so glad you didn't take any notice of me. Kiss. Kiss.'

After he'd complied with her command he said, 'I've told your da I realise we can't marry. Just to put his mind at rest, you know.'

Megan almost fell from his arms with horror. 'But . . . don't you want to?'

'Of course, but we've got to be subtle about it. Careful, come up with a plan.'

'But you said you had a plan?'

'It was a stupid one. I was thinking of us pretending to go for a walk and coming back married, not much good as a basis for a happy marriage. We'd never forgive ourselves.'

Her eyes began to fill with tears.

'Not tears, Megan, please. I'll come up with something. For the moment he thinks he's won, so at least his mind is at rest. I've left you a present on the kitchen table. Goodnight, love.'

Rhodri held her face between his hands and kissed her lips, not with his usual hungry passion, but gently and with respect. 'Goodnight. Sorry you're so tired.'

When he got home the phone was ringing. It was Megan, to thank him for the perfume and to say she'd be round for a meal tomorrow night wearing bucketfuls of it.

Chapter 9

Dan climbed the steep hills to Beulah Bank Farm later that same week. Over the stone humpbacked bridge, then through the trees and finally out into the farmyard. Megan was waiting for him at the kitchen door. 'Hello, Dan! Come in the house first, we've got delayed this morning and Gab has just gone to sort the cows out for you.'

'OK.' As he walked into the kitchen he said, 'I didn't realise Gab Bridges worked for you.'

'Just this last week or two. The other man did a moonlight flit, no warning no nothing, so Gab came to give us a hand for a while but I think it might be permanent. There's not enough work or money for six sons on one farm.'

'I see. How many head have you?'

'Twenty, that's all, not enough pasture for more, you understand.'

'That's a lot of work for you.'

'Not really, we manage. Go in, see Da for a while, he misses company.'

Dan thought about what Rhodri had said about Mr Jones being a malevolent, embittered, old fraud. Better approach with caution, he thought.

As he half-expected, Dan was greeted with a terse question. 'You up to this TB testing job?'

'And good morning to you, Mr Jones. To answer your

question, yes I am. All in a day's work to me, and at least the rain's held off. How are you this morning?'

Mr Jones paused while he contemplated whether or not Dan's brisk manner constituted impertinence but he didn't get a chance to retort because Dan went on.

'It's a long climb up here but well worth it when you get here. Wonderful spot to live.' Dan crossed the room to look out of the window. He could see right down into the valley and just, but only just, see the nearest roofs of houses in Barleybridge.

'Not if you can't get out.'

Dan turned back from the window and asked, 'What stops you?'

Mr Jones snorted his anger. 'Are you blind? Can't you see I'm handicapped?'

'Of course, but why should it stop you going out? Megan drives.'

'And make an exhibition of myself? I'm not one to like putting on a spectacle for everyone's amusement.'

'I doubt if they'd even notice you.' He went to sit down. 'I remember once going to the amusement parks in Florida with my wife and seeing "the handicapped" as you call yourself, going on the rides. They didn't care two hoots about being manhandled on, they were too busy having a wonderful time. Some of them in far worse nick than you. Just needs a bit of courage, and I'm sure you're not short of that.'

Megan came in to sit with them. 'Dan, I've been meaning to say, we'd love your Rose to come to see us one day. Would she, do you think, and bring the baby? Come for tea?'

'I'm sure she would. She'd love it. If it's not too much for you, Mr Jones . . . you being handicapped.'

Mr Jones, used to more deferential treatment, snorted with anger for a second time that day. 'So long as the baby doesn't grizzle all the time. What is it?'

Megan answered. 'A boy, Da.'

'Lucky man. You need two or three more the same.' He looked at Megan and she flushed.

They heard the back door open and a voice bellow, 'OK Meggie, my love, we're all set.' It was Gab.

Dan got to his feet. 'I'll get my boots and then we'll start. Lovely day for it, out of the wind.' He winked at Megan and went outside.

Gab had organised the run and the crush, set the farm lad to getting the first cow into it, and was marking off the list. 'Number!'

'One two five.'

Dan had his syringes ready and took the blood. He heard something of a commotion, but he was concentrating hard and ignored it. When he took a breather for a second he saw that Megan had brought her da out to watch and he was seated booted, behatted and blanketed on a chair, out of the wind. Dan smiled to himself. There was more than one way of skinning a cat, he thought.

When they'd finished, Megan wanted him to stay for coffee but Dan declined. 'No thanks, Megan. I've got a busy day ahead. Must press on. I'll tell Rose about the tea invite. Thanks for it, she loves getting out to meet people.'

'Good. We'll look forward to that, won't we, Da?' But her da was getting ready for the journey back to his own chair and he ignored her.

Dan asked Mr Jones if he'd done it right?

Mr Jones proffered a grudging compliment. 'For a young strip of a lad you didn't do badly. I'll give you that. Come along, Megan, get a move on.' He flung off the blanket and grasped Megan's arm to help him rise to his feet. Dan took his other arm and between them they got him into the house. Mr Jones thanked him for his help.

'A pleasure. Any time. Good morning, Mr Jones.'

Seated back in his chair, Megan's father said, 'Arrogant beggar, he is. But he does a good job, I'll say that for him.'

'He's well respected in Barleybridge is Dan. He's an excellent vet. Even your arch enemy Lord Askew approves of him.'

'Does he? Wouldn't call that a recommendation coming from him. The fat, thieving, manipulative . . . Where's the blanket for my legs?'

'I'm just putting it on, see?' She draped the blanket over his knees in the way, from long experience, she knew he liked the best.

'I need a hot drink, Megan.'

'I'll put the kettle on, but first I need a word with Gab.'

'You're a good girl to me. Don't think I don't appreciate you because I do. I've a fancy for . . . Never mind, it'll all be too much for me.'

'What will, Da?'

'Nothing.'

'You know how I hate half sentences. Just tell me.'

He pressed his lips into a straight determined line and then relented. 'That wheelchair you got and I refused to use.'

'Yes.'

He shook his head. 'No, never mind.'

'Are you wanting me to get it out?'

Belligerently he replied, 'No. No. Even if you do, I shan't sit in it.'

'I see. Won't be long.' Nevertheless, later that morning, she got the wheelchair out from under the stairs and gave it a dust and left it out in the passage to the back door. When she was in the kitchen preparing lunch for Gab and her father she heard him closing the downstairs bathroom door and knew by the noise his slippers were making that he hadn't gone straight back into the sitting room. Putting her eye to the crack of the door she saw him inspecting the wheelchair. She heard him tut-tutting and complaining. 'Pretty pass things have come to. Huh!' Megan realised he was coming into the kitchen, so she went back to washing the lettuce for the sandwiches.

Her da stood propped against the door frame catching his breath. 'I'll eat in here with Gab. Make a change.'

'Right.'

Gab came in at the stroke of twelve, washed his hands at the sink and took his place at the table. A huge hulk of a man, the twin by twenty minutes of Gideon and the oldest of the Bridges's brood, he had his mother's light blue eyes, and the sandy hair and the long, thin, hook nose of his father.

'Thank you, Meggie, my love.'

Her da grunted disapproval of 'Meggie' but had the sense to say nothing, for without this man to help on the farm they'd be in deep trouble. Good farm hands were rare nowadays, so he made an effort to begin a conversation, but Gab would have none of it. He ate every sandwich on his plate and then began eyeing Mr Jones's plate so ravenously that he felt compelled to offer him one of his. 'Here we are Gabriel, *Megan*'s made too many for me.'

Gab devoured that and then began on the fruit cake. When he'd eaten two big slices of that he moved on to the bowl of fresh fruit. He then poured himself two successive half pints of cider from the big jug Megan had put out, drinking them without a pause, then he stood up, said, 'Thanks, Meggie, my love.'

As he left the kitchen, he turned back to look at Megan and Mr Jones caught the look Gab gave her; an alarming mixture of love overlaid with deeply felt lust, which shocked him. Megan, busy peeling a peach, didn't notice, but when she realised Gab hadn't gone she looked up to see if he needed a word about something and blushed to the roots of her hair when she read what was in his face. He'd undressed her, in his mind, but not like Rhodri did with love and tenderness. This was something quite different. He'd *stripped* her. Mentally she re-dressed herself, prayed her father hadn't noticed, and concentrated hard on removing the stone from her peach. Gab abruptly turned towards the door, opened it and was gone. Megan's da said, 'I'm . . . going . . . for a lie . . . down.' Placing both hands on the table he heaved himself to his feet.

Megan said, 'I'll get your inhaler, you sound as though you need it.'

Mr Jones nodded. Damn the man for looking at Megan like that. How dare he? As she came towards him carrying his inhaler he looked at her with new eyes, and saw for the first time in his life just how attractive she really was, the red hair, those large tender eyes, the proud carriage of her head, the slender, expressive hands: she was attractive, so very attractive, no wonder Gab had looked at her like that. He could see why now. His daughter! The subject of such . . . lewdness. He'd have to watch him. Better still he'd advertise for a man, and get rid of him that way.

But it was easier said than done. The current downturn in farming had meant that young men were seeking work in the towns and leaving farming far behind them. So they were stuck with Gab, until times changed. Megan's da had seen the other Bridges boys when they'd all been going in to Weymouth together one Saturday night and had called to pick up Gab. They'd filled the kitchen and, to a man, they'd plainly showed their appreciation of Megan. There wasn't one of them who could be trusted one iota more than Gab, so he couldn't even swap one of them for him.

Rose called for tea one afternoon as Dan had promised. 'Are you sure, Megan, that Jonathan won't be too much for your father?' she'd enquired on the phone one day that week.

'Absolutely certain. Please come, Rose, we do want you to. Winter's coming on and we feel the need for company. That sounds as if I'm being rude to you, but it's true we do. I've got a present for the baby and I'd love to give it to him myself. So, yes, we'll see you Tuesday.'

Rose instinctively knew how desperate Megan must be feeling, with an invalid father and a lover she longed to be with. Not much of a recipe for happiness. No, sir!

When she got there she found Mr Jones ensconced in his chair looking grumpy and outfaced by her coming. But she was determined he wasn't going to find her lacking in respect and affection.

Rose shook his hand and keeping hold of it, impulsively bent forward to kiss his cheek. Despite himself, he enjoyed her vital femininity and her open friendliness. 'Hi, Mr Jones! What a pleasure, I've heard all about you from Danny.'

'Have you indeed? Not much to the good, I expect.'

'Indeed, it was. He said you'd been out to watch him TB testing and that you'd approved of him.'

'I did, but he's an arrogant beggar. I can see it won't bother you though, you're tough enough and shrewd enough to be able to cope with him, aren't you? So where's this baby of yours?'

'I've left him in the kitchen, I didn't know if . . .'

'Bring him in. I want to see him. We never get babies visiting us. Go on, girl, bring him in.'

So Rose went back to the kitchen, picked up Jonathan's travelling seat and carried him in. He was looking particularly like Danny today and she loved him for it. She held the seat so that Mr Jones could see him without having to get up. As he looked at him Jonathan opened his eyes and stared straight at Mr Jones. Two little hands waved haphazardly about, he yawned and then pulled a face as though he was concentrating very hard on something that was worrying him.

'Why, there's no mistaking who he belongs to. My word I've never seen a little chap looking so much like his father. Just look at that expression, see? Just like Dan, that is. Isn't he a grand baby? Megan! Where's the present?'

'Coming!' Megan came in from the kitchen carrying a teapot in one hand and a parcel in the other. 'Here it is! It's more fun for adults at the moment but he'll grow into it.'

With Jonathan on her knee, Rose opened the parcel and out came a fluffy white toy sheep. 'Oh look, my darling, look what Megan's bought you!'

'Turn her over and look at her tum,' Megan said.

There was a long slit down the length of the sheep's stomach and, when Rose put her fingers inside, she could feel something in there. When she pulled at it out came a small fluffy black lamb. Then another one all white this time and then another white with a black face. She gave a delighted cry of surprise each time one appeared. 'Oh, Megan! Where did you find this?'

'In the posh toy shop in Barleybridge. I couldn't resist. I almost bought one for myself.'

Rose pushed the three lambs back in again and pulled them out one after the other. 'I could do this all afternoon! It's absolutely splendid and thank you very much indeed. Very appropriate for a vet's son.' Clutching the sheep and Jonathan, Rose stood up and kissed Megan and then kissed Mr Jones again. 'Thank you very much. Isn't it lovely? I'm so pleased with it. He'll love it when he's bigger, and can do it by himself.'

Unexpectedly Mr Jones said, 'If I'm careful I could hold the baby, couldn't I?'

Without hesitation Rose placed Jonathan in his arms. Megan went to the kitchen to bring in the rest of the tea things. Rose sat back in her chair and watched in silence. Mr Jones, in a world of his own, didn't speak a word. He simply sat looking at the baby in his arms as though he'd never seen a baby before. His crippled hands clumsily stroked Jonathan's cheeks, cuddled his little feet, which were fidgeting about, and tried to get him to hold tight to a finger. Then he cleared his throat and said huskily without looking up, 'You are lucky, my dear. He's perfect. Here, take him, before I drop him.'

Rose got up, took the baby from him, and looking down at him she said, 'Have you no grandchildren?'

'No. Nor likely to have. That fool of a son of mine hasn't the slightest interest in having a family at all. It's all glitz and glitter with him and he gets plenty of that in London. As for Megan, she can't marry when she has me to look after.'

Before Rose could answer Megan came back with a loaded tea tray. The business of pouring tea, handing out plates, cutting cake and consuming it took time, and Rose still hadn't found the right moment to put in a word for Megan and Rhodri to Mr Jones by the time Megan was clearing their tea things.

But she did notice that Mr Jones was beginning to tire.

'I think I'd better be making tracks. Any minute now this son of ours is going to be shrieking for his food. I wonder . . . Mr Jones . . . could you find the time to come to our house for a cup of tea one afternoon? Just for an hour, if Megan can spare a few hours?'

Megan stopped what she was doing and waited, fully expecting that her da would say no. But to her surprise he said the opposite. 'If you can be bothered with an old man, yes, I'd like to. Thank you.'

'Good! I'll ring next week and we'll plan a day. Lunch perhaps, too? Will that be all right with you, Megan?'

Before Megan answered Rose, they heard Gab calling. When he didn't get an immediate answer he came on into the sitting room in his stockinged feet. He loomed in the doorway. 'Sorry, didn't realise you had company, I just need some help with ordering some more feed, please, Meggie, my love. Don't know your supplier and we're nearing the end of what we've got. Must do it today. Afternoon, Mrs Brown. Nice to see you.'

Rose smiled at him. 'Hi! Gab. It's nice to meet you. Dan said you were helping out.'

Megan picked up the tray. 'Yes, you're right. I meant to order it last week and never got round to it.' She headed for the kitchen carrying the tray, and as she went to pass Gab, still standing in the doorway, he took the tray from her and gave her a long, hot, lustful look, which wasn't lost on Rose. Without moving her head she turned her eyes to see if Mr Jones had noticed and he had; he looked livid.

'I'll be off, then.' Rose gathered her things together, picked up Jonathan and said, 'I'll give you a ring, promise. I'm so glad you said you could come. Be seeing you, Mr Jones.' Rose went into the kitchen to thank Megan.

Gab was seated at the table with Megan beside him studying a file. 'I've come to say my goodbyes. I'll ring next week when I know what Dan's doing, and we'll make a date for lunch. Perhaps Saturday. Is it all right me asking? I didn't know how your father would feel.'

Megan looked up from studying the file. 'It's fine, no one's more surprised than me that he wants to go out. Thank you very much.' She gave Rose a smile of thanks, and it was still on her face as she pointed something out to Gab who wasn't looking but was occupied with admiring Megan's hair. Again Rose caught sight of the desire in Gab's eyes and wondered if Megan recognised it for what it was.

''Bye, Rose, thank you for coming. 'Bye, Jonathan.'

''Bye, Megan. Thank you for asking me. The tea was lovely. 'Bye, Gab.' She left the kitchen, went down the short passage and out into the farmyard to get into her car. A frisson of apprehension shot through Rose, which she tried hard to shake off, but couldn't. She'd seen desire in men's eyes herself many times, but never with the hint of threat which she recognised in Gab's look. Megan was a stunner. Who would have guessed there was such sweet beauty hidden away in that remote farmhouse? No wonder Rhodri had fallen for her. No wonder at all. But Gab!

From the depths of his chair, after Rose had gone, Mr Jones watched Megan dusting crumbs from the table she'd used for serving the tea. 'Isn't that Rose a lovely girl? So kind to want to be bothered with a crippled old man. It will make a change. Yes, a very pleasant change. Fresh she is, New World fresh. That Dan's a lucky man. Don't know how he's managed to get her. He wasn't exactly at the front of the queue when good looks were given out.'

'Not many people are.'

Megan's da didn't tell her how he'd realised what a beauty she was, didn't want to rock the boat. He was damned if she upped and left. Damned to a procession of 'helpers' or else a nursing home and he wasn't having that. No, she'd just have to wait.

Dan shifted Jonathan round so he could see his face. 'Darling, I certainly won't tell Rhodri. He's far too wound up about the situation. If he finds out, he'll probably murder Gab. What a mess! What with Megan's biological clock ticking away and Rhodri fit to die for her and Gab obviously fancying her like crazy, things could be hotting up.'

'Mr Jones knows it too. He was livid.'

Dan looked up at her and asked if Mr Jones was willing to come for lunch or had he to be coerced?

'Willing. Very willing. I was amazed.'

'So am I.'

'He's an old sweetie really, just in so much pain and so resentful of not being able to do what he wants, which is farming, he can't help but let it spill out into every corner. He treats Megan like a servant, but what alternative has either of them?'

'Not much. I bet you're the first person to say he's such a sweetie.'

'You should have seen him with your son. Watch out, he's being sick!' By the time they'd cleaned him up and Dan had changed his trousers and Rose had given the baby her favourite recipe for wind, and then they'd got him to sleep, the evening was almost over and they gave no further thought to Old Man Jones, except for Rose to say that she was going to solve their problems.

'Rose! You're not to interfere! Promise!'

Eyes wide with innocence, she agreed she wouldn't interfere, just help things along a little. Sitting up in bed during the night, feeding Jonathan while his father slept the sleep of the righteous, Rose thought how to bring it about. She could make a beginning by inviting Rhodri for lunch at the same time as Mr Jones and Megan. No, that would be too obvious. Or she could ask other people she knew and then the larger group would make it not quite as obvious. No, that would be too much for Mr Jones. All those people. No. What she'd do was encourage him to go out more and then he would have less time to brood and more time to see how the other half of the world lived. He needed cheering up. The whole balance of his life wanted rejigging. Brightening. Freshening up. Revitalising. And she was the person to see to it. Yes. Coming here for lunch would be a start. But as she put Jonathan back into his cradle, sated with milk and almost asleep, Rose remembered the glittering of Gab's eyes and the lust in them, and hoped Rhodri's and Gab's paths would not cross.

Chapter 10

It was, however, Rhodri's afternoon off the following day and he and Megan were taking the chance to shop in Barleybridge. He couldn't find her when he first arrived at the farm, but he did find Gab in the nearest field, mending a fence.

He was lifting a huge hammer with the greatest of ease and raining blows on a new fence post. Rhodri watched the rhythmic strokes of his powerful arms with admiration. Strength like his was amazing. 'Gab! Hi!' He guessed Gab would answer without the slightest shortness of breath.

The post as secure as he could make it, Gab rested the mighty hammer on the ground and turned to see who'd called his name.

'It's you. If it's Meggie you're wanting she's inside getting ready.' The light eyes appraised Rhodri. 'Business brisk?'

'Yes, thanks. And you?'

'Busy, you know, always something to do on a farm. Nice autumn though. Easy to get jobs done when the weather's good.' Gab eyed him again with a speculative look. 'Lucky for you Old Man Jones is having a good day. He cramps your style, doesn't he?'

'What do you mean?'

'Having that old git ordering you and her about. She never has a minute.'

'I know. He doesn't order me about.'

Gab leant on the post he'd just put in, his chin resting on his hands. 'He does. He tells you marriage isn't on the agenda.'

'Who told you that?'

'Obvious, isn't it? All he needs is a . . . *man* with a firm hand to tell him where to get off.'

Rhodri felt at an immediate disadvantage. 'Does he indeed? Well, thanks for the advice.'

Gab nodded his head towards the house. 'She's coming.'

Both men watched her walk across to them. Rhodri saw his beautiful lover walking towards him. Gab saw the swing of her hips, her slender ankles and her red hair blowing in the wind. To avoid getting her shoes dirty Megan didn't walk through the gate into the field but stood on top of a small stone wall alongside the gate and waved. Rhodri looked at Gab intending to say he'd be seeing him sometime, but the words stopped in his throat when he saw the lecherous look on Gab's face. A furious rage welled up in his chest. How dare Gab harbour thoughts like that about his Megan? She was his. Absolutely his and his alone.

He snapped out, 'You'd better get back to your fence mending, Gab,' and looked at the darkening sky, at the heavy grey clouds lumbering across from Beulah Bank Top. 'Looks like rain. Get on with it, man.' He waved cheerfully to Megan, his heart like a stone in his chest.

Gab's answer was, 'Get stuffed.' He waved to Megan himself and shouted, 'Meggie! Where's that lad? I need another pair of hands or I'll not get done before milking.'

On the wind came Megan's reply. 'OK.' She got down from the wall and went into one of the outbuildings from which the lad emerged in a second and hurried across the field to Gab.

Rhodri grimly strode towards Megan, focusing his eyes on her lovely welcoming smile knowing it was for him, and him alone. Childishly he made a show of kissing her so Gab could see she belonged to Rhodri Hughes. When they were in the car fastening their safety belts Rhodri said, 'You know Gab?'

'Of course.' She knew what he was going to say.

'Does he ever try it on?'

He noticed her slight hesitation but she said, 'No. Of course not.'

'He looks as if he might, but he'd better not.'

Megan turned to look at him full face. 'He won't. I shan't let him.'

'You've noticed his face then when he looks at you with those greedy eyes of his.'

'I have, but he won't.'

'Does your da know?'

'Of course not. He's not that perceptive.' She turned to look out of the car window. 'If we don't get off the afternoon will be gone and I shall be needed back for Da. Start her up, Rhodri, and don't fret. Trouble with the Bridges boys is there's too many of them and too few suitable girls. They fancy anyone in a skirt.'

'You're a stunner you see, that's why I worry.'

'And I'm his boss and pay his wages, better wages than he's had since he left school, I bet. Thanks for the compliment, though. Are we going or are we staying?'

'Going.' Rhodri revved up and charged out of the farmyard. They were over the humpbacked bridge in no time at all and speeding into Barleybridge. While Megan was choosing some lingerie, Rhodri excused himself and slipped away to buy a gift for her. He chose a manicure set in a leather case crafted into the shape of an old-fashioned cigarette case. He knew how she loved to keep her hands as immaculate as she could.

On the way back in the car he handed it to her. 'Present for my lovely.'

Out of the corner of his eye he watched her face as she opened up the box it was in.

'Why, Rhodri, that's lovely. I've never had one of these. It's just beautiful. Thank you.' Megan kissed his cheek, twice. 'Thank you.'

'When you use it think of me.'

'I think of you every day, my darling. All day.'

They'd almost reached the humpbacked bridge and Rhodri decided to stop there for a short while. 'I won't come in when we get back. You'll have enough to do. Let's pull in here and talk.'

'OK.'

When he'd parked the car Megan said, 'I like sitting on the slope down to the stream, there's a big flat boulder in just the right place . . .'

'Do you come here often then?'

'When I'm sick of the house and Da, I come here to get away. Escape it all . . . for a while.'

Rhodri felt immeasurably sad. 'Well, let's then.'

So they sat huddled tightly together on the stone watching the busy stream attending to its own affairs. 'This stone's only just big enough for the two of us.'

Megan grinned. 'Cosy though.'

'Oh! Yes. It is.' His arm tightened around her shoulders. 'Could stay here for ever.'

'Too cold.'

'We're sheltered from the wind.'

'Nice place to make love, though.' Megan chuckled. 'Slope's a bit steep. It'd be something of a challenge, wouldn't it?'

'Have to mind you didn't finish up sliding down into the water.'

Megan laughed. 'You're right there.'

He loved to hear her laugh, there wasn't enough of it in her life. There would be if she married him.

Megan shuddered.

'Cold?'

'No, just a weird feeling. Premonition or something.'

Abruptly Rhodri got to his feet. 'Time to go.'

Megan looked up at him. 'You sound as though you felt it too.'

'No. Not me.' He hauled Megan to her feet and made an effort to kiss away their strange feeling of something about to happen. 'What was it you felt?' He gripped her hand to help her up the slope to the road.

'Just nothing, really. I'm being silly.'

He opened the car door for her, made sure she was comfortable and then went round to get in his own seat. As they drove up between the trees, he could feel her discomfort settling on him too. He tried to force it out of his mind but couldn't. Not her da? Not something happened while they were out? He checked the car clock. They'd been exactly two and a quarter hours.

As he put on the hand brake he said, 'I won't come in. I'll wait till you wave to say your da's all right.'

Standing with his back against the car, he watched her unlock the door and disappear inside. Then she came to the door again and waved. So it wasn't that, then. The old sod was still alive. So what was it? He blew her a kiss and she returned it and then closed the door. He didn't know when he'd ever felt more alone than when the door closed behind her. Loneliness, like great waves of shocking pain, rolled over him leaving him desolate. It would be tomorrow morning before he spoke to another living soul. What kind of a life was that? He started up the engine, and was about to drive away when Gab came out of a stable door and went to open the back door of the house. He called, 'Meggie, my love. I'm off.' He'd better not go in or . . .

Rhodri heard her say from somewhere inside the house, 'OK. See you in the morning, Gab.'

There was something dashing about Gab, something lean and handsome and . . . what was the word? Virile. Earthy. Like that gamekeeper in that book . . . what was it? He'd recall it when he wasn't thinking about it. But he was just like him.

Politely Rhodri waited for Gab to get in his scruffy little car, more fitted for the knacker's yard than the road, and drive away. When he'd gone Rhodri thought, Gab sees more of her than I do, and remembered the peculiar feeling they'd both had sitting by the stream that ran under the humpbacked bridge. No, he really was being stupid. He bet Dan didn't have such daft thoughts. No, not Dan. Dan would have found a solution. But he was damned if he could. Dan would have compromised on something or other, and had Old Man Jones eating out of his hand. That gamekeeper. Yes, that was it. D.H. Lawrence. *Lady Chatterley's Lover.* That was who Gab reminded him of.

His worries were still with him the next morning. Everyone else seemed focused, busy, enthusiastic; he was preoccupied with thoughts of Megan which were gnawing his innards, rendering him useless. But the arrival of his third client rapidly emptied the forefront of his mind. It was Adolf, Mr Featherstonehough's Rottweiler. A soaking wet Adolf.

'Good morning, Adolf, good morning, Bert. You've been fighting Perkins again, haven't you, old chap? I can tell. Kate's been throwing water over the pair of you, hasn't she? You're not looking too perky, Adolf. What's your problem?'

Mr Featherstonehough answered on Adolf's behalf. 'It's the old problem. That lump in his groin. Only this time it's worse and well . . . see what you think.'

'Ah! I'll have a look.'

Rhodri felt around Adolf's groin with trepidation. He knew what Adolf meant to his owner: the whole world. But the news wasn't good.

'Let's see, how old is Adolf now?' Rhodri flicked the records through on the computer and found Adolf's name. 'He's almost twelve?'

'That's right. And as good as ever till these last few weeks. But he's lost heart. If it hadn't been for Kate's bucket of water Perkins would have had him for breakfast this time.'

'Do you get the feeling he's in pain?'

Mr Featherstonehough couldn't bring himself to answer. 'No. No. Not pain exactly. Well, to be honest . . . yes . . . I think so. Yes, it's in his eyes, it's as if he's asking me to help him. And the way he behaves. Laid with his eyes shut but not really asleep, and I hear him prowling about in the night.' He bent to ruffle Adolf's ears and did it with deep affection.

Rhodri said to Adolf, 'Excuse me,' bending to feel the lump in his groin again. It appeared to be much more extensive than the last time. 'I think I'm going to keep him in and do some X-rays.' He looked up at Mr Featherstonehough and very slightly shook his head. 'It may not be as bad as I think but . . .'

'Be honest with me, Rhodri, no beating about the bush. I need it straight from the shoulder.'

'I have an idea the lump has spread. We said when we operated a year ago that we didn't know if we'd got absolutely everything cut out. I'm afraid it looks as though we haven't.'

'I see. Well, he's almost twelve. If he was younger would you operate again?'

'Can't say anything until I've seen the X-rays.'

'Bad as that, is it?'

Rhodri nodded.

Mr Featherstonehough ruffled Adolf's ears again. 'I shall need to see the X-rays to convince myself.'

'Of course.'

'Adolf's been a grand dog all his life. I shall miss coming here. We'll miss Perkins and his damned fighting. Miss my wet trousers.'

'You could always get another.'

Mr Featherstonehough slowly shook his head. 'Not fair to get a dog when you're not sure you'll see it through its life. No. Might get a rescue cat though. My wife always wanted a cat, but we couldn't have one, not with this old codger, nor with old Fang either. They both hated cats. I'll leave him with you. I'll come back for him. Tomorrow, eh?'

'That's right. Tomorrow, first thing.'

'I shall want to be with him when . . . you know . . . at the end. If it turns out that . . .'

'Of course.'

The X-rays confirmed Rhodri's worst suspicions. He

got Mungo to take a look and the two of them stood together shaking their heads. Dan came in and joined them. 'Who's is this?'

Without looking at him Rhodri replied, 'Adolf's.'

'Mmm. Looks like very bad news. How old is he?'

'Almost twelve, he is.'

Dan said, pointing to the huge mass of the cancer, 'Curtains for Adolf then.'

Rhodri turned to him. 'You're a hard-hearted beggar, you are. Colder than ice, that's what.'

Mungo added, 'Practical might be a better word. He is right. It's all too late for Adolf.'

'I know that! I have got eyes, but is there any need to say it quite so bluntly?'

Dan apologised. 'Sorry, very sorry. Didn't mean to be unfeeling.'

'Unfeeling! You haven't got a thoughtful bone in your body, see.'

Mungo interrupted. 'Steady, Rhod, Dan doesn't know Adolf like we do.'

As though Mungo had never spoken Rhodri continued. 'This dog is well loved both at home and at this Practice, we shall miss him, all of us. But you, having no heart, don't have an inkling what we mean.'

Mungo's lips went into that thin line, which anyone who'd crossed him could have recognised, but Rhodri was too eager to put Dan in his place to notice. 'You're a damned nuisance you are, always right, sticking your nose in where it's not wanted and putting everyone's back up. This is none of your business. I know what I have to do, just needed Mungo to confirm it for me.'

'Dan, I wonder if you'd care to leave us now? Did you have something to say to me?'

Dan hesitated. 'I did. But it can wait. I apologise, Rhodri, I wasn't trying to tell you your job. Sorry.' He closed the door quietly behind him and left to start his calls.

Mungo waited for the sound of his brisk footsteps to die away and then turned to Rhodri. 'I've a full morning of appointments, so I can't see you till about one. In my office. I've a few words to say to you.'

He also left, going first to collect his list of appointments and the client files along with them. In reception he saw Bert Featherstonehough waiting patiently. Without warning Perkins hurtled down the passage from Mungo's flat door, straight as an arrow into reception and to where Adolf always preferred to sit. He put on his brakes when he realised Adolf wasn't there, stood for a moment studying Mr Featherstonehough and then placed a paw on his knee. Mr Featherstonehough bent forward to stroke his head and Perkins forgot his manners and licked his face.

'Well, now then, Perkins, young fellow m'lad, he's not here, is he? No, he isn't, you're right. And I think you know what's the matter. You've been a good mate to my Adolf, haven't you?' Perkins snuffled in his ear. 'Well, old lad, you won't be getting Kate's bucket of water over you again, I think, perhaps. Unless there's been a miracle. My Adolf's going to that doggy heaven where the rabbits all run slowly and the sun always shines. Yes, indeed.'

How Mr Featherstonehough kept himself from breaking down no one knew, for they were all close to tears. It felt as though a chapter in the life of the Practice was ending. Perkins accompanied him into Rhodri's consulting room, which he well knew was not allowed, and was briskly removed by Rhodri, but no one had the heart to stop him sitting outside Rhodri's consulting-room door.

Stephie whispered to Joy, 'Do you think Perkins knows?'

'It looks like it. Dogs are very perceptive, some sixth sense, you know.'

'Poor Perkins, no more fights with Adolf. I shall miss him.'

'So shall I.'

Mr Featherstonehough came out of the consulting room, ramrod straight, and marched to the main door, like the old soldier he was, looking neither to right nor left. One of the waiting clients half rose from their seat intending to say something consoling to him, but sank back down again when they saw how close to breaking down he was. As for Perkins he watched his friend disappear through the main door and then stood up and walked slowly into the back and up the stairs to Miriam for comfort.

When Stephie went to get a clean uniform from the laundry room she happened to glance out of the window and saw that Mr Featherstonehough's Volkswagen Camper was still parked outside. He was sitting in it staring out of the front window like a man made of stone.

'Should we go out to him do you think, Joy?'

'No. He's tough, regular in the military police, worked with army dogs till he was forty. He'll come to terms with it in his own way.'

'He'll be lonely when he goes back in the house and there's no dog there.'

'Of course, but knowing him he'll do something about that before too long.'

Stephie thought about that and then said, 'I expect you're right. Can't have been easy for Rhodri.'

'No. It's all he needs at the moment. Putting Adolf down. Poor Rhodri.'

Mungo knew the value of Rhodri's experience in the Practice and had no intention of asking him to leave but he did know he had to be firm. There must be no more being tough with clients and no more of this unpleasantness to Dan. He took off his reading glasses when Rhodri came into his office and leant back in his chair. 'Sit down. I've had a long morning and so too have you, and we both need our lunch hour, so let's not beat about the bush. How did Bert take it?'

'Very well. Said his goodbyes and marched out like the good soldier he is. Everything well held in, no tears, no breaking down. But underneath . . .'

'I expect he'll be a while getting used to the idea. If it were Perkins . . .'

'Exactly. You wanted to see me.'

'Rhodri, you know how much we value your experience? I don't want to lose you, either by you giving notice or me suggesting you find another post, but I really do have to say that I can't tolerate this business of you being at loggerheads with Dan. He's an excellent asset to the Practice and you must agree about that. He's bringing in more equine work than I'd ever hoped possible so not only his expertise but the money he's earning through equine is improving our finances no end. We can't expect that everyone will get on with everyone else just because they work together, but this vendetta with Dan is becoming childish.'

Rhodri strove to interrupt but Mungo held up his hand

to silence him. 'I won't have it. Do you understand? It's all over nothing.'

'It isn't all over nothing. He dealt with that crazy dog Bingo and then examined the cat and more or less told me what I needed to do to save it, when it should have been either me or Graham or Valentine who should have done it. He's arrogant, he's always right and . . .'

'Yes?'

'And he seems to have everything I want.'

'What's that?'

Rhodri shrugged his shoulders, he'd look a fool if he said he wanted a wife and a child like Dan. That he wanted some of Dan's 'get up and go'. Some of his bluntness. That it was sheer jealousy motivating the vendetta.

'Is there nothing to be done about Megan? Can't you marry her and go live there and sort it that way?'

'And have to tolerate that dreadful old beggar every day of my life?'

'God, man, the house is big enough, you could make him rooms of his own. Surely?'

'He wouldn't have that.'

'Wouldn't he just. Well, if he wants taking care of all the rest of his life the compromise can't be all one-sided. Megan's a great girl and very attractive, I can see why you want to marry her, but . . .'

'Yes?'

'I do think that all this business is what is really at the root of your attitude recently. Something has to get sorted. I won't tolerate it much longer.' Mungo placed his fingertips together and looked at him very directly. 'You may be envious of Dan but with some effort you can be in the same position as him, with a lovely wife and a family. However, in the meantime, no more being abrupt with clients and no more fuelling this vendetta with Dan. I know he's outspoken, but at heart he's a very fair-minded, kindly man doing a good job, and well liked. Just like you.'

Rhodri looked at his hands as they lay on the desk. Well liked? Kindly? Fair-minded? Well, yes, he, Rhodri, was all of those. And in his better moments he knew Dan was all of that too. 'You're right. I'm starting to become a bit cracked over it all. Yes, you're right.'

'I know I'm right. Get your personal life sorted then and we'll all feel the benefit. Thank you for dealing so well with old Bert. I need my lunch.' Mungo got to his feet and Rhodri did too. 'No hard feelings?'

Rhodri shook his head. 'No hard feelings. You'll have no need to speak about it again.' But in his heart he knew he was defeated before he'd even begun. There wouldn't be a solution for him and Megan so long as that selfish old man lived.

That selfish old man as Rhodri had called him was being just that. Demanding and irritable and making Megan feel shredded. She kept her patience as long as she could, hoping that the bad mood would pass but eventually she snapped.

'Da! That's the tenth time you've called me in all over nothing. I've work to do even if you haven't, please let me get on with it.'

'I think that's the cruellest thing you've ever said to me. How can I work? I want to but I can't. And don't get in the habit of answering me back. I don't deserve it.'

'You do. This morning, you do. It's only nine o'clock

and I'm worn out and I've a day's work to face. You're not being fair to me.'

'Fair? What's fair about the state I'm in, eh?'

Megan simply looked at him intensely.

'And you can take that sullen look off your face, I don't need that this morning.'

'I'm thinking of getting some help in.'

'I'm not having strangers wandering about this house pretending to flick a duster and costing a fortune. We're all right as we are.'

'We're not. And I wasn't thinking of someone to dust.'

Mr Jones's face went almost purple with rage. 'To do what, then?'

'To put you to bed at night and get you up in the morning and do your ablutions and stuff. A nurse, kind of.'

'A nurse? Absolutely not. That would be the end of me trying hard to be a person instead of an invalid. I try, damned hard too.'

'Don't try to appeal to my better nature, I'm reaching the end of my tether, but I don't suppose that's occurred to you. There's only Mr Jones in the whole wide world who's allowed to do that. Well, I'm telling you, Da, it's me who's done for, me who's exhausted, me who's—'

'What's got into you, girl? That Rhodri been at you again, trying to get you to marry him? Believe me, marriage isn't all it's cracked up to be, and I should know.'

Megan knew just where this was leading: into a tirade about her mother. But Megan had witnessed her mother weeping in the kitchen when her father was out in the fields. Knew about the physical revulsion her mother felt, the hatred when he'd raised his hand to her, never striking her but leaving her with the threat of it. The compassion

173

Megan felt for his predicament flew out of the window on days like this.

'Da, for heaven's sake, don't start down that line. I'm sick of it. Now, I'm getting on with my work, you'll have to read the paper while I do.' She turned to leave the room, knowing he'd think of one more thing as she left.

'Don't forget my morning coffee, I—'

'When I'm good and ready, Da.' As she crossed the passage into the kitchen she heard him shuffling about on his table for his glasses and the rustle of the paper as he picked it up. For two pins she'd escape this very day. Leave him to rot. She looked round the kitchen and thought, there's nothing here that can't wait until tomorrow. She'd do it, just for the day. She put out on the worktop all the things for lunch, put the kettle on to boil for the coffee and then raced upstairs to get changed.

'Here we are then, Da, coffee with a piece of your favourite shortbread. I've left everything out for lunch, I'll have a word with Gab before I go.'

'Where are you going?'

'I don't know yet, but somewhere, because if I don't I shall go mad.'

'But what about me?'

'I've told you, I'll ask Gab to keep an eye.'

'But I don't want Gab to keep an eye I—'

'Just for today. Be seeing you.'

As she opened the door to go find Gab before she left, she heard him say, 'When will you be back?' but she didn't answer.

Gab was taking a break in the old tack room and his eyes lit up when he saw her in the doorway. 'Hello, Meggie my love, what can I do for you? Dressed up and off somewhere to see that feeble Welsh lover of yours, I've no doubt.'

'Right first time, but he's not feeble, not feeble at all. I'm leaving Da. Everything's out for lunch, could you see to him for me, Gab?'

Gab stood up and moved closer. 'Of course.' He put a hand on the door frame, just above her head, which placed him only a foot away from her. Looking into her eyes he said, 'Wish I was coming with you. Need a chauffeur? Eh? Though we'd have to go in your car, couldn't ask a lovely girl like you to ride in my old ramshackle thing. My, but you're beautiful. This morning there's a light of rebellion in your eyes and well do I like it.'

Megan pushed his hand off the door frame. 'Much more from you and I shall tell your mother about you and your fast ways.'

A slight blush had come on her cheeks and Gab revelled in it. 'Ooh! You wouldn't! She's fiercesome, she is.'

'So am I. Now make sure the lad does some work today. I caught him in the hay loft yesterday, in the middle of the morning, reading an obscene publication.'

'It's what boys do at his age.'

'Well, not in my time, not when I'm paying him to work. See!' She prodded his chest to emphasise her point and found her hand being taken to his mouth and kissed. 'Stop that, Gab! You need the money and I need you for the work and that's it. Full stop.'

Megan turned on her heel and marched to her car. The drive into Barleybridge cooled her temper. It was a wonderful morning and here and there shades of autumn were on all the trees, just enough to let you know winter wasn't far away. First she went to find Rhodri, an unprecedented move on her part. In the car park she met a neighbour. 'Hi there, Megan, come to see Rhodri, have you? He's busy, but I expect he'll find time for you!'

She met a receptionist from the medical practice just coming out of the main door, who put down her dog and said, 'Hello, Megan. How's your da at the moment? Keeping well?'

'Very well, thanks.'

'He's a lovely vet that Rhodri of yours, treated my Duke something lovely he has.' She twinkled her fingers teasingly at Megan and went round to the car park.

Honestly, thought Megan, your life isn't your own. They know everything. After a talk with Joy, who didn't seem to be her usual happy self, and a natter with Mungo, she began to feel like a person again and seeing Rhodri lifted her heart to such an extent that she kissed him in full view of the waiting clients and embarrassed him to death. But she didn't care and neither did he when he thought about it. They lunched at the Askew Arms, and thought about going away for a weekend together so they collected brochures from the travel agents. They were standing outside discussing where to go when Rhodri looked at his watch and said with horror, 'My God! I should have been back a quarter of an hour ago!' They fled hand in hand for the car park, zoomed down the slope to the exit with more speed than sense, and then raced off down the road to the Practice.

They were greeted with a round of applause by the clients in reception which embarrassed them both.

'He's getting as bad as that Scott, he is.'

'Where've you two been then?'

'I don't know, what it is to be in love.'

An old man, with a grin on his face, asked Megan, 'Does your father know you're out?'

Rhodri beat a hasty retreat to his consulting room, slipped on his white coat and when he saw who was the first on his list he almost groaned. 'Goliath Costello.'

Megan apologised for their late arrival to Joy, but she simply laughed and said, 'Don't worry, I'm glad you've put a smile on his face, he's badly in need of it.'

'I know. Something has to be done.' But she didn't enlighten Joy about what it should be.

Megan's last words echoed around Joy's head long after she had left. Had the time come to do something positive about Duncan being missing, but was he actually *missing*? Or had he kind of mislaid himself for a while because he needed time alone? He'd been dreadfully distraught and exceedingly frank the night she'd admitted she *tried* to love him. What a stupid, hurtful thing that was to have said.

When Joy got home that night she searched frantically for his passport, first in the place they always kept them, namely the secret drawer in his desk, but it wasn't there. They'd both renewed their passports at the same time so she checked her own and saw it was another two years before they needed renewing again, so it wasn't because he'd sent his off for renewal. But he wouldn't anyway without hers. So the truth dawned on her: he'd decided before he left that he might go abroad. A grown man in his right mind was free to go where he wished. It didn't mean he was in danger, did it?

Money! Did he have access to money? She checked the small amount of post, which had accumulated since he left. They'd always been scrupulous about not opening each other's post, but she overrode her feelings on the matter and stuck her thumb in the flap of the envelope from his bank and took out the statement. He'd withdrawn all the money and closed the account. This was when she began to think she should contact the police.

The next morning she went straight up to the flat to find Miriam. Mungo, she knew, had already gone downstairs to begin work so this was her chance. She found Miriam still at the breakfast table reading the morning paper.

'Hello! What can I do for you, Joy?'

'Just need a word.' Perkins hurtled in to have a word before she could say anything. 'Hello, my best dog. And how are you this morning?'

She found comfort in his greeting but it did nothing to lighten the pain in her heart.

Miriam put down the paper. 'Tea?'

Joy shook her head. 'Tea, no. Sympathy, yes.'

'What's the matter?'

'It's Duncan.'

'Yes?' Miriam realised Joy didn't look her usual self this morning and dreaded what she might hear.

'He's gone.'

Relieved, Miriam said, 'Oh! Is that all? He often does. How many times have you told me that? In the middle of a project, can't sort it, goes out for long walk, comes back. Resolved! Hey presto!'

'He's been gone for days and days. Taken his passport, clothes, and never got in contact once.'

'Why?'

'We had a row.' She told the whole story in detail and then, surprisingly, broke down in tears.

Miriam pulled a tissue from the box on the window sill, and handed it to her. 'He is a grown man, well used to surviving on his own. Accustomed to solitude. Just because he's taken his passport doesn't mean he's gone abroad. He's taken it just in case he decides to, I expect.'

Joy looked up at her and said sharply, 'Don't take it so calmly. He's a missing person, don't you understand?'

'But, Joy—'

'Never mind "But, Joy". That's what he is: a missing person. I just want to know where he is. If he's all right. You'd think the least he could do is ring me.'

'Joy! Joy! You should never have asked him to have sympathy for Mungo, of all people. No wonder he disappeared. He's probably sitting in some mountain hut somewhere in Switzerland, enjoying the sun, eating his breakfast, wishing you were with him.'

'Ever the optimist.' Joy wiped her tears away. 'I'm going to the police. Just to say he's kind of missing.'

'If it makes you feel better, you do just that. Take photographs in case.'

'Do you think he's laid on a mortuary slab somewhere and no one knows who he is?'

'You've watched too many TV hospital dramas, you have, Joy Bastable. He's got his passport, you said so yourself. Of course he's not, but if it puts your mind at rest then go to the police and inform them.'

'I will. At lunchtime.'

'Go now. I'll keep an eye downstairs. Look, I'm fully dressed, I'll fling the breakfast things in the dishwasher and be down there in two ticks.'

'Don't tell them where I've gone. Say it's a doctor's appointment. OK?'

'OK.' Miriam stood up, hugged Joy and said, 'Why shouldn't they know, though? You've a right to be anxious about your husband, surely? Go in our bathroom and adjust your make-up. I feel quietly confident he'll be all right. There's no need to worry.'

The police took it calmly too. Her husband was adult, in his right mind, and free to come and go as he chose. But yes, they'd keep an eye. Let them know if he came back. Description? Ah! A photo. Good. Well, it was on the records now, madam. With a lovely lady like you to come back to, he'll soon be home. Don't worry.

What else could she do but worry? The fool. In her heart she knew she'd have a long wait. Why on earth should Duncan *want* to come back to her? She looked in her rear-view mirror at herself. She didn't look like a lovely lady this morning . . . more like an old hag. To have said she *tried* to love him! She was such a fool. As she swung into the Practice car park, Joy braced herself to face everyone.

Chapter 11

Dan was on veterinary duty at the weekly cattle market, so Rose had arranged to collect Mr Jones and take him to see it. He couldn't remember the last time he'd been to one and was up and about early to make sure he didn't delay Rose. Megan was flustered, hoping against hope that he didn't turn vicious on Rose as he did on her; some mornings the slightest thing could set him off. But he appeared too enthusiastic about his trip to bother being aggravating.

'You'll be all right on your own today? I'll be back before lunch though.'

'I shall be fine. Absolutely fine. You go and enjoy yourself. More toast?'

'I think I will. Now you're sure Rose will have room in her car for me? And the chair?'

Megan nodded. 'Of course. I've told you, they have a huge Mercedes estate. They've room for two wheelchairs.'

'Is the baby going, did she say?'

'No, the cleaner's taking care of him.'

'Pity, I'd have liked to see him. Rose is a lovely girl. Full of zest about everything.'

'She's very beautiful too. Such poise. Yet she doesn't rub your face in it like some people would do when they know they're lovely to look at.'

'Can't think why she fell for that ugly beggar. She could have had anyone she liked.'

'Da! He isn't ugly. Not at all. Just a bit craggy. He's lovely when he smiles.' Megan paused with her teacup almost at her lips and looked far away into the distance. Her da looked up and saw what he called her 'Rhodri look' on her face. He was about to say something cruel that would hurt her, but he changed his mind. He'd realised she was just as beautiful as Rose but she hadn't been given the opportunity to glow with love like Rose had. And that would make the difference. And why didn't she glow with love? He didn't get time to answer his own question because Rose was at the door calling, 'I'm here. Are you ready?'

They left for the market in a flurry of fitting in the wheelchair. Had he got his blanket for his knees? Would he need a hat? Should he . . .? Impatient of Megan's concern he said abruptly, 'Let's be off, Rose, or it will all be over.'

Rose kissed Megan goodbye and whispered, 'Have a quiet morning to yourself.'

Megan waved them off and went indoors, glad to be alone.

Rose parked her car in a space reserved for the disabled and got Mr Jones out and ensconced in his chair. He was so eager to see what was going on he didn't complain once about her ineptitude with the wheelchair nor the fact that she hadn't Megan's strength when it came to helping him out of the car. Mr Jones could taste the sounds and sights of the market before he could even see it, and he was looking forward to a reminder of life as it used to be.

He relished the goat pens, admired the cows, studied

the chickens, ducks and geese, saw some pigs he rather fancied, and thoroughly enjoyed listening to the farmers and the farming community exchanging news and views.

They spotted Dan after a while near the sheep. He was arguing with a farmer about a dozen or so sheep in a pen in front of them. 'I'm sorry, I'm saying this for the last time, these ewes are not fit. I have to insist you withdraw them from the sale.'

The farmer, Bernard Wilson, a big burly man, unshaven and unkempt with a noticeably prominent broad nose, folded his arms across his chest and said belligerently, 'I'm damn well not listening to a load of soft in the head do-gooding tripe. There's nothing wrong wi 'em that some good food won't cure.'

'I shall need to examine each one and if I find that any of them are unfit to travel then I'm afraid I shall have to put them down.'

'Put them down! You damn well will not.' He squared up to Dan, prepared to fight for his rights.

Tad Porter materialised beside Dan. 'I might have known that lot were thine. They're rubbish and tha knows it.'

'Since when 'as Tad Porter known better than me. I've been in't sheep business for forty years and I say there's nowt wrong wi' em.'

'I'd shame to own sheep in that condition.'

Phil Parsons erupted from nowhere shouting, 'You're at it again then, Bernard. I knew them were yours the minute I clapped eyes on 'em. Rubbish, they are. It's neglect that caused that lameness and there isn't a peck of flesh on 'em.' Phil leant over and reached into the pen, digging his fingers into thick fleece and feeling the spine of one of the sheep. 'Skeletons they are. Skeletons.'

Bernard put up his fists. 'And you can mind your own damn business. Yer can't even see 'em wi' that balaclava over yer eyes.'

Phil shouted, 'I may not make a fortune from farming, but I do know neglect when I see it. He's right, is Dan, they're not fit for sale. Cruel neglect, that's what.'

Tad Porter, puffing on his pipe, drew a powerful pull of smoke into his lungs, released it in a pungent cloud then said, 'Trouble is, Bernard, tha's idle. Phil's right, it's nowt but sheer neglect.'

Dan hadn't heard Tad speak in such long sentences ever before and sensed he was deeply stirred by the condition of the sheep, though there seemed to be another bone of contention mixed with his anger. Dan said firmly, 'You know as well as I do they are not in good condition and I've half a mind to get the RSPCA involved.'

By now a small crowd had gathered, hoping for some excitement to add an extra thrill to their day. There were murmurs of agreement from the crowd and someone who looked as though he might be an animal rights activist waded in with, 'Criminal! That's what. He shouldn't be allowed to keep animals if he can't care for them better than this. It's my opinion he should be prosecuted. Are you willing to put the wheels in motion?' He addressed his question to Dan, but before Dan could answer, Bernard had planted an almighty fist on the man's nose, knocking him back into Tad and Phil and scattering them into the crowd. Blood poured from the man's nose, splattering on anyone close to him. Bernard roared, 'And you can keep your nose out of it, too. I know you from before, you're another of them do-gooding activists.'

Dan intervened. 'Now, now this can all be settled quite amicably. Let's not get too excited.' Bernard advanced on

Dan, who nimbly skipped out of his way, hands palm upwards. 'That's enough. We can't have a brawl in the middle of the market. I'm doing my job to the best of my ability and in all conscience I cannot allow these animals to be put up for sale. They are in such poor condition it amounts to neglect, like Phil said.'

Tad Porter stepped forward. 'It's not the first time he's brought sheep unfit for sale. He's done it before, but no one does anything about it. Even the RSPCA can't pin 'im down. You go for 'im, Dan. And while you're at it, look at 'is dogs.' In a quiet aside, Tad volunteered to take care of Bernard's sheep for a couple of months, get them up to scratch, sell them and give Bernard the money. 'Can't abide to see animals neglected like this, I may not like the chap, but his animals aren't to blame for that. It's a genuine offer. I feel real sorry for the poor old sods. You tell him.'

When Dan put Tad's proposal to him, Bernard exploded. 'Definitely not. I'm not a charity case. Far from it.' He took up his belligerent position again, arms folded, chest stuck out, bottom jaw jutting. 'Do your worst.'

The activist, having stemmed the flow of blood from his nose, said thickly through the clots of blood still blocking his nostrils, 'There's Richie! Come over here, you're needed. We'll see what the police think to this. I'll have him for assault.' He vigorously beckoned the inspector over.

Dan had had no intention of involving the police but it was now too late. Richie, whom he'd met at Bridge Farm, was coming across.

Mr Jones rubbed his hands with glee. 'I haven't had such fun in years.'

Rose wasn't quite so sure. She didn't count it as fun to

see her beloved under threat from a bully like Bernard Wilson, and was, truth to tell, relieved to have the inspector on the scene. The activist wanted Bernard prosecuted for grevious bodily harm, and insisted on his right to have him charged, but Dan declined to get involved in charges about neglect, preferring to approach the whole matter on a long-term basis of ensuring Bernard was supervised much more closely and, dare he use the word, educated into a positive attitude rather than being under threat of prosecution.

It all fizzled out after a while because the inspector had to make notes and Bernard, seeing he was about to be arrested if he didn't calm down, lost his belligerent edge and was positively meek and mild. Only Phil Parsons and Tad Porter remained to see it through.

Phil said quietly, 'His dogs, he breeds beagles, are a disgrace. Disgusting conditions. Broke my Blossom's heart once when she fancied one and went to have a look. Filthy they were. The RSPCA had a go at him a year or so back, he improved for a while but they're as bad as ever I bet. Honest. He advertises pedigree puppies for sale in the newspaper, but I bet there isn't one that's in good nick. I'm off to the trailer for a coffee, want one?'

Dan nodded. Phil asked Mr Jones and Rose if they wanted one too and they both agreed. He came back with a tray laden with paper cups steaming with coffee, wooden spatulas instead of spoons, and a mountain of packets of sugar. Very pointedly he'd brought one for Richie too but not for Bernard Wilson. Tad Porter insisted he paid for his own. Phil refused his money. 'Don't be daft, there's no need.'

'I won't be beholden to anyone. We're all of us doing badly, you can't afford to be generous.' He pushed the money into Phil's jacket pocket. Phil said gruffly, 'There's no need for that.'

Mr Jones and Rose took their coffees to a quiet corner and Rose sat down on a wall to drink hers. 'I guess I'd no idea being a vet could be so . . . well . . . lively.'

Mr Jones gratefully took a sip of his coffee and then said, 'You've no idea how much I've enjoyed myself this morning. I haven't been to a market for . . . well, I can't remember when, and I want to thank you for taking the time. You've made an old man very happy.'

Rose patted his arm. 'I've an idea you're not much older than my stepfather, so less of the old.'

'Where is he?'

'Coming to England next week on business. Privately, I think it's an excuse to see Jonathan. He's so proud of him, you'd think he was his own grandson. Which he is in a way, but not really.'

Mr Jones stared ahead at the auctioneer working his way down the pens. 'I miss out on life, you know. Megan can't marry, because she has me to look after and as for my son, well, he won't marry in a thousand years. He's . . . you know.'

Rose thought she knew what he meant and simply answered, 'I see.' The tension between them was relieved by her mobile ringing.

'Rose, here.' She listened then said, 'Right, I'm on my way.' She snapped her phone off and said, 'Sorry, got to go. Jonathan needs feeding and won't be pacified with a bottle. I'll tell Dan. He'll look after you and see you home. I should have expected this.' She stood up from her seat on the wall, and Mr Jones thought yet again what a lovely girl she was. So elegant. And so . . . well, beautiful.

'That's all right, my dear. I'm sure Dan will take care of me. Hurry home. And thank you.'

'I'll find Dan for you—'

'No. No. That's all right, I'll find him myself.'

'Are you sure, I don't like leaving—'

'Of course I'm sure, I *can* manage this thing you know. Megan can always come for me if needs be.'

Had Megan witnessed her father's surprising spurt of independence she would have been astounded. But at that moment she was more than occupied with the situation she was facing. Her dogs were not allowed to sleep in the house, but had warm, snug beds in one of the unoccupied stables. From time to time she cleared out the stable, washed their bedding and today, while her father was out, she was painting the inside walls to keep them fresh. She was wearing an old scarf around her head, because she always managed to splash paint everywhere and most especially on herself, an old pair of black wellingtons kept specially for the purpose, old cotton trousers and a shirt that had seen better days. This job she could do without his continual interruptions and she was busy singing while thinking about the coming evening when she and Rhodri were going to a classical concert in the old town hall.

She'd promised herself to make plans that would free her from her daily obligations to her da, but so far had not come up with any ideas. Bending down, Megan painted the last corner on the third wall and then turned the ladder round to paint the wall with the window and the door in it. She was adjusting the ladder to enable her to reach the topmost part of the wall when Gab appeared in the doorway.

'Here, let me do that.'

'No, thanks, Gab. I'm fine. I'm enjoying doing a job without a single interruption from Da. It's a pleasure, believe me.' Megan smiled at him so he would know she wasn't being uncooperative out of unfriendliness. The dogs eddied around Gab's legs in greeting, he bent to acknowledge them and ruffled their ears, and chucked them under their chins. 'Great dogs, these. They know who is and who isn't welcome, don't they?'

'They do.' Megan placed the bucket of paint on the top step of the ladder and climbed up to begin painting. 'They're old and they're wise you know. Gyp is nine and Holly ten, you wouldn't think so, would you?'

'They still work the sheep like young 'uns, though. You'd never think . . .' A splash of Megan's paint landed on his sweater.

'Oh sorry! Here, use this old cloth to wipe it off.'

But as Gab took the cloth from her hand he gripped her wrist. She looked down in surprise and saw that look on his face, which he kept specially for her when her da wasn't looking. A blazing look, a daring, passionate look that unnerved her. There was something crude about it, and a boldness of which nothing good could come.

'That's enough, Gab.'

'No, it's not enough, it isn't even the beginnings of enough.' His grip tightened.

'Gab! Let go.'

'Come down.'

'I said, let go.'

'I said, *come down*.'

'I won't, Gab. Please. Don't make a scene. Please let go.' He didn't so she tried to twist her arm free, but it made him grip her even tighter.

Balancing on top of the ladder she couldn't put all her

strength behind pulling her wrist away so she climbed down, but he mistook her reasons, thinking she was doing it in response to his demand. As her feet touched the ground he wrapped an arm around her waist and bent his head to kiss her. It was a ruthless kiss, which numbed her lips and stifled her breathing. Megan pressed both hands against his chest and pushed hard.

'Ahhh! I like reluctance, it enhances the chase.' He bent his head to kiss her again but this time she twisted her head away so he couldn't. 'It makes me all the more determined.'

'Damn you, Gab. Let me go. If you don't I'll—'

'Yes?'

She realised she had nothing to threaten him with. 'Just leave me alone. Please.'

Gab released her. 'You've no idea how I feel about you, have you? It hurts like a great pain in here.' He banged his fist on his chest as he spoke. 'Day in, day out. Unbearable. I need you, like a plant needs sun for its very life. I ache for you.'

'However much you feel, it won't get you anywhere.'

'Why not?'

'You're not my type.'

'Not your type? I'm the eldest son of a farmer who owns acres of land, and even you have to agree I'm attractive to women. I'm a good catch. Do you not feel even the tiniest little bit of something for me? I can have any girl I choose, you know, but it's you I want. Come on, Meggie my love, it's the lad's day off, your da's out, so why not? Let me show you what loving can be like. You won't be able to get enough of me, if you give me a chance. Believe me, I know.'

Gab pressed her hand to his lips and then he kissed her

wrist, then the softness at the curve of her elbow and then the hollow of her throat, and Megan, briefly yielding to his persuasive lips, could sense the the truth of him saying he could have any girl he chose.

'Ha! The ice maiden begins to melt.' He kissed the hollow of her throat again and nuzzled his face into her neck while his lips pressed kisses on her warm skin. He lifted his head and looked intensely into her eyes. His hand strayed to the buttons at the neck of her shirt and began fumbling to undo them. That was when she came to her senses. Her hand holding the paint brush full of paint jerked into life and she smashed it as hard as she could into his face. Gab, blinded by the wet paint, was so startled he let go of her.

Megan, in charge of herself once more, followed up her attack on him with a vicious punch to his throat. He backed off coughing and complaining. Wiping off the paint as best he could without a mirror, he began to laugh, a roaring bellow of a laugh till his face grew red and he had to stop. Propped against the door frame he gasped. 'By heck. You're a harridan, you are. But it excites you, resisting me, doesn't it?'

'No. You disgust me.'

'You mean you're disgusted with yourself for fancying me, just then, just a tiny little bit. I felt a small surrender, I did.' He grinned a lopsided grin, which confirmed for her his attraction to women. He was going to add something but they both heard the sounds of a lorry turning into the yard so Gab stuck his head out of the door to see who it was. It was the feed.

Megan climbed the ladder again, dipped the brush in the can of paint and continued working on the rough stone surface of the stable wall. She trembled inside herself, shocked at finding just how vulnerable she had been for that moment. Her mobile rang, so she rubbed her hand on her trouser leg and fished it out of her pocket. 'Hello?'

'It's Da here. I'm ringing to say I'm lunching with Dan at the Askew Arms so don't worry about me.'

'You are?'

'Yes. He's bringing me home afterwards, Rose has had to go home to feed the baby, you see. Are you all right?'

'I'm fine, thanks. Have a good time.'

'You sound funny, odd like.'

'Bit breathless, I'm at the top of the ladder painting the dogs' stable. Enjoy, as Rose would say.'

'I can come home.'

'No. No. There's nothing the matter at all. Be seeing you. Enjoy. 'Bye, Da.'

Megan stuffed the phone back into her pocket, picked up the paintbrush again and carried on with her painting. By the time the lorry driver and Gab had unloaded the bags of feed, she'd put the last brush stroke on the wall and was ready for lunch. She stood for a moment admiring her handiwork thinking there was something enormously satisfying about completing a job like this. Washing out the brush under the outside tap Megan thought about her da having lunch with Dan.

But her father wasn't thinking about her at all as he sliced through a very tender piece of steak. 'I must say, Dan, I do appreciate you taking time to have lunch with me. Most considerate. What's happened about the chap with the sheep in such poor condition?'

'I've put three of them down. The rest are just about well enough to travel back. I've officially reported him.'

'So you should too. They were a disgrace to the farming community.'

'Tad Porter's taking them on, and he'll sell them and give Bernard what he gets. More wine? There's no love lost between them, but being a farmer Tad puts the animals' welfare first, even though he finds profit a thing of the past.'

Mr Jones proffered his glass to Dan with a nod. 'Thank you.' He took a sip. 'Remarkably good wine cellar they must have.'

'It was Lord Askew who introduced me to this wine. It's a good choice, isn't it?'

'You've dined with Lord Askew?'

Dan agreed he had, but only the once. 'He paid for it too, even though I was rude to him.'

'Can't stand the chap, myself.'

'You have to know how to handle him. Believe it or not I think he desperately wants to get on with people but doesn't know how.' Dan saw Lord Askew approaching their table.

'The man's a damn fool.'

Dan tried to catch Mr Jones's eye to warn him Lord Askew was coming up right behind him.

'A damn fool he is, that Lord Askew. A big, fat, blustering, self-opinionated fool. I've no sympathy for him.'

Dan cleared his throat, looked behind Mr Jones and said, 'Good afternoon, my lord.'

Mr Jones paused and then slowly put down his fork and painfully turned his head to look behind him, thinking Dan was joking. But, by God he wasn't. For once in his life Idris Jones was dumbfounded.

'Afternoon, Brown. Saw you in the market, thought I'd lunch with you, but you have a guest.'

'You'd be most welcome . . .' Dan moved his chair to make room.

'No, no. Be so kind . . . to introduce us.' He nodded at Mr Jones.

'This is Idris Jones, Beulah Bank Farm.'

'Never seen you here before.'

Lord Askew received a brusque reply. 'You're right, you haven't.'

Lord Askew moved forwards and offered his hand to Mr Jones and pumped it with comradely vigour. 'Good afternoon to you. You do right to get out and about despite your infirmities. Stunts the mind, makes one inward looking, selfish even, and one's view of life becomes . . . distorted . . . don't you know, if one doesn't make the effort. You'd better mind this chap,' he pointed at Dan, 'he's dynamite once he gets on your case. He'll have you climbing mountains before long. Enjoy your lunch.'

The restaurant manager, appalled by what he knew Lord Askew must have overheard, had been hovering nervously during this conversation and was relieved to be free to lead Lord Askew to the table he'd reserved for him.

Mr Jones commented, 'Hmm. He must have heard me.'

'He did.'

'Hmm. More of a gentleman than I gave him credit for.'

'Shall you climb mountains?'

'All depends what mountains you have in mind.'

Dan hesitated knowing he must choose his words carefully. 'I was thinking of . . . no, no. It doesn't matter.'

'Speak up, man.'

'I was thinking of a colleague of mine, lovely chap, sincere, who deserves a wife, and he's found a lovely girl he'd like to marry. But she can't marry him.'

Mr Jones put down his knife and fork, dabbed his mouth with his napkin and leaning back in his chair asked, 'Might I know this girl?' He raised his eyebrows at Dan.

'She's a stunner, an absolutely lovely woman, and deserves a happy life. You know, love and children and such. I can heartily recommend it. Believe me I can. Heartily.'

The waiter came to clear their plates. 'His lordship recommends the almond torte, sir. He said to say.'

Dan agreed. 'Then the almond torte it shall be and for you, Mr Jones?'

'The same.' When the waiter went away to get their pudding Mr Jones said, 'Has Rhodri put you up to this?'

'If he knew what I was saying he'd more than likely choke me to death. We don't get on. Neither professionally nor socially.' Dan smiled half an apologetic smile and waited.

The pudding had arrived before Mr Jones answered him. 'It's none of your damned business this. It's between Megan and me. Look at me, go on, really look at me.' He waited while Dan looked at him. 'I need her at home with me, I can't manage on my own, so that's an end to it.'

'That's selfish and what's more you know it.'

'How dare you speak in that tone to me?'

'Someone has to and today I'm your man. The days when elderly parents kept one of their girls at home to care for them in their old age are long gone and good riddance I say. Megan has as much right to a life of her own as your son has. He's disappeared off into the night leaving the farm and you, without, I suspect, so much as a backward glance. So why shouldn't Megan disappear too?'

'Because she knows which side her bread's buttered, that's why.'

'There are other ways of going about it. What Megan needs is more help with her workload.'

'Like?'

'Help with the house, help to look after you. It's all possible with a bit of thought on your part. You could organise it for her, you haven't lost your faculties, your mind is razor sharp.'

'Hmmph.'

'Lovely pudding.' Dan raised his glass in the direction of Lord Askew and thanked him with a nod of his head. Lord Askew looked enormously pleased.

'I won't have coffee.'

'Right. I'll get the bill, time I was back at the Practice anyway.'

'I'll get a taxi then, can't stand much more of your sermonising.'

'I'll get shot down in flames if Rose finds out I didn't take you home. So please, allow me.'

Dan swung the wheelchair out from the table and went out of the restaurant paying the bill as he went. 'I promise not to sermonise all the way home, but think about what I've suggested.'

'Hmm.' And that was all that was said all the way back to Beulah Bank Farm.

That afternoon, Megan's da spotted some small flecks of dried white paint on Gab's eyebrows when Gab called in for his cup of tea in the kitchen, and he wondered if there was a reason for Megan sounding out of breath when he'd spoken to her on the phone. Purposely he invited

Gab into the sitting room for a word when he was about to leave for the day. 'You're a good worker, there's no mistake about that. You've put more hours in than I expected and it's much appreciated, I shall give recognition to the fact in your wage packet.'

'Thank you, Idris. Thank you. It's a pleasure working for Megan and for you. I'll say goodnight.' He came back to ask if Megan was around. 'I've a message for her.'

'Upstairs, getting ready to go out, and she's running late.' Before Megan's father could say no, he couldn't go upstairs, Gab had gone, pounding up the stairs two at a time. Gab found her on the landing, in her dressing-gown, searching for something in a cupboard.

Megan looked up startled. 'What do you think you're doing coming upstairs?'

Gab ignored her indignation and came straight to the point. 'Not fallen out with me about this morning, have you?'

'Actually, I'm very angry about it. There's to be no repetition, you understand?'

'There won't be. I promise.' But the insolent grin on his face belied his words. 'See you in the morning. Half past five. I'll come and give you a knock if you like.' Again those lustful eyes slid from head to toe of her. Again that disarming grin, the joy of so many girls.

Megan gave Gab a disdainful look, found the shoes she was looking for, slammed the cupboard door shut and went into her bedroom, closing the door behind her.

Gab laughed to himself, ran back down the stairs to find Mr Jones in a fury waiting for him at the bottom. 'I did not give you permission to go upstairs. Under no circumstances do you go up there ever again. Your place is the farm. That's where you belong. Right?'

Gab sprang to attention, saluted and said, with an insolent grin on his face, 'Yes, sir! Three bags full, sir!' He bounded out of the house obviously unscathed by Mr Jones's anger.

Chapter 12

Going home in the early hours from a night call Dan's headlights lit up someone weaving about in the road ahead of him when it was almost too late to take evasive action, and at the last minute he had to swerve to miss. A gateway came conveniently into view and he drove into it, thankful he hadn't hit whoever it was. Switching off the engine, Dan grabbed his torch and got out. His torch picked out a person now scrabbling helplessly in the road, trying to get up.

At the same moment, Dan heard a car coming from the opposite direction and waved his torch back and forth on the road to prevent the man being run over. As the vehicle drew near he saw it was Phil Parson's old van. By the light of his torch he realised Blossom was in the driver's seat. She jumped out leaving the engine running and the van in the middle of the road and shouted, 'Why Dan! It's you! Who's this?' Dan shone his torch on the person in the road and both he and Blossom said at the same time, 'Bernard Wilson!'

He was stoned out of his mind and reeking of alcohol.

Dan shouted, 'Bernard! It's Dan Brown from the veterinary practice. Can I give you a lift home?'

Bernard sat up, clutched Dan round his knees and mumbled, 'Taken a wrong turning. Where am I?'

Blossom answered him. 'On your way to Applegate

Farm and the Caravan Park.' To Dan she said, 'This isn't the first time. Since his wife did a runner he's been on the bottle more often than not. He came to us one night and Phil made him sleep it off in a stable, wouldn't have him in the house. Phil has a drink but I've never seen him the worse for wear.' She gave Bernard a light kick with her foot. 'Get up, you daft ha'porth.'

But Bernard didn't get up. He said, 'Eh! I can't be. Applegate P-p-park Caravan, you say?'

'You are. Shall I give you a lift? Come on. Get up.' Dan put his hands under Bernard's substantial armpits and tried to heave him up but couldn't quite manage it, so Blossom volunteered her help.

'I'll take him home. I can lie him down in the van. I've done it before.'

They each put their hands under Bernard's armpits and together they staggered across to the van with him, his feet trailing on the road. Bernard protested. Blossom opened the back doors of the van and with an almighty effort they got Bernard in, lying him flat on his back on the mattress amongst the pink and white fluffy pillows. Blossom said, 'Couldn't be comfier, now could he?'

'Well, no. But I'm coming with you, you'll need someone to get him out at the other end.' Dan stood looking at Bernard laid in Blossom's boudoir of a van and wondered.

Blossom said, 'She left him destitute, you know, she took a load of money with her, he's never picked up since. In his own way he loved her. Poor chap.' She shut the van doors with a shattering, grinding clang, closing them on Bernard shouting loudly, 'Badger's Lot! First stop Badger's Lot. Hurry up. Badger's Lot. Home, Jameth and don't thpare the hortheth!'

Blossom giggled. 'Wait till I've turned round.' Blossom gave a masterful demonstration of how to turn a sluggish, out of condition van round in a narrow road, sprung it into second gear and moved off with Dan following, hoping Bernard would not retch his entire night's drink up on Blossom's fluffy pillows. He daren't begin to imagine what she'd been up to that night, returning home to Phil in the small hours.

When they opened up the van on arriving at Bernard's farm he was still singing his heart out, rolling about on the pillows, merry and exceedingly happy. Dan grabbed his ankles and pulled him to the edge of the van floor and then he and Blossom reached in to grab his arms and get him upright. As he straightened up he said, 'Go on, then, Blossom, my love, give us a kiss. Ten pounds for a kiss. Go on then. Ten pounds for a kiss.'

Blossom roughly pushed his head away from her face as his pursed lips drunkenly searched for her mouth. 'Not when you stink of beer. You know the rules. Ready, Dan?'

'We need the door open first. Let's see if he has a key.'

'He never locks up. It'll be open.' Together they headed for Bernard's house door, staggering under his weight as he was now almost unconscious with sleep and drink.

The door was not only unlocked but wide open. They squeezed in through the doorway and Blossom directed Dan to Bernard's bedroom. 'Thank God he sleeps on the ground floor, we'd never have got him up the stairs in this state.'

With the light switched on and coming in from the fresh night air Dan not only saw but smelt the state of the house. He'd seen some sights in his travels around the world but he didn't think he'd seen anywhere that matched the downright neglect and degradation of Bernard's kitchen. He'd thought Blossom's own kitchen was ghastly but this . . . They had problems getting through it because the three of them kept tripping over things left abandoned on the floor, slipping on old food spilt carelessly and left to rot, and Dan was sure he'd spied a fat rat sneaking behind the cooker as they passed. Oh God! he thought, not rats too. Inside the house! They emerged into the hall where Dan unintentionally kicked a score of empty beer bottles, which dribbled their dregs onto the filthy threadbare carpet as they rolled about, adding to the general stink of the place.

He and Blossom finally heaved Bernard onto what passed for a bed; a greasy mound of sheets and blankets reeking of Bernard's unwashed body. Blossom pulled off his boots and heaped the blankets on top of him. 'There you are, Bernard, sleep it off. Goodnight, old man. Goodnight.' She patted his shoulder, shook her head in despair and made to leave.

The two of them, Blossom and Dan, stood outside Bernard's back door looking up at the night sky. Blossom said, 'Magnificent, isn't it? Puts everything into perspective, doesn't it, looking up at a night sky. All those millions of miles out there that you can't get your head round. Anyway, must get back.'

'Phil all right?'

'Oh yes! My night out tonight. He's used to me being late.'

Dan opened his mouth to say he didn't know Barleybridge had the kind of nightlife that kept one out on the tiles till this hour, but shut his mouth before the words were out.

'Something should be done about Bernard.' Blossom hooked her hand in the crook of his elbow. 'Every bit of him's in a mess. Especially his dogs. He's a great chap if only he didn't drink so much. He'll be all day getting over that skinful. Goodnight, Dan. Thanks for being a good Samaritan.' She reached towards his cheek and planted a kiss on it with her ruby red lips. 'Goodnight! You're a great chap. One in a million. My Phil thinks the world of you and so do I.'

She swung up into the van, her slender legs and her very neat bottom a temptation for any full-blooded male. Dan thought what a strange mixture she was. At once a tart, a good wife, and by the looks of the back of her van a . . . no, she couldn't be could she? . . . But where had she been till this time of night? Still, he'd never have got Bernard home without her. He remembered the rat and shuddered. Thought about his home and his own lovely bed and Rose snuggled beside him, warm and comforting and sweet smelling. As he turned for home, he looked forward to spending what remained of the night in bed with Rose and hoped to tempt her to stay there for at least part of the morning.

But the next day when Dan went in to the Practice at lunchtime he was a man of action again. First he had a word with Mungo concerning what steps he should take about Bernard.

'Want to keep the officials out of it, if we can. He's a desperate man, needs a good woman, but no self-respecting woman would take him on in the state he's in.'

Mungo retorted, 'We'll be running a marriage bureau for farmers next. Just watch your step, Dan. There is a limit.'

Dan eyed Mungo and thought, What's got him out of his pram this morning? But he ignored the sarcasm. 'Can I take Rhodri with me to look at the dogs? He puppy farms you know. Beagles.'

'I think that would be a good idea. But not too much of the social work, Dan. We're not a charity.'

'I appreciate that, it's the animals' welfare I'm most interested in. We can't stand by and just let it happen. That would be irresponsible on our part.'

Mungo sighed. 'It would. Yes. Not too many hours though. Like I said . . .'

Together they both added, 'We're not a charity,' and laughed.

Dan went to find Rhodri. 'Have you time to spare today for going with me to see Bernard Wilson's kennels?'

'You mean you're actually asking me to go with you, actually asking me for help?' The sarcastic tone of his voice couldn't be missed.

'Yes. You've told me more than once to keep to my side of the Practice so I am. In any case, you're much more au fait with dogs than I am. After all, it is your field of expertise. I understand they're being kept in appalling conditions. Could all be hearsay, but I've an idea it isn't.'

'Someone brought a puppy of Bernard Wilson's in a few months ago. I didn't reckon much to him – too thin, flea ridden, riddled with worms, you know the kind of thing. I'd be glad to come. Very glad indeed.'

'Excellent. Bring something with you, whatever you think might be needed. I'm more interested in his sheep after an altercation in the market about the condition of some he brought in for sale.'

'Right. I've no operations this afternoon, if you're free?'

Dan nodded his agreement, and within the hour they were on their way to Badgers Lot and Bernard Wilson.

Rhodri had refused to go in Dan's Land Rover so they were travelling in Rhodri's own Citroën. To break the ice Dan commented on how much he liked it.

'It suffices.'

'More than suffices, it's great. Comfortable ride too.'

'Yes.'

Badgers Lot was a turning off the main Weymouth Road. The lane was narrow and in places the tarmac had worn away, but with Barleybridge having had a dry summer the ruts weren't too bad, though Rhodri's suspension took a bashing as they passed the open gate to the farm.

'Good grief! Those ruts.'

'I'm afraid that's symptomatic of what we shall find when we get there. Though to my knowledge he's never called us out all the time I've been at the Practice, so I don't actually know. He was blind drunk when Blossom Parsons and I took him back home last night. I've no idea what state he'll be in this afternoon.'

Rhodri didn't answer, giving the whole of his attention to the preservation of his adored car. But as they reached the farm buildings he said, 'Oh my word! What a mess.'

Corrugated iron sheds were in a state of imminent collapse. There were stables with gaping holes in the roofs where the tiles had fallen away. The surface of the farmyard had sprouts of weeds growing between the cobbles, a stable door swung bleakly on its broken hinges. Bernard's old lorry stood lopsidedly, one tyre completely flat. But the silence was the weirdest thing. A deep, deep silence in which only the gentle purr of the engine of Rhodri's car could be heard.

Dan hoped he wasn't going to find anyone dead. He'd been there, done that, and he didn't want to face it again.

But he didn't have to. Bernard was in the kitchen, sitting at the table drinking tea from a mug. A gigantic teapot, once brown and shining and welcoming, now streaked with old tea stains and even older dust, stood on the table and Bernard was refilling his cup from it as they went in.

'Visitors! By hell! Visitors! Busybodies more like. Come to see if I'm drunk, have you? Well, I'm not.'

Dan spoke up. 'Dropped you off last night. Found you in the road. Come round?'

Bernard eyed him up and down. Slurped some more tea into his mouth and having swallowed it said, 'It was you? Thought it was Blossom Parsons.'

'Her too, we happened to arrive at the same spot at the same time and took you in hand. Feeling better?'

Bernard nodded. 'Grand woman that Blossom. Grand loving woman.' He slurped at his tea again and asked Rhodri what he wanted.

'Well, boyo, I've come to see your dogs.'

Sensing interference, Bernard, slowly and with great control, asked, 'Why?'

Rhodri stepped back a pace. 'To check if they're all right, see.'

'Joined the do-gooders, 'ave yer?'

'No. But I'm a vet and I can't bear to see neglect.'

'Who said anything about neglect? Not me. I suppose I've no option seeing as there's two of you. They're in the sheds. Not fed 'em yet, only just woken up. That was my next job.' Bernard stood erect by levering himself up via the kitchen table. He was a mountain of a man, bulging in all the wrong places with his pugnacious, heavily jowled

206

face set just how it had been over the sheep in the market. He lurched out of the back door into the farmyard.

To their horror Dan and Rhodri realised Bernard was leading them to the sheds. They exchanged glances but said nothing. Once inside the sheds they could distinguish through the gloom several runs carelessly constructed from chicken wire. In them were dogs of all ages wading in their own filth. The stench was appalling. It was difficult to see through the gloom if any of them needed attention. Above one run the roofing had fallen in allowing the rain to penetrate. It was mud-filled and young puppies were listlessly paddling about in it. There were wretchedly dirty feeding bowls standing about, bereft of food, and worse, no drinking water anywhere.

Dan stood silent, hurt beyond belief. Rhodri's heart was pounding with distress. Dan flashed him a warning glance, which Rhodri minded to heed. Taking a deep breath he said, 'It seems to me you've not been well, Bernard. Otherwise you wouldn't have let it be like it is.'

'Tha's polite if nothing else. Yes, I've been ill, you could say that.'

'Managing on your own?' Dan enquired.

Bernard nodded.

Rhodri shouldered the responsibility for action. 'I see there's one stable that's still got the whole roof left on it. How about if we clear it out and I'll sort out which dogs are OK and we'll put them in there. Dan, you can wash out the bowls and Bernard you get the food ready for the bowls when Dan's finished. Also water, if you please.'

'That stable has nowt in it at all, 'cept a load of old sacks from years back,' Bernard volunteered.

Dan raised an eyebrow at Rhodri but he didn't notice, so to inspire Bernard, Dan began his job by collecting the bowls. The worst job was Rhodri's. He carefully removed any dogs who appeared reasonably healthy and carried them across to the stable he'd decided upon. Bernard was right, it was full of old sacks. Rhodri kicked them aside, thinking he'd keep them clean to use as bedding. Ten dogs, of all ages and in varying degrees of neglect were put in the stable. The rest Rhodri carefully examined; two breeding bitches, old and in such poor condition he would be doing them a kindness by putting them to sleep. This left eight young dogs all about five or six months old, which Bernard had bred but obviously had not been able to sell, and no wonder.

Dan appeared with a stack of feeding bowls and a plastic washing-up bowl he'd spotted amongst the rubbish in the corrugated iron shed. He'd cleaned them all, and filled the plastic bowl with fresh water. 'Where's Bernard?'

Desperately distressed by what he'd found Rhodri said, 'I can't believe this. There's two I want to put down, because they're worn-out breeding bitches, too many litters, too little food, and looking at this motley lot, three have dicky hearts, three are so thin because of starvation and worms I don't know whether to put them to sleep or let Bernard give them a second chance.' Rhodri pointed to one. 'That pup's got deformed legs, due, I've no doubt, to too much inbreeding and too little calcium over the years. So he'll have to go. I think Bernard should be prosecuted.'

'He's coming. Put that one to sleep that's deformed, he can't be helped, he's leading a miserable life and can only get worse. Let's give the others a chance.'

Bernard arrived with an enormous bucket of feed for the remaining dogs. Rhodri gave himself no time to think.

'These two bitches, I want your permission to put them down.'

'Nay! Them's my two best bitches.'

'*Were* your two best bitches, Bernard. They've worn themselves out breeding for you. Two litters a year, was it? The first before they were a year old? Eh? For what, seven years? Eh?'

Bernard put down the bucket he was carrying. 'Sometimes.'

Rhodri raised his voice in anger. 'It's criminal, Bernard. This one I'm putting to sleep because he'll never find a home crippled as he is. You should never have let him live, it was cruel. These I'm hoping, with your help, to build up into handsome little dogs. They're well marked, someone will want them. They all need worming absolutely without doubt. I'm deeply grieved.' He shot such a woeful look at Bernard that he looked embarrassed.

'I don't want 'em like this. It's that I haven't been well, and things have gone from bad t'worse. Just needed some help. You know.'

Rhodri nodded. Silently he got on with worming the dogs he wanted to save, organising Bernard to dig a hole to bury the ones he'd put down, and then between them they emptied another stable that only required plastic sheeting to cover the place where the tiles had slid off the roof and it made a safe, warm, clean place for the younger dogs to be kept.

Finally, the dogs got fed and watered and the hessian sacks, stored for years, were shaken out and used to make reasonably satisfactory bedding for them.

Dan looked at his watch. 'Time we went. We've made a start for you. Tad's got your sheep, and we've done what we can today for the dogs. Either Rhodri or I will be back tomorrow afternoon to see the progress you've made in erecting an outside run for these dogs so they can move out of the stables and into the fresh air and be able to get some exercise.' He glanced at Rhodri hoping he had his approval and said, 'We don't want to get the authorities involved, but by God, Bernard, Rhodri will have your guts if you don't improve your standard of care of these dogs. Won't you, Rhod?'

'Absolutely.'

They were both silent for a while after they left Badger's Lot and then Rhodri broke it by saying, 'I don't think I've seen such systematic cruelty in all my life. Downright appalling, it was. And the strange thing about dogs is they don't bear grudges.'

'I thought they were all very quiet, very subdued. I think if we hadn't gone there today some would have died in the next few days. They might still die if we don't give him support. The chap's completely lost heart. You should have seen his sheep! Thanks for coming with me. Thanks for your expertise, too. I've nothing but admiration for the way you kept your temper when you were so angry.'

'He's a mental case really.'

'What good will it do anyone if he ends up in hospital?' Dan cleared his throat and looked out of the window for a moment and then said, 'I reckon his stud dog has already died. Otherwise where is he?'

'Hadn't thought about that, but I bet you're right. He must have had his own stud dog, no self-respecting breeder would want him taking his bitches for mating when they were in such bad condition. He must have had his own.'

Dan decided on a change of subject. 'Old Man Jones enjoyed the market the other day.'

'Yes, he did. Full of it when I went to see Megan. What he needs, really.' He fell silent while he negotiated the dreaded roundabout just outside Barleybridge. 'Can anyone tell me why they have to make a roundabout where you can go either way round it? I think the transport planners should be lined up and shot.'

Dan chuckled. 'Too right. Will you go tomorrow?'

'I will. My half day today so I'll drop you off now, and then I'm going to see Megan.'

'She's worth fighting for. Old Man Jones might be coming round to getting Megan some help. I put the ball in his court at lunch.'

'You did?'

'Told him he was no fool. I said his mind was razor sharp . . .'

'Too right, it is. In more ways than one where Megan's concerned.'

'Rose is taking him to a game fair at the weekend. She's determined to get him out and about.'

'That's wonderful.' By now they were parked in the Practice car park. Rhodri turned to look at him and spoke without any of the resentment his voice frequently held when speaking to Dan. 'We do appreciate Rose taking him out. By the time Megan's done the farm work and the cooking and things and attended to her father she hasn't any spirit left for taking him anywhere at all. Anyway he wouldn't go even if she could find the time, but he will with Rose.'

Dan thanked him and added, 'Tell you what, Rhod, you'd better watch that big beggar Gab, he's got "stud" written in large letters on his forehead.'

Rhodri's mind absorbed the shock of hearing his own

fears voiced and then he replied, 'Well, I wouldn't have put it quite like that, but I do know what you mean.'

'If he decided to act upon his feelings Megan wouldn't have a chance, and Old Man Jones couldn't do anything about it if he did.'

'Get out. I'm off.' Rhodri revved the engine up with spirited determination and Dan leapt out, thinking if he didn't he'd be at Beulah Bank Farm before he could draw another breath. As he shut the car door he said, 'I'll leave Bernard to you, tomorrow.'

Rhodri nodded and the wheels were turning before Dan had shut the door.

Rhodri reached the humpbacked bridge and as he passed over it he thought he'd caught sight of Megan's jade cardigan out of the corner of his eye. He braked, reversed, parked and jumped out. He went to lean his arms on the wall of the bridge and look over. He was right, it was Megan, lost in thought, gazing at the stream, as it bubbled and dashed along over the stones. She hadn't realised he was there and for a moment he enjoyed watching her. She'd fastened her hair back with combs so it hung down her back but off her face, so he could see her profile unhindered. There was a loveliness about her that almost made his heart stop beating. The sun wasn't shining but it seemed to him that she glowed without its help. His heart flipped into action again, but he still didn't let her know he was there. What Dan had said about Gab sprang into his mind. God! If ever he . . . He'd better let her know he'd seen her. Rhodri found a small loose shard of stone on top of the wall, picked it up and threw it into the water, looking forward to her brilliant smile as she looked up and recognised him.

But he didn't get what he expected.

Instead, the face he saw when she looked up was filled with a kind of bitter determination as though she was steeling herself to keep a grip on fear. Then when she saw it was him, relief flooded it and he was rewarded with a wan smile and a wave of her hand.

He was down the slope and beside her in a moment, his arm around her waist, hoping to dispel her mood. 'My afternoon off. Would have been here earlier but I went with Dan to a cruelty case. Kiss?' Rhodri squeezed her tightly to him and kissed her temple, because she still hadn't looked at him properly.

Megan's arm crept round his waist and they stood silently staring at the water. She couldn't tell him. Couldn't find the words, not the right ones that would explain why she was here in her private paradise, trying to come to terms with the dreadful afternoon.

It had all begun when her father had had an altercation with Gab about some minor neglect of the farm work, so minor that in fact the reason for the upset had become quite lost in the subsequent turmoil. The three of them were in the kitchen eating lunch, her father having taken to eating with her and Gab at lunchtime to make sure, as her father had put it, there couldn't be any nonsense from Gab.

They'd both ranted and raved about it to begin with but then more pressing matters emerged and Gab became exceedingly angry.

'Look here, Idris, I'm not a common or garden farm hand for you to take to task, I'm the eldest son of a well-to-do farmer, helping you out. That's all. Helping you out. I could walk out of here this minute and leave you to it. Up to milking, are you, up to going up the hill to the sheep, checking they're OK? Rounding them up. Marshalling the dogs? Eh? I don't think so, bit of hedging and ditching, unloading the feed bags? Up all hours in the lambing season? Eh?'

Mr Jones didn't have an answer to all that.

'Getting the cows in the crush for TB testing? Are you up to that? I don't think so.' He paused expecting an answer, and when he didn't get one, continued his tirade. 'In that case, if you've nothing to say, don't come criticising me from the comfort of that armchair of yours. Meggie and me manage very well, don't we, Meggie?' He took her hand and held it and she couldn't pull it away.

'Please, Gab, let go of my hand.' She said it so quietly, so gently, that anyone else would have done as she asked immediately. But not Gab. No, not Gab. He held it even more tightly and said to her da, 'Mr Jones, this daughter of yours, I want to marry her. I'll live here and when you get as you can't even walk about, I'll carry you wherever you want to go. I'll look after you, in a way that that Welsh lover of hers isn't willing to do. How's that for a promise? I'd be a fine asset for this place. Very useful to have about, and I'd care for Meggie here, like no one else could. So, I'm telling you I'm marrying her and she wouldn't be unwilling.' He looked round the kitchen as though he already owned it.

'Marriage! To an ape like you? I don't think so. Ha! Certainly not! She's here and here she stays.'

'Exactly! Here she stays with me, the three of us together.' The tone of his voice was eager. 'You'd have some fine healthy grandchildren, I'd see to that.'

Megan had shuddered and he'd felt it because he was still holding her hand. 'She won't admit to it but she can't wait. That poofter of a Welshman couldn't stir a rice pudding never mind Meggie. She's mine is Meggie. So what do you say? Come to think of it, you haven't much choice.'

Megan's da replied, 'I'd sell the farm first.'

'Oh! Brave words, those. Brave words. But only words. In the present climate you'd get nothing like its value.'

Megan's da got to his feet. 'Megan, help me back to my chair in the sitting room. I've had enough of this.'

Gab released her hand and she took her da back to his chair. As he sat down he whispered fiercely, 'I would, you know, I'd sell it first.'

'Don't worry, I'm not marrying him whatever he says.'

She'd waited to hear Gab leaving the kitchen and when he'd gone she'd tidied up the lunch things and made the dinner for the feral cats. They were waiting for her, stood about at various vantage points, eyes glinting. Only six today. Briefly she wondered where the other two were, but she opened up the stable door and put down two bowls of food. They always waited outside, fearful of being trapped, but it was Megan who was trapped because in the gloom of the stable she hadn't noticed that Gab was standing in there waiting for her. Her heart leapt into her throat and she thought, he knows my movements as well as I know them myself. As she turned to go out he took her arm and pulled her to him. 'I meant it. I really do. You and me. This farm. We'd make a go of it.'

He reached out and snatched at the stable door to close it.

Megan struggled to free her arm.

'Gab, please don't. You can't make me marry you. You really can't.'

'Then I'll leave. This minute. Right now.' He folded his arms across his chest and waited. By now the cats had gathered their courage and were standing by the door, the bravest daring to squeeze their way in.

Her heart sank at the prospect if he left. 'Forcing my hand is no way to make me want to marry you.'

'I could always tempt you instead.' He'd looked at her with that passionate look she'd grown to dread.

'Well, you won't. Sorry, Gab, but you won't. You'll find someone one day. Believe me.' Out of the corner of her eye she saw the cats trying to get in. Matter-of-factly she'd said, 'Now, the cats are getting desperate. Come on. Let them in.'

Some of the determination went out of him and he looked less the passionate suitor and rather more the determined supplicant. 'I won't give up wanting to marry you. And I'm not leaving. I think enough of you to know what it would mean if I weren't here. I love you, Meggie, like I've never loved anyone before. I've said it plenty of times to girls, but only because I knew that was what they wanted me to say, never because I really *loved* 'em. But with you it's different. I haven't even looked at another woman since I came to work here, if that's any recommendation. Faithful. That's what I would be. Staunch and faithful. I'd do what was right by you, and I'd work this farm, till they'd all be jealous of our success. You and me together.'

He took her into his arms, despite her resistance, and kissed her with such passionate ferocity that she knew instantly that his kind of loving couldn't ever be right for her. When he'd stopped long enough for her to draw breath she said, 'It's no use, Gab, it's no use.' Gab looked down at her with a kind of raging disappointment in his eyes that frightened her. He strode out of the stable across the yard and into the milking parlour, leaving her exhausted and emotionally spent. That was when she'd abandoned everything she'd meant to do and come here to her private paradise to recover.

Eventually Rhodri said, 'What is it, love? Needing five minutes to yourself?'

'Yes.'

'Shall I leave you here then? Or can I give you a lift up to the farm?'

'Don't leave me here. I'll come.'

'Before we go, tell me what the matter is. Please.'

No reply.

'Is it your da playing up again?'

No reply came, but her arm tightened round his waist. Rhodri held on to her and waited.

'I'm being ridiculous. It's time I pulled myself together.'

'You're never ridiculous, and you don't need to pull yourself together, you're the most pulled together person I know, see.'

He turned her to him and hugged her, but after a moment she drew away from him. 'It's Gab.'

Oh God! thought Rhodri, recollecting what Dan had said. He asked as gently as he could, 'Is it, love? What's he been doing that's upset you?'

'He comes closer every day. You could say, and this sounds stupid, he's getting a hold on my mind. I know he's wanting to . . . oust you.'

'But what's he *doing* to make you feel like that?'

'Nothing. Not really.'

'Well then, perhaps you're overtired, things always seem worse when . . .'

Megan stood away from him, her eyes blazing with indignation. 'I'm not in my teens, Rhodri. I do know what I'm talking about. Don't belittle me by saying I'm tired, I'm always tired. I've a massive sleep debt, but it doesn't mean I've lost my senses. Far from it. I'm acutely aware of him and his need of me and I don't like it. If I sack him then I've everything on the farm to do myself and I can't, simply can't, take on any more work. I need him like a drowning man needs a lifebelt. So don't suggest it, unless you have a viable alternative.' Megan flaring up as she did only made Rhodri think she must have good cause.

'Are you sure he's done nothing?'

Her temper cooled instantly but all Megan could say was that he came too close to her, all the time and had in fact kissed her, the more angry she got with him the more daring he became, mistaking her anger for passion.

'Passion!'

'He thinks every woman he meets finds him irresistible. And I can see why. He is irresistible. That's the trouble.'

'Irresistible? My God! I'll kill him.' Rhodri clutched Megan to him and held on to her till she protested. He released her saying, 'Megan, get in the car. Your da in?'

'Of course, what else?'

'We'll make him a cup of tea and then you leave me to talk to him.' He gripped her hand as they climbed the slope up to the lane, stowed her in his front passenger seat and, still breathing heavily, climbed in on the driver's side and revved up the engine. Beating in his brain was the word 'stud' till there was nothing else in his head but that.

They roared up to the farm. Rhodri parked beside Gab's crumbling heap of a car and in his fevered imagination he thought, That sod will be like his own car by the time I've finished with him. Gab was nowhere to be seen, so they went into the kitchen and prepared a tea tray together. Rhodri carried it into the sitting room to find Mr Jones waking up from his afternoon sleep, stretching as best he could and yawning too.

'Good afternoon, Mr Jones. Nice bright day for September.'

'But there's a chill in the air, we can't forget it's autumn.'

'You're right there. Now here's your tea. We've timed it nicely. Who's this mug for, Megan?'

'Gab. Pour it and I'll take it into the kitchen for him.'

Rhodri, grateful Gab didn't drink his tea in the sitting room, said generously. 'Cake too?'

Mr Jones answered him. 'Of course. Cake. He needs to be kept sweet, does Gab, we can't manage without him.'

'I wish you could.'

Megan went out with Gab's tea and cake and didn't come back.

Rhodri took his opportunity. 'Look, Mr Jones, I'm feeling very concerned about Gab. I feel, no, I *know* he's a threat to Megan, and I want something doing about it.'

'I've tried to find someone else but I can't.'

'Do *you* find him a threat to her?'

Mr Jones hesitated and then said, 'Has she said so?'

'This afternoon.'

Mr Jones put down his cup of tea. 'He's getting too familiar with her. I can see that, and far too cocky.'

'Will you agree to us marrying? That would put a stop to it, I'm sure.'

'Absolutely not, Rhodri Hughes. I need Megan here with me and that's that. Good try, Rhodri, good try.'

'And you're willing to put her in jeopardy for your own selfish ends?'

'He won't dare make a move on her, not with me here. Believe me. I have his measure.'

'What I fail to understand is that you bought this farm in the full knowledge that you wouldn't be able to do the work yourself. I can't help but ask why.'

'I'll tell you why. Howard, that's my son, Megan's brother, is one of those who lost his job in the city overnight. There was an ugly fraud case and it meant they had a complete clear out of anyone even remotely connected with it. Howard was one of them. He claims he had nothing to do with it, but I have my doubts, he's easily led. He'd a massive mortgage on his flat, and no money coming in. So he rented the flat out and came home. Came home! To Wales, and did nothing but moan about how isolated we were. Can't imagine why he thought it was any different from when he'd grown up there. He was at a loose end, not knowing what to do so I suggested he took up farming. I said, it's a thriving business, hard work but the returns are there, so why not? He leapt at the chance but said he had to be nearer London, so he could be up there in a couple of hours at the most. I was so delighted he'd come home and was willing to farm I agreed to move. We sold up and came here. We'd been here three months and I was beginning to think it was working out well, after all he'd been brought up with farming and as a boy he'd loved it. Then, out of the blue, he got a call from one of his so-called friends with the promise of a job and immediately he went back to the city and the life he preferred, leaving me and Megan to carry on as best we could. That's why we're here, and as Gab so rightly said only this afternoon, to sell up now would be sheer idiocy.'

'I didn't realise. Megan never mentions him.'

'No wonder. Such a betrayal. She can't bear to say his name out loud. She was distraught when he left. So was I.'

For the first time since Rhodri had known him Mr Jones's eyes filled up with tears.

Rhodri stood up and made the feeblest of excuses. 'I'll get some more hot water, I expect you'd like another cup?' Not waiting for an answer he went to the kitchen primarily to make sure Megan was all right. She was. Gab was sitting at the table with her, concentrating on his tea and cake.

'Here comes the Welsh lover. Hot-foot, ardent and up for it.'

Rhodri objected to his familiarity. 'For a start, you can shut up, nobody asked your opinion. More tea, Megan?'

'Oh! The worm has turned.' Gab laughed and, imitating Rhodri's Welsh accent, he said, 'More tea, Megan?'

'That will do, Gab. If you've finished, you'd best get back to work.' Megan glared at him as she spoke, but it only invited Gab to be even more confrontational towards Rhodri. He stood up, bent over towards Megan and said, 'Right, Meggie, my love, I'll be off then. Milking calls.' Then he darted towards her and kissed her on the lips and with a jeering glance at Rhodri he went out. But he hadn't bargained for Rhodri leaping into action at this affront to his male pride. Before he knew it he and Rhodri were wrestling out in the passage. The noise they made brought Mr Jones to the door of the sitting room.

Unfortunately for Rhodri, his anger had made him reckless; he'd disregarded how big and how fit Gab was. The fight was unequal in every way. Gab was a head taller, and much stronger than Rhodri and if it hadn't been for Megan picking up a tin tray in the kitchen and hitting Gab on the side of his head with it so he was momentarily stunned, there would have been an ignominious ending to the fight for Rhodri.

Breathing deeply Rhodri stood back and Mr Jones shouted, 'Get out! Get out the pair of you. Fighting in my house. I won't have it. Gab, pull yourself together. It was a mere tap she gave you. Get on with the milking, that's what you're paid for.' He was gripping the door frame by this time and his breath was rasping in his throat, his chest visibly heaving with every breath he took.

'Da! Da!' Megan rushed to his side, all thoughts of the threat of Gab gone from her mind.

Rhodri opened the back door and almost kicked Gab out. 'Get back to doing what you know best.' There was a very satisfactory feeling for Rhodri as he said that. He slammed the door shut so hard the house echoed with the noise.

Mr Jones could no longer castigate him, for he was incapable of speech. Megan got him back in his chair and gave him his inhaler. Rhodri took the tea tray out, put the cups and plates in the dishwasher, lined the tea cannister up with the other kitchen jars, put the sugar in the cupboard, and sat down to wait. There would be no point in going to see if he could help Megan with her father, his presence would only make matters worse.

What he didn't like was the realisation that had hit him when he saw Gab kissing Megan. Out of the blue he could understand what it was Megan was talking about when she said that Gab was irresistible to women. He was. He had a kind of sexy charm to him, a sinewy, physical, powerful sort of attraction, and Rhodri hated him for it. His own part in the drama appeared useless if not downright pathetic. He admitted to himself that Gab was more of a man than he.

He heard Megan's footsteps coming towards the

kitchen. Rhodri stayed silent, trying to pick up on her state of mind so he wouldn't say the wrong thing.

As soon as she shut the kitchen door she burst out, 'What made you do it? Honestly, Rhodri, I thought you would have had more sense. You'd better go home, while I see to Da.'

'He's got to go.'

Horrified, Megan said in a loud whisper. 'I'm not putting Da in a home. What are you thinking of?'

'No, no. I meant Gab.'

'Oh! I see, of course. Find me someone else to do his work and he'll go, till then I've got to stick with him.'

'Right.' Rhodri didn't dare offer to kiss her before he went. 'I'll be off. I'll go to Kate's drinks party by myself, then?'

Megan nodded. 'She'll understand I can't come. Give her my good wishes. 'Bye, Rhodri.'

She went out of the kitchen leaving the door wide open for him. So that was it. He was dismissed and he couldn't even have the pleasure of her company at Kate's leaving party. All he had to look forward to tomorrow was visiting Bernard Wilson to check on the dogs. Big excitement that would be. He was so angry about the whole situation at Badgers Lot he knew he'd have to keep his temper in check or else Dan would have something to say if he lost it and made the whole situation even worse than it was. He paused by the back door, debating whether or not to say goodbye to Mr Jones, but decided not to. He went out into the yard hoping against hope he wouldn't bump into Gab before he left. He'd been such a fool to pick a fight with him. Thank heavens Megan had saved his skin. A little smile escaped and lit up his face at the thought. She was resourceful if nothing else, but how much better it would have been if he'd won the fight though. That would have put that damned Gab in his place. As it was . . .

Chapter 13

As it was, Megan spent a large part of the night awake worrying about her da and about Rhodri and wondering if she and he would ever be safely married to each other. That likelihood appeared even more remote than ever, if that were possible. There wasn't any sense in alienating her father by getting married without telling him; in any case she wanted to have friends and family about her to enjoy their day. Not some hole in the corner event as unmemorable as going to the supermarket or visiting the doctor.

Megan felt mean and shallow sometimes when she thought about her da. Much as she loved him, much as she wanted him to be happy there were times she pondered on his selfishness and wished . . . no, she wouldn't indulge herself. If only Howard would help, would come home even if only for a weekend, just to relieve the pressures on her. A phone call once a week did nothing either for her or her da. You'd think a brother would show more interest, if only for her sake. She turned over in bed, thumped her pillow to make it more comfortable, and closed her eyes again.

But opened her eyes immediately and sat up, thinking she'd heard someone trying the front door. Her clock said twenty past five. Twenty past five? The fleeting thought that she'd forgotten to lock up last night passed through her mind, then she heard a foot on the stairs. Then another. It wouldn't be Da, he never came upstairs. Megan reached for her dressing-gown, put it on while still in bed, got out and stood behind the door listening. As she tied the belt there came a tap at the door right by her ear. Megan was so twitchy she actually jumped and clamped a hand to her mouth to stop herself from calling out in fright. But the stealthy movements of the person the other side of the door now centred on the door knob which she saw was being turned, slowly but surely. She stepped back to allow the door to open and a head appeared. It was Gab. In a loud whisper he said. 'Meggie, my love, like I promised, I'm giving you your early morning call.'

Gab didn't actually step into the bedroom but he did wait for an answer. 'Meggie? Are you up already? Meggie!'

Seething with a mixture of temper and fright, Megan answered, 'I'm up. Thanks.'

She heard him chuckle, then say, 'Cup of tea ready for you in the kitchen in five minutes. OK?' The door shut and she was left with a pounding heart and fury boiling up inside her. How dare he? How dare he? What was worse, how had he got in?

She found out when she finally got down into the kitchen. He was standing there, bold as brass, his sandy hair spiky and tousled, his light blue eyes boldly hypnotising her with his direct glance, his shirt neck wide open exposing his bare muscular chest, and their large back door key tauntingly displayed on a chain around his neck.

'I said I would. And I did. I'm a man of my word, you see.'

'Give me that key. Please.'

Gab dodged to the other side of the table. 'Come and get it!'

The singsong tone of his voice incensed her. 'Don't play your stupid games with me. Give me that key. Now.' She held out her hand and waited.

'If you want it, come and get it.' He grinned that attractive grin of his and for a split second she . . . his eyes sparkled as he recognised her hesitation for what it was. 'Come on. Come on.' Gab beckoned with both hands. Softly he whispered, 'You want the key. You come and get it. I'll exchange the key for a kiss. That's fair, isn't it?' Again those inviting, beckoning hands.

'Stop playing the fool. You'd no right to take that key. Give it to me.' But she daren't get close to him.

His eyes roved over her, drinking in the essence of her, draining her will power from her in a way Rhodri never did. 'Even at this early hour you're beautiful. There can't be another woman in the whole world so beautiful at this time in the morning as you. You're a sight for sore eyes.' Gab removed the chain from round his neck and held it out to her. 'Here you are, Meggie my love.'

'Lay it on the table. Go on. On the table.'

With a show of reluctance he did as she asked. He placed it carefully down, arranging it delicately as though it were a great treasure. 'I didn't take your key, I had another one made, at the key cutters in the precinct when I went to get my hair cut yesterday afternoon.'

Megan slipped the key from the chain. 'Here, this is yours. So where is our key, now?' She laid the chain on the table again, the key itself held tightly in her hand behind her back.

'Hanging where it always hangs, on the wall in the passage.'

The tension between them was so strong it was almost visible.

He drank his tea down, his eyes never leaving her face. 'That's better.' He nodded his head towards the door. 'Milking. OK?' He paused for a moment, his hand on the knob of the kitchen door and looked again at her with eyes full of passion. She sensed the intensity of his feelings beating at her. 'I shan't be satisfied till you and me's married. I don't mind your da. It won't bother me it being a threesome, but he won't cower me like he does that Rhodri. If I say, then I say and that's that. Must go.' Before he closed the door, he looked at her with triumph in his eyes.

The lad rapped on the window as he went by with the cows to the milking parlour and it broke the spell. Megan went to the window and watched him and Gab fooling about on their way to begin the milking. God! If she could find someone else, even half as energetic as Gab, she'd take him on this minute. What worried Megan was his magnetism. She knew full well if she hadn't met Rhodri first . . . she would have been in his arms in an instant. That was the danger. Pull yourself together, Megan, she thought. He's a farmhand, that's *all he is*.

Megan sipped her tea. Nevertheless, she thought, he's an attractive devil. She allowed herself to think about him for a moment. Life would be exciting, that's for certain. Her da would have the asthmatic attack of all asthmatic attacks, though, if she said she was marrying Gab. Or would he? There was no gainsaying the fact that Gab's father had a huge acreage, an enormous farmhouse in an enviable position, with amazingly rich pasture land so in actual fact he wasn't just a farmhand . . . the lights flickered as they always did when the milking machine was switched on. The flicker snapped Megan out of her mood. Tea for Da. He'd be waiting, waking early, like farmers always do. As she poured his tea she wondered if this was all it was to be for the rest of his life? She would so have enjoyed the party last night, and Rhodri would have enjoyed it more if she'd been there. They would have left early and gone to Rhodri's and made love. She looked around her kitchen and felt it enclose her like prison walls.

'Good party last night, Kate! Thoroughly enjoyed myself!' Dan dashed past reception and into the staff office at the back. 'Rhodri in?'

Kate, trying desperately to rally her resources after her late night and the excitement of the party, called out, 'No, not yet.'

Dan called over his shoulder 'OK. If he doesn't come before I go, remind me to leave a message for him.'

Kate busied herself organising the appointments for the small animal clinic and printing out the call lists for the farm vets.

Dan came back in. 'My list? Please.'

'You've an emergency at Applegate Farm. Came in five minutes ago. Sounds urgent, but then when Blossom calls it always is. Go there first. The rest is more or less routine.'

Dan picked up his list and said, 'Tell Rhodri I want to know how Bernard Wilson and his dogs are doing, and does he need me to call?'

'Right.' Kate added a note to Rhodri's list, at the same time answered the phone and hoped Annette wouldn't be too long before she got there. Surely she couldn't be blaming the road-works again.

Dan hurtled off to Applegate Farm decidedly pleased with life. Phil Parsons was leaning over his farm gate awaiting his arrival. He'd obviously purchased a new balaclava, for this one was tweedy and brown, but with the two self same slits for his eyes and a bigger one for his mouth. 'About time.'

'Sorry, came as quickly as I could.'

'Come on, then. Come on. It's Star. Right off colour, he is. I'm worried sick.'

As Dan pulled on his boots he asked how the pygmy goats were doing.

'Grand. When you've seen to Star you can 'ave a look at 'em. Hamish is doing a grand job with 'em, and Blossom's right taken with 'em too. Come on, before it's too late.'

'What are the symptoms?'

'You tell me, that's what I pay you for.'

Dan held up a placatory hand, went through the farm gate and headed for the byre where Sunny Boy the bull had always been. He felt quite a pang that it wouldn't be him he'd be attending.

Star, the new occupant of the first-class byre at Applegate Farm, was looking uncomfortable. Dan approached with caution, gently making Star aware of his presence and noticing with approval that his head was tethered firmly, both sides, to the two-foot thick wall.

Phil muttered, 'He's tethered, not taking any more chances. It breaks my heart to see him like that but after Sunny Boy gored Hamish . . . well, I can't take the risk.'

'How is Hamish?'

Mystifyingly Phil replied, 'You'll see after.'

By this time, Dan was in Star's stall using his hands to feel him all over. 'When did this start?'

'He looked a bit uncomfortable last night, Hamish said, not himself you know, but nothing specific. This morning he's worse and hasn't eaten a bite. Not even his favourite snack.'

'What's that?'

'A bag of crisps.'

Dan had to laugh. 'A bag of crisps! Honestly, Phil, I can't believe it.'

Phil chuckled. 'It's his favourite, honest. Loves 'em. Do nearly anything for a bag. Has t'be plain, doesn't like them artificial flavours.'

Dan shook his head in disbelief. 'You've not been giving him anything else strange, have you?'

'Absolutely not.'

'Well, I've taken his temperature and he has got a slight one, which shows things are not quite right. I'll stand here for a bit and watch him. There, look, did you see him look down his flank? There's something causing him pain.' Dan placed his fist on Star's left flank and stayed silent.

Phil whispered, 'Are you doing a bit of faith healing or something? Laying on of hands, like?'

Dan didn't answer, but concentrated hard. Then he said, 'Watch!' and Star glanced down his flank again as though anxious. 'I think he might have something lodged in his rumen because every time it contracts it's making him wince. Got a piece of planking? About five or six feet long?'

Phil, thinking Dan must have taken leave of his senses, disappeared and came back a few minutes later with the required piece of wood. 'Will this do?'

'Excellent! Now you stand the other side of him and pass the wood through and you hold your end and I'll hold mine and when I say lift, lift as hard as you can up against his body.'

'Here! Just a minute, what are we doing?'

'We'll put pressure on his body right where it counts and if it causes him pain, which we'll know by his reaction, then I shall know my diagnosis is correct.'

'Oh! Right!' Still convinced Dan had entirely lost the plot, Phil waited for the signal.

Dan bellowed, 'Lift!' and the two of them heaved the plank of wood up against his body and Star grunted, loudly.

'Just what I thought. Once more to make sure.'

'Well, I'd grunt if someone was heaving a plank up against my insides.'

'Now!' Poor Star grunted again, and lifted a back leg.

'We're right. He's got a piece of wire or some other solid object jammed at the point of his rumen, and he feels it when the rumen begins to contract from that end, and we make him feel it when we push the plank up against him.'

Full of hope Phil asked, 'Maybe it would pass through him with a pint of castor oil? Do you think?'

'No, absolutely not. We've got to get it out.'

In a feeble voice Phil asked, 'You mean, putting your arm up his arse?'

'No, cutting him and pulling it out through his side. It's the only way.'

Phil clung to the top of the stall gate. 'Hell's bells. No, you can't mean it.'

'I do. If I'm going to save him.'

'Think of the risk.'

'Think of the risk if I don't.'

'Knock him out for a few minutes, you mean?'

'No, an injection to numb the whole area and do it while he's standing here.'

'Oh God! Will you need 'elp?'

'An extra pair of hands would be helpful, yes.'

'I'll get Blossom, she's better at this kind of thing than me.' A distraught Phil shuffled off to the house, feet dragging as though taking his last steps on his way to hell.

Blossom appeared in the doorway of the byre wearing a spanking blue-and-white striped butcher's apron over her skimpy clothes, vivid pink rubber gloves on her hands, and her peroxided hair wrapped tightly in a tea towel that had seen better days.

'I've come. Phil's sitting by the fire, stroking the cat and praying.' Her glossy ruby lips broke into a conspiratorial smile. 'No nerve for this kind of thing. Where do we start?'

'Are you sure? It's not pleasant and I've no idea what I shall find when I get in there. He's certainly got a temperature, which will mean a lot of infection and possibly a smell when we get inside.'

'Women are tougher than we look. The main thing is to get Star better. He can't go on as he is. So . . .' She held out her pink rubber hands and they were as steady as a rock. 'See . . .'

'Right then, we'll begin. I shan't say please or thank you or will you, I shall give commands and you'll have to act on them. First, I need a bucket of hot water and some soap to clean myself off now, and again halfway through the operation.'

'Right. I'll get that straightaway.'

Blossom survived the initial opening up of Star's flank, and really admired Dan's stitching technique when he sewed a pocket of Star's rumen to his skin to keep the sack in place and enjoyed watching as Dan made an incision into the rumen, but it was when he put his arm deep down inside, right up to his armpit and was obviously searching about for the foreign body that Blossom came over faint. She clutched hold of the sty wall, swallowed hard, took some deep breaths and was sufficiently in charge of herself to be able to appreciate Dan's shout of triumph as he brought out a huge, crooked, rusty nail, which he examined and then placed carefully on the windowsill of the byre.

'Oh my God! Was that what it was? This nail?'

'In a very painful place. Don't pick it up, I need you to stay clean. I'm stitching next.'

'No wonder he had stomach-ache.'

Blossom pulled herself together and helped Dan disinfect himself, passed him the appropriate needles for stitching up, and didn't really relax until Dan was giving Star a pat of approval.

Dan couldn't have had better help if he'd sent for Bunty to assist him. 'Thank you, Mrs Parsons. You've done very well. Quite remarkable. I wonder, have you trained as a nurse?'

Blossom gave him a wry smile. 'I know it's hard to believe but I have. However, I got caught in a patient's bed one night, Sister found me and went berserk, and I was dismissed. Served me right, it wasn't the first time. But there we are.' She shrugged her shoulders. 'I loved it while I was there, but . . . you can't have everything, can you? I'll go tell Phil, if he hasn't passed out by now. Thank you, Dan, for what you've done. Marvellous.' Her ruby red lips broke into a wicked smile, she twinkled her fingers at him and left.

Before he left, Dan went to find Phil to ask for a look at Callum Tattersall's pygmy goats. He found him leaning on the gate of a small field. A brand new shed had been put in to act as a night shelter, and there busily supervising Hamish tidying it up were the goats, Sybil with her kid at her side.

Phil nodded towards Hamish and shouted, 'Put your shoulder to it, it'll be dark before you've done.'

Hamish looked up, grinned and shouted back, 'Come and give us a hand, then!'

Dan's eyebrows shot up with delighted surprise.

Phil nudged Dan and said quietly, 'Surprised? I bet you are. I told you he'd speak before long, didn't I? Well, it was these here goats that did it, believe it or not.' Phil kept his voice low and told Dan the whole story. 'We came to collect 'em that day, you know, when poor old Callum snuffed it . . . anyway, we knew, Blossom and me, that Hamish was getting close to talking, but he couldn't quite make it. We could see, you know, he was on the brink. Well, he was delighted with the goats and especially the little kid; she was only about two weeks old, wasn't she? Well, that night he went out to make sure they was asleep and comfortable like, it being their first night and he was ages. Blossom said I should go out and check up on him. So I did.'

Phil paused for a moment, unable to carry on speaking. He dug in his pocket and brought out some titbits for the goats, clicked his tongue at them and they came running across to him.

'There you are. That's it. All gone. So, there he was, sitting in the night shelter on the floor in the straw, rocking back and forth with the little kid fast asleep on his lap, holding her like you would a baby, talking away like I don't know what. All like baby talk, you know. I was amazed. Couldn't believe it. All of a sudden he realised I was there and he looked up and smiled and said, "Isn't she beautiful, Phil?" Just as if he'd never been dumb. I just said, "She is that." Then we locked up and went in. I don't mind telling you I was gobsmacked. Soon as we got in Blossom asked him if he wanted hot chocolate or Horlicks before he went to bed, thinking he'd point to the jar like he always did, but he *said*, "Horlicks." Well, she was that overcome she burst into tears. Since then he's talked, almost nonstop. So, you see it was something about that little kid that must have gone right to the very heart of him and kind of healed him up inside.'

'Has he been able to tell you why he couldn't talk, what it was that clammed him up?'

'No. But we were talking the very next day about another kid being due soon, you know, and how we were looking forward to it and Hamish said out of the blue, "He killed the baby, right there, in front of me." And he wept, such terrible grief, like I've never heard before. Broke Blossom's heart it did, and mine, I can tell you. So what that means I can't bear to think, but I reckon it'll all come out in the wash one day. Some kids have rotten lives, don't they? Rotten.'

'Poor chap. But he's happy here, Phil, you must be doing a good job.'

'It's Blossom mainly.' Phil straightened himself up and said, 'Thanks for Star, sorry I couldn't help. By the way, I've given Bernard Wilson a hand to make new runs for his dogs, and I've more or less promised I'll buy one of the young ones off him for Blossom, it'll be one less for him to feed. But don't tell her, it's a surprise for her birthday.'

Rhodri phoned Dan on his mobile later that day and asked him if he had time to go see Bernard Wilson and his dogs. 'I'd promised to call today but I've a road accident come in and I can't leave till I've finished operating and it's a major op, so I don't know how long I shall be.'

'So long as it's all right with you?'

There was a short hesitation and then Rhodri answered, 'Yes, of course it is.'

'Right I'll go, leave it with me. Good luck with the op.'

'Thanks, it's tricky. Crushed ribs. Do or die job.'

'Good luck, then.'

Dan called at Badgers Lot and as he pulled into the farmyard he was greeted by the sound of barking, and an ancient vacuum cleaner grinding away in the farmhouse. He couldn't see Bernard outside so he rattled on the back door of the farmhouse.

The noise of the vacuum stopped and the door was opened by a large woman who looked like a female version of Bernard, except she hadn't got a three-day growth of beard. Instead she had a smooth, fat, rosy country face, with frank, no-nonsense eyes and unfortunately for her, Bernard's bruiser of a nose. 'Yes?'

Dan took off his cap. 'Good afternoon, I'm Dan Brown, Veterinary Surgeon, called to see Bernard's dogs.'

'I'm Hannah, Bernard's sister. He's gone to the feed place, back soon. Feel free to go look, I've shut them all in the stables, 'cos Bernard's cleaning the runs when he gets back. I'll get on if you don't mind.'

Dan thanked her and went to see the dogs. As he turned to cross the yard he noticed a rat trap standing under the kitchen window with two vast rats in it. Hannah's voice boomed out from the door, 'And he's those two to kill when he gets back. The mucky devils that they are.'

'Right!'

The runs had been well constructed, they were large and afforded the dogs plenty of room for exercise. He opened the double doors of one run, closed them safely behind him and opened the top half of the stable door for a view of the dogs. There was a light switch by the door post and Dan switched it on. Today he was greeted by noisy young dogs, not quite as healthy as he would have liked, but a vast improvement on how they'd looked a week ago.

They were rolling and tumbling about, wrestling energetically with each other. One came to the door scrabbling to reach him, Dan bent down to stroke his head. 'Now then, young man, you look better than you did. Bernard been taking care of you, has he?'

Before he got an answer to his question Bernard's old lorry rumbled into the yard loaded with feed bags. Bernard climbed out and came across to speak to him. 'Afternoon, Dan.'

'Afternoon, Bernard. Just happened to be going past.' He nodded his head towards the open stable door. 'You've done a good job. They're looking better.'

Bernard came into the run and hitched his bulk onto the stable door in the space left by Dan. 'By hell! That Blossom Parsons has got something to answer for. She rang my sister, she did, they knew each other when they were nurses together. Told her I needed 'elp.' He jerked his head in the direction of the house. 'The blasted woman's come and she's turned my house upside down. Says she intends living here. "*We're both lonely*" she says.'

Dan studied what Bernard had said and then replied, 'She looks to me as if she'll take care of you all right. Meals and such and you have to admit the house was . . . worse than a pigsty.'

Bernard looked at him. 'Yer nothing if not outspoken, you. Upset all my arrangements, she has.'

'But I bet you've nice clean sheets on the bed and the kitchen's spotless. You've a lot to be thankful for, Bernard.'

'Ummph. Depends how you look at life. Says she wants to put a shower in, so I says if you pay for it you can, thinking she'd back off, but did she? Did she hell as like. Right, she says, I will, when I've got this place cleaned up to my satisfaction, I'll get a plumber in.' Bernard shook his head in disbelief.

Dan decided to change the subject. 'These dogs are beginning to look better. I'll just have a look at the others and then I'll be off.'

'I even have to take my boots off before I go in the kitchen. Says she wants a porch building over the back door so there's room for my boots and farm clothes undercover.' He grunted and groaned at the prospect but Dan could tell, though Bernard wouldn't ever admit to it, that he was quite liking being looked after.

Hannah's foghorn voice boomed out from the back door. 'There's these two to see to.' She was pointing at the rat trap. 'Hurry up. And then there's the dogs' runs to clear up. When you've done that there'll be a nice bite of fruit cake and a cup of tea ready. I'm gasping. How about you, Dan?'

Dan shook his head and refused on the grounds of pressure of time.

Hannah had to have the last word. 'And there'll just be time for you to walk the young dogs before dark, Bernard. I've got some lengths of rope ready, so be sharp about it.'

'Wouldn't mind but she's poured all my beer down the sink. Not a drop, she says, till I've done all the jobs that need doing. Poured it down the sink! How can a man function without his beer, I ask you?'

Dan surveyed Bernard's well-rounded stomach and said, 'Before long you'll be as thin as a whippet!'

Bernard snorted his disapproval, let himself out of the dog run and headed for the rat trap. Dan beat a hasty retreat. If there was one thing he loathed, it was rats. He shuddered, put the Land Rover in first and headed off towards Porter's Fold, the last of his calls for that day, chuckling to himself about Hannah's clean sweep of Bernard's house. She was just what the man needed, was Hannah. He had a good farm with acres of good land, all it required was diligent application and it could become quite a goldmine.

When Dan had finished his last call he went back to the Practice to check in. The waiting room was half full and Kate was behind the desk talking to a client. They both broke off when he approached.

'Hi, Dan! Finished? There're no more calls. Joy says go home if you like. Zoe and Colin have already finished. Slack day today.'

'OK. Will do.'

The client took her credit card from the counter, saying, 'See you Monday, Kate, half past nine. 'Bye.'

'I shan't be here Monday. This is my last day. I'm off to college next week.'

'No! Really. You got in then?'

Kate gave the client one of her winning smiles. 'I did.'

'Will you come back here when you've qualified?'

'I honestly don't know. We'll have to wait and see. They might not want me.' She gave a bubbly laugh and the client laughed too.

'It would be lovely if you could. Good luck, then.'

'Thanks! Be seeing you.'

Dan said good afternoon to the client and then asked Kate if Rhodri was still about.

'He is, but he's not in the best of moods. The dog, you know the road traffic accident? Well, it died. He's awfully upset about it.'

'Oh! Sorry about that. I'll go find him.'

Dan caught up with Rhodri in the staff room and found him in the depths of despair, slouched on a chair, staring into space.

'Sorry, Rhod, about the dog. You did say it was do or die. We can't win every time.'

Rhodri stirred himself. 'No, we can't, but it would have been nice to have made it with this one. Mungo gave a hand but it was no good.'

'Ribs, you say.'

Rhodri nodded. 'Caved in, they were. The owners were distraught.'

'I've been to Bernard's for you. His sister has turned up and is making Bernard's life a living hell. She's cleaning up, trapping rats, and generally organising him with every intention of staying put.'

Rhodri sat up. 'That's a plus then. Just what he needs. And the dogs?'

'Doing much better. The young ones were rolling and tumbling about and beginning to enjoy life.'

Rhodri nodded. 'Good. Good.'

'He could make a go of it, you know, breeding dogs. Nice little earner if it's done properly. And with that sister of his behind him . . .'

'He could. But he'd have to do a sight better than he is now if he's to attract enthusiastic buyers.' Rhodri gave a heavy sigh. 'I wouldn't buy one off him at the moment.'

'What's up, Rhod? It's not just the dog dying, is it?'

Rhodri stood up. 'You don't want to know my troubles.'

'That's for me to decide.' Dan deliberately planted himself on a chair and made himself comfortable.

Rhodri sat down again but stayed silent. Then opened his mouth as though he was going to speak, closed it and then changed his mind again. 'My ferret, you know, Harry, I found him dead this morning. Old age, you know. And this dog dying on me hasn't helped. I've had Harry since he was a few weeks old. We knew each other so well, and he could still surprise me.'

'In the scheme of things Harry going is really quite a small thing . . . You—'

'Small thing? It might be to you but it isn't to me. That's your trouble, always seeing things in black and white. I wonder sometimes if you have a heart at all.'

'Oh I have, indeed I have, but you need to get your priorities right. I think Megan is far more important. I saw Gab in a shop in the town the other day. The assistants were round him like bees round a honeypot. You can see why, where women are concerned us lesser mortals can't hold a candle to him.'

Rhodri was standing up looking out of the window by now and ignoring Dan's remarks. He was thinking of Harry. Of how, that morning, Harry had not come to the bars of his cage when he'd gone out to bring him in the house for a run before he left for work. Of how he'd dreaded opening up Harry's sleeping quarters, guessing what he'd find. But there he was, his eyes wide open, his mouth open, his lips drawn back in a grimace, and dead. He'd picked him up and held him to his cheek to remind himself of the feel of him and for a last goodbye, but it simply wasn't Harry any more, he'd left already for wherever it was ferrets went at the end of their lives. There'd never be another Harry, he couldn't bear another parting like this.

'Rhod?'

'Sorry. We were talking about Megan, weren't we? I don't need you to tell me that. Megan herself admits how attractive he is. Not that *she* finds him attractive, but she knows he is, which he is and I wish he wasn't. You don't know of a farm hand in need of a job, do you? Because that's what she wants, someone to replace Gabriel Bridges.'

'I don't, no, but I do wonder if you should persuade Megan to marry you and you say that you'll live at the house with Old Man Jones.'

Dan thought Rhodri would explode, the expression on his face was so outraged as he turned from the window. '*Live* with that conniving, nasty old beggar? Not likely.'

'But when he sees he's not threatened with being left on his own or having to go into a nursing home, he'll come round to it. Heavens above, the house is big enough. I bet it would be possible to make quite separate living quarters. You and Megan in one part and him the other. He's scared he'll be no longer in command of himself, no longer in charge of his life and all that. You've got to try to see it from his point of view.'

'You haven't had him raise his stick to you and miss hitting you by a hair's breadth. That is humiliating, see.'

'I can believe that, but that's what I'm saying: he's not given up on himself and isn't likely to, so you do some compromising and I think he is enough of a man to do the same. He'll want to match up with you because you're treating him as though he's a man and not an embittered invalid. It's not giving in, Rhodri, on your part, it's using your brain. He's a tough chap, as well you know, so it's the two of you at loggerheads.' Dan clenched his fists and banged his knuckles together imitating the two opposing forces. 'You're just as stubborn as he is in your own way, Rhod, but it's for you to make the first move.'

'It's just the thought of living under the same roof. I have this picture in my mind of us getting married and living in my house, see. On our own. That's what I wanted above everything, to *rescue* Megan.'

'But he wouldn't be in *bed* with the two of you, would he? It would be you and Megan at the other end of the house. Just think of that. Every night in bed together.'

Rhodri blushed bright red. He looked away out of the window again and quietly asked, 'Would you compromise like that for Rose?'

Dan nodded his head. 'I'd find it very difficult, if not impossible, but for Rose's sake, yes, I would. And believe me, her mother would be twenty times more difficult to live with than that old man, because she's chosen to be a bitch for absolutely no reason at all. And think, you'd be better placed for keeping an eye on Gab too, there is some merit in that.'

'Do you know, you're right there.' Rhodri became seized by the idea. 'I could rent out my house to someone, live at Beulah Bank Farm married to Megan, and see how it all pans out. It's not the solution I would have preferred, but you've made me see it's better than nothing at all.' Rhodri pounded his right fist into the palm of his other hand and looked triumphantly at Dan. 'You've persuaded me, I don't know how, but you have.'

'I'm sure it would take the edge off Gab's obsession too, her being married.'

'Oh yes. I think it would. Why have I never thought

like this before? I can't believe I've been so blinkered. Of course old Jones is frightened and quite rightly so. The poor beggar.' Rhodri paused and then said, with a wry smile on his face, 'It crosses my mind he won't live to an old age, will he? Not in his state.'

'Now Rhod, now Rhod, I didn't put that in my equation.' Dan wagged a warning finger at him. 'But it is a thought.' Then he burst into laughter.

Rhodri caught the infectiousness of it and laughed too. 'By God! I'll do it. Yes, I will.'

'You're a wise man and kind with it.'

Rhodri smiled and said, his voice full of excitement and energy, 'I'm off to propose.'

Chapter 14

He did just that with flowers, a bottle of champagne and the engagement ring he'd bought months before. Halfway there he rang her on his mobile and suggested she walked down to the bridge to meet him because he had something special to say.

She hadn't got there by the time he arrived so he sat in the car admiring the emerald and diamond ring he'd bought her. It sat so beautifully in its box, contrasted so well with the black velvet lining, it almost seemed a pity to take it out, but he knew how much better it would look on her finger. The oblong emerald caught the rays of the sun and dazzled him, to say nothing of the wonderful sparkle of the diamonds surrounding it. Apart from his house and his car, it was the most expensive thing he'd ever bought.

Rhodri looked up when he heard her quick step on the tarmac of the road. His heart leapt. Having her da under the same roof seemed a small price to pay for such a prize. He closed his fingers over the box.

They held hands as they walked down the slope to the edge of the stream. Silently Megan drew his attention to a kingfisher poised alertly on a stone just above the water's edge. His bright eyes shone in the sunlight as he made to fly off, changed his mind and then in a flash he was gone. Rhodri tried to follow his darting flight down the stream and thought what a good omen it was to have seen such a rare sight. It gave him courage.

'Megan. I've decided. I want us to be married and I'm willing to live at the farm with you and your da. I've always imagined that you would come to live with me in my house, always thought it was the only way, because I wanted to rescue you from slaving for your da, Sir Galahad to the rescue, you know, but I realise that's not possible, so I thought if he saw I was willing to compromise then he might compromise as well, if that's possible.'

She said nothing, but he felt her fingers tighten on his.

'So, I've bought you an engagement ring. I love it and I hope you do, but if you don't I'll gladly exchange it for another one. It's an emerald with diamonds round it and it will suit I'm sure but, as I say, if it doesn't then that's all right by me and we'll go back to the jewellers. Of course, it may not be to your taste so if it isn't ... well we'll change it. I don't mind in the slightest.'

'Rhodri! Hush! Show me.' His hands were shaking so much he couldn't open the box. Megan placed a gentle hand on his and said, 'Darling! Why the nerves?'

Rhodri, filled with hope, calmed his racing heart and opened the box. Megan gasped with pleasure when she saw it, a gasp so genuine he knew instantly that she loved it. It slid on her finger as if it had been designed especially for her. She held up her hand and admired the fire in the diamonds and the wonderful, deep, flashing green of the emerald. In a hoarse, reverent whisper she said, 'I love this. Absolutely love it. If I'd been with you I'd have chosen this very ring myself. And I want to say how much I appreciate you offering to live at the farm. It's a big sacrifice and I realise how much you must love me to make it. I'm proud to wear a ring given to me by such a loving man, such a dear, kind man like you. It's an honour, it truly is.'

Megan flung her arms around Rhodri and she kissed him like she'd never kissed him: gone was the sweet tenderness of her kisses, replaced by a wild, fierce loving, the depths of which he had not seen before. This was a Megan full of a deep, rousing passion. When she gave him time to draw breath he said, 'Put me down! Put me down!' Then clutched her tighter than ever and kissed her frantically. When they stopped kissing from shortage of breath Rhodri burst out with, 'Harry Ferret died today.'

Megan released herself from his arms and said, 'Well, honestly! That's nice! Harry dies, so suddenly you're willing to come to live at the farm. Would you prefer to stay where you are and get another ferret instead of me?'

Rhodri took her seriously and shook his head sorrowfully from side to side. 'It's been an awful blow losing Harry, but no I shan't get another.'

'I suppose that's some consolation even if I, obviously, come second best.'

'Now, Megan, you know I don't mean that, what I really meant to say was . . .' Rhodri saw she was laughing and knew he'd dropped himself right in it. 'Sorry, I didn't mean it to sound like that. I'd have proposed even if he hadn't died this morning.'

Megan's eyes filled with tears. 'I know. I shall miss him. I'm so sorry, love. It must have been dreadful.'

'I knew it was coming, he hadn't been himself for a few days. Not interested in anything and not a pest when he was out, so I knew.' He turned away from her and bent to retie his shoelace so his voice was muffled. 'It won't be easy for me coming to live at the farm, but I'll do my best.

Perhaps if I'm willing to compromise on what I would have preferred, your da might too.'

'Don't spoil a lovely moment talking about how stubborn Da is. Let's go tell him. Better still, ask his permission.'

'His permission?'

'His permission to marry his daughter, see.'

'Ahhh! Right.'

He stood outside the sitting-room door, nervous beyond measure, knowing he musn't make a mess of asking permission this time, knowing he must do it thoroughly and properly and most of all humbly but firmly. He felt Megan's hand push him right in the middle of his back as she whispered, 'Go on, he can't bite.' Oh no? Rhodri pushed open the door.

He put the ring in its box on the table beside his chair. 'Good evening, Mr Jones.'

A bent twisted index finger pointed at the box. 'What's this?'

Courage came to him when it was most needed, and he spoke without a stammer, plainly and forthrightly. 'An engagement ring. I've asked Megan to marry me and before you say anything, I've asked her on the understanding that we live here, in this house after we're married. I know there might be difficulties, but I realise you can't live on your own and I wouldn't want to deprive you of your daughter and maybe if we both try to be civilised we would manage quite nicely. It's what I want. It's what Megan wants and we both hope it's what you will want. So, I'm asking for your daughter's hand in marriage, and I hope you'll give us your blessing.'

Mr Jones didn't reply.

Rhodri, running out of steam, sat down abruptly and

waited patiently, and when he still didn't speak he suggested he should open the box and have a look at the ring.

'You open it.'

So Rhodri did and Mr Jones for once in his life was quite taken aback. 'Has Megan seen it?'

Rhodri nodded. 'Just now.'

'She likes it?'

'Loves it.'

'I see.'

He seemed very calm and Rhodri became anxious that it might be the calm before the storm. He closed the box and put it in his pocket. 'Well?'

'She's very precious to me. Never realised how much till a week or two ago. Always felt boys were more important in a family, see. Then I saw that Gab, of the lustful eyes, admiring her and I thought, no, you're not getting this precious daughter of mine.' He paused, looked up at Rhodri, with what passed for a smile for Mr Jones, and said, 'I wish we had champagne in the house, we need to crack a bottle open.'

'Great minds think alike. I've just put one in your fridge.'

'What are you waiting for then? Open it. Never mind waiting for it to chill. Go on, boy.'

Rhodri stood up. 'It's all right with you, then?'

'I wouldn't be opening champagne just for fun, now would I?'

'Thank you.' Rhodri put out his hand. 'Let's shake on it.' Mr Jones extended his arm and they shook hands.

His heart bursting with love and complete delight that he'd finally got Old Man Jones on his side, though he'd never actually said he could marry Megan, not in so many words, Rhodri charged at the kitchen door, flung it open and shouted, 'Crack open the champagne! Your da says . . .'

Seated at the table drinking tea was Gab with a face like thunder.

Looking back on the whole episode that night before she slipped into what proved to be a fitful sleep Megan cringed at the horror of it. Immediately before Rhodri had flung the door open with such heartfelt delight, Gab, in a wild burst of silent anger, had broken every stem of the flowers Rhodri had given her and flung them in the waste bin. When he'd returned to sit down his hands shook so violently they were almost beating a tattoo on the table, and the tea was jumping out of his mug at every beat. She wished she'd never told him.

Megan had leapt out of her skin when the door had bounced open and revealed Rhodri standing there, his face glowing with his overwhelming happiness. There must have been much less than thirty seconds of silence but it felt an age and then Gab, with a snarl on his face like that of a cornered fox, said, 'You'll never have a moment's joy, Meggie. Never! I'm the man for you. I've told you before and I'm telling you now, you're mine. *Mine*, do you hear!' Gab had got to his feet and in one surprising fluid movement had skirted the end of the table, grabbed her by the arms and kissed her full on the lips. Taken so completely by surprise it was a moment before Rhodri took action.

He'd run round the end of the kitchen table to prise Gab's arms from Megan, but Gab held her in a vice-like grip. She struggled to escape, fearful for Rhodri's safety, but neither he nor she could get her away from him. Gab threw his head back and gave a tortured roar, 'Leave her be! She's mine!'

Megan's da came in. 'Let her go! Do you hear me? Let her go!'

Gab shook her like a terrier with a rat, till her brains felt as though they were thudding against her skull. 'Listen to me! Listen to me! You're mine! Mine! Do you hear?'

Megan cried out, 'Please, Gab! Please stop.' Gab's fury fell away from him just as quickly as it had come. What all three of them were fearful of was the anguish of his eyes and the violence of his shaking body. For a moment he stood there looking at them standing in a tight cluster by the table. He spun on his heel and headed for the kitchen door in a wild zig-zag as though his legs didn't belong to him, muttering to himself. Megan knew he was in love with her, that he was passionate about her, but she had never realised just how deeply he felt. She was terribly shocked by his reaction to her engagement, shocked to the core.

They listened for his next move. His car ground and whined as it always did as he strived to start it up, then it fired and he roared away out of the yard.

No one spoke.

No one moved.

Till Megan pulled her frock straight.

Her da picked up his walking stick from the table.

Rhodri tried to pull himself together.

In a strange, high voice Megan said, 'I think we'll have tea and leave the champagne till later.'

Her da said, 'Thank God he's done the milking before he left.'

Rhodri said, 'You're not having him back after that, are you?'

'No! Put a drop of whisky in mine, Megan.'

Megan put a drop in each of their cups and carried them through into the sitting room.

For two hours they'd debated how they'd manage the farm without Gab, and whether or not they should tell Mr Bridges exactly why he wouldn't be allowed back.

In the end Megan's da had said firmly, 'I shall tell him. In fact I'll tell him right away. Pass me the phone, Rhodri. Please.'

Before Rhodri had found the number in the telephone book there was a loud knocking at the door.

They'd looked at each other in turn, uncertain what to do. 'Who's that?' they said. 'Who's that?' 'Is it Gab?'

The hammering began again, so Mr Jones said, 'Rhodri, would you be so kind as to answer the door?'

Megan recalled the fear she'd felt in her bones when she heard Richie Jamieson's voice in the hallway. What did he want with them? Questions had raced through her head, one after the other.

The inspector had removed his hat before he spoke and they all watched him intently as he smoothed his ruffled hair. 'I might as well come straight out with it. I'm sorry to have to tell you that Gabriel Bridges has been shot. As you apparently were the last people to see him we wondered if you wouldn't mind making a statement?'

Rhodri flinched at the word 'shot', feeling this was one shock too many. He licked his dry lips before he spoke. 'When you say shot, do you mean he's *dead*?'

'No, but it would appear he's very close.'

The inspector had taken statements from all three of them. They'd each described the events of the evening as they saw them, trying desperately to be accurate. Finally the question came. 'Rhodri. Did you leave the house at all? For any reason.'

'No, I met Megan at the bridge and then came on here and I have never left the house at all. I've not even gone into the yard, since I got here.'

He asked both Mr Jones and Megan if they could verify that.

Mr Jones tapped his stick on the floor. 'Richie, I don't quite know what you're getting at with that question, but I can tell you that Rhodri has never left the house, not for a second. If he had he would have said so, when you asked him.'

The inspector smoothed his hands over his hair. 'Do you own a gun, Rhodri?'

'No, never.'

'Mr Jones?'

Megan's da shook his head. 'I do not. I will not allow them in the house.'

'Megan?'

'Never, ever. I know nothing about guns.' The awful suspicion the inspector was inferring made her ask, 'Tell us exactly what you mean when you ask us if we have guns and have we left the house?'

When the inspector answered he emphasised each word very deliberately. 'Mr Bridges says that if Gab had shot *himself* he would not have missed. He's very adamant about that. He would have done the job properly he says, him being a crack shot.'

Mr Jones was horrified. 'It isn't an attempt at suicide, then? You're sure about that?'

'Not had time for forensics to come up with any firm evidence. Just making inquiries.'

'Where was he found?'

'Well, Mr Jones, he was found in one of the Bridges's barns with the gun beside him. None of them had any idea he'd been in the house, that he'd got his gun out of their special reinforced gun cupboard, gone out to the barn and used it. The first they knew was when they heard the shot. They went out and found him. Stunned, they are.'

Megan broke down in tears. She kept repeating, 'All because of me.' Time and again.

Then her da spoke with more vigour and conviction than he had for a long time. 'Get Megan a brandy, Rhodri, please. Megan, you're not to blame. He knew full well that you and Rhodri were . . . well, together and wanting to marry. It most certainly wasn't your fault, because you never gave him any encouragement. Now, pull yourself together and drink that brandy. Go on. I want to hear no more of you being to blame. You're not. Now inspector, we've told you all we can, may we be left to ourselves?'

It was a polite way of putting it and the inspector could find no more reasons for staying so he'd agreed he would leave. 'It may turn out that the evidence proves he tried to commit suicide in which case I shall trouble you no more. Mr Bridges was so certain, you see, that he wouldn't do any such thing. Not Gab. Don't fret yourself, Megan. All may turn out better than we think. I'll be in touch.' Then the inspector had left the house.

Later, Megan flung herself over in bed, and tried to sleep but all the time, racing through her head, were the events of the evening and they wouldn't go away. She'd had no idea that Gab was so intense about his feelings for her. No idea at all, well perhaps that was not strictly true, because she'd felt a response to his advances more than once, which she'd hurriedly squashed knowing he wasn't right for her, but for this to happen ... She went downstairs to make herself a drink only to find the kitchen light on and her da boiling a kettle.

'Da! Why didn't you shout for me? I would have come down and made you a drink. You know that.'

Mr Jones put an arm around her shoulders. 'I'm not entirely useless, my dear, not quite anyway. You've been through enough tonight, I can't ask any more of you. I'm making the tea, is that all right?'

'Yes, but I can do it.' She tried to intervene but he would have none of it, so they sat in the kitchen drinking the first cup of tea he'd made in years. 'I shan't make a nuisance of myself when Rhodri comes to live here. I'm making plans.'

Megan reached across the table and touched his hand. 'There's no need to make any plans. We'll be all right. Believe me.'

'But I am. You and Rhodri deserve me making plans. You don't need an old chap like me on the scene all the time. We all need privacy and I shall see the two of you, and I, have it.'

'Thank you, Da, I do love him, really, really love him, you know and he loves me. So very much. We're going to be very happy. Living here was his idea, not mine. He's always fancied us being together at his house you see, but ... anyway ...'

'I appreciate him thinking of me, and in return I've to do my best for both of you, because I want you to be happy.'

Megan had stood up, put an arm around his shoulders and squeezed him tight. 'Gab saying we'd never be happy, he's wrong, isn't he?'

'The man was out of his mind when he said that. Take

no notice of him. I'm determined you'll be happy. Somehow I just needed Rhodri to take that one step forward to make me see daylight. I'm sorry I've been so unthoughtful, cruel almost—'

'No, Da, never cruel.'

Rather sharply Mr Jones replied, 'Don't tell me what I am. I know I've been cruel. Now drink up and then bed and we'll see about Gab in the morning. You and I, we'll go together and sort things out.'

The following morning Rhodri had a long string of appointments and he couldn't let his clients down, so he arrived at the Practice early and was waiting to start his day. After the night he'd had he was in no mood for tender loving care for anyone but Megan.

He'd buried poor Harry when he'd got home from Megan's: in his garden, in the dark, with his sitting-room window open and his CD player blaring out Jeremiah Clarke's *Trumpet Voluntary*. It seemed appropriate for such a time. He'd stood for a moment, silent and introspective, brooding on the day he'd had, a day of unbelievable contrasts. The road-accident dog he couldn't save, Dan turning his mind round so completely about living at the farm, proposing to Megan and her absolute joy when she saw the ring he'd bought her. Then the pleasure of Mr Jones's acceptance of him, though it was his due after all, and then the horror of Gab and the possibility in Richie Jamieson's mind that he, Rhodri Hughes, the epitomy of stern moral values, might have tried to *kill Gab*. It made him shudder when he thought about Gab's desperation. He felt he kind of owed Gab something, he'd be creative about that tomorrow, because Gab wouldn't actually die if it wasn't as serious as first thought. No, Gab was tough, he'd survive.

Rhodri looked down at the fresh mound of earth covering Harry. Poor Harry Ferret, no more walks, no more unravelling of the loo roll, no more finding him hidden fast asleep under a cushion. No more Harry burying his busy nose and whiskers in his jumper. Poor Harry. He'd miss him. The final flourish of the trumpet ended. Rhodri had cleaned off his spade, shaken his Wellingtons off on the back door mat, propped the spade against the wall and gone in to bed and sleep.

So, here he was about to begin another day, his first as a betrothed man, engaged to be married to the light of his life. For a moment he indulged himself by thinking about breakfast in the kitchen with Megan each morning before he left for work and how that would set him up for the day, and smiled to himself.

Goliath Costello was the first client on his list. He opened his consulting room door and called out, 'Good morning, everyone, Goliath Costello, please.'

Miranda leapt from her chair and dashed in with Goliath. 'Have you heard about the eldest of the Bridges? Been shot he has, according to the police, in one of their own barns. Honestly, who'd do a thing like that? A lovely young chap like him?'

'I did hear. Booster for Goliath, is that right?'

'Yes. Can never remember which one is which of those boys, they're all so alike. Ben, Gab, Gideon, Simeon, Joe and . . . what's the other one, all out of the Bible, I know! Elijah, no, that's not right, I know: Joshua. Poor chap. Never done no harm to anyone, Gab hasn't, but to shoot him in his own barn! I ask you.'

'There, that's Goliath sorted for another year. How's his behaviour, is he still messing all over the place?'

Miranda looked up at him, eyebrows raised. 'What?'

'I said has he stopped messing all over the place?'

'Goliath? Oh yes. I realised you were quite right when you said he was top dog, so after that, when he did it, I started picking him up by his scruff and growling at him and shaking him, like his mother would have done and chucking him out the door and completely ignoring him and it worked. So, they say the police are hot on the trail. I mean why would one of the Bridges boys want to kill *himself*. I've just had a thought. Was it over that Jones girl? You know her, don't you? From Beulah Bank Farm? Lovely looking girl. Have you heard any more news, is he still holding his own?'

'I don't know.' Rhodri, completing the data on the computer for Goliath, wished she wouldn't go on about it. 'That's it, then. Be seeing you, Miranda.'

'I reckon it's a *crime passionnel*. That's what. I reckon some boy got jealous of him, followed him home and shot him. With his own gun though, that's a bit much, isn't it? They could at least have used their own.' Miranda looked at Rhodri for some response and realising she wasn't going to get any, finally decided to go. 'I'm off then. 'Bye!'

His next client, surprisingly, was Mr Featherstonehough and in his hand a brand new cat basket. 'Spect you're surprised to see me?'

'I am. But it's very pleasant. Who's this?'

'This is Cleo. About six months old she is, I think, and I've come to have her checked over and to see about having her spayed, that's if she needs it. I don't know, you see.' He lifted her out of the basket and placed her on the table. 'Now, isn't she beautiful? My late wife's name was

Cleo, so I've called her after her, seeing as she'd always wanted a cat and couldn't have one.'

Rhodri admired Cleo. She had the most unusual deep amber, slightly slanted eyes set in a pointy, elegant face and her fur was the colour of milky coffee. She pranced about the examination table in a most delightfully giddy manner. 'My word, but she's a very pretty cat. A bit of the oriental about her in her face. Where did she come from?'

'Found her under a bush in my garden, sheltering from the rain, lost and alone, fed her a couple of days, advertised I'd found her but no one came forward so I took her in. She's a bundle of love she is.' He kissed the top of her head and looked at Rhodri slightly shamefaced and embarrassed.

'Can't see any sign that she's been spayed, but she does seem very young to me. I shouldn't guess her to be more than eight months.'

'I don't want no toms after her and all that business.' Mr Featherstonehough placed Cleo back in her basket. 'I miss him you know, Adolf, I mean, the great beast of a dog that he was. I can't quite forget him, you know. Still listen for his claws on the kitchen floor, or I think I can hear him scratching the door to come in. It's hard, but she's beginning to fill the gap.' He patted the basket.

'It's bound to be hard. I mean, you had him for almost twelve years, that's a long time in anyone's life.'

Mr Featherstonehough rapidly changed the subject. 'Talking of life, have you heard about Gab Bridges? Terrible, isn't it? They say he's blown half his face away. Have you heard that?'

'I understand things are not quite as bad as first thought. They say he's been very lucky, and they've every hope—'

'Can't understand why he did it.'

Rhodri answered as non-commitedly as he could. 'Love life gone to pieces, I understand.'

'Ah! Well, poor chap. See you Tuesday.'

And so it went on, client after client, all with their own theories as to what might have happened, the stories increasing in intensity and wild supposition as the day progressed. Even Alan Tucker, newcomer though he was, had theories to air when he came in for Bingo to have his foot looked at.

'Thought we'd come to the country for a quiet life and what do we find? A near murder within weeks. Are they clients of yours? I expect they must be, them being farmers. 'Course that's the trouble, isn't it, farmers with guns all too easily available. It's his front left foot, it's swelling up and he's limping. They say the Bridges boy's close to death. Poor chap, at his age. What an ending. I did hear they thought he'd interrupted some poachers and they'd shot him. They say he shot at them first but missed. Blood! Never seen the like, you could have taken a bath in it, they say. It's a what?'

'A thorn or a needle gone right into his foot between the pads, here look, it's gone in slanting and very deep. He's very sensitive about it. Must be painful.' Rhodri crouched on the floor and held Bingo's foot so Mr Tucker could see. 'See, I think I can get it out with tweezers. Will he be all right, do you think?'

Mr Tucker, uncomfortably reminded of the incident in the waiting room with the cat Muffin, agreed he would. 'He's settled down now in the new house. No problem. That cat! God that was embarrassing.'

'Hold him tight with his head well away from me. That's it.' Rhodri gripped hold of the end of whatever it was and pulled. Bingo stood for him as though carved from stone.

It was a sewing machine needle Rhodri finally extracted from his pad. 'There we are. You're a good patient, Bingo. Very good. Don't walk him on muddy ground for a day or two, help prevent infection, see. If he's still limping badly two days from now, bring him in and I'll take another look. It should be OK, though, but you never know.'

'Thank you, Mr Hughes. Thank you. You don't know anything about this Bridges boy then?'

'I know he isn't going to die, that's a fact, and you can tell anyone you meet the bullet didn't go into his brain. Skimmed it by a millimetre. Good morning, Mr Tucker.' Rhodri patted Bingo on the head. 'You're a good dog, Bingo, nice to know.' Bingo looked up at him, his fine dark eyes viewing Rhodri benignly. 'I'll give him an antibiotic to fight any infection. Right? Bit of Rhodesian Ridgeback in him, is there?'

Mr Tucker smiled. 'Bit of everything, I think.' He turned to leave and then turned back. 'The cat, was it all right?'

'Couple of stitches and some frayed nerves but otherwise absolutely fine.'

'Good. I'm glad. Good morning and thank you, Mr Hughes.'

The waiting area had buzzed with rumour all morning and if a client hadn't known about it when they came in they did before they left. When he took his break Rhodri rang Megan but there was no reply so all he could do was leave his love to her on the answer machine.

That was because Megan had driven Mr Jones to Bridge

262

Farm and they were sitting in the kitchen around the big old pine table with the five boys and Mrs Bridges.

'My Billy's at the hospital, he hasn't left since they took him there.'

'What's the situation today?' Mr Jones asked.

'It is not nearly as serious as they first thought. The bullet has skimmed his brain down the left-hand side and come out again. He had a scan last night and they're very hopeful he'll make a full recovery. Half an inch the other way and he'd have been . . .' Mrs Bridges took a deep breath and gained control of her trembling voice.

'So, Mrs Bridges, I'm sorry to talk about such painful things but we do need to know the truth. We are involved. Have you any more news about who shot him, if indeed that was the case?'

All five of the boys went on red alert at the thought that Gab had fired the gun himself but Josh, ever the peacemaker, said quickly, 'Later today they'll be able to tell us.'

'I can tell you it certainly wasn't Rhodri, he was with Megan and me in the house and never left it after Gab had gone. We're truly very distressed about it all. Please believe me.'

At the mention of Megan's name the Bridges boys all looked at her and she flushed at their scrutiny.

Mrs Bridges said, 'You've no call to be upset, girl. I knew he was in a bad way over you. I told him you were promised, but he wouldn't listen. Gab's tough, he'll pull through.' Her bravery was all the more commendable when you saw that her normally bonny face was drained and aged with her anxiety.

Megan said, 'I'm so sorry about it all, Gab was terribly upset when he left, I'd just told him Rhodri and I had got

263

engaged. He took it very badly. He couldn't stop shaking. That would be why . . . he missed. Him shaking . . .' Her voice trailed off.

Josh asked how they'd managed the milking this morning.

'I did it with the lad.'

Mrs Bridges tut-tutted. 'Well, then you shouldn't have, my dear. One of our boys will be there this afternoon and take over Gab's work till we see how things go. So don't you fret . . .'

The back door burst open and in came Mr Bridges, haggard, unshaven, tousled. He gasped when he saw eight faces looking at him. 'What about work? Done everything, have you? And what are you two doing here?'

Before anyone could answer him, Mrs Bridges stood up and went to him. Looking up into his face she asked so softly they could barely hear. 'Come now, Billy, tell his mother how he is.'

Billy looked down at her, the belligerence set aside for the moment. 'Well, he's coming round, Adele. Like they said, it's not nearly as bad as we thought at all. The bullet missed his brain by only a hair's breadth, and they emphasise it's early days, but things are looking very good. That's why I've come home for a shower and some food and a change of clothes. So he'll be back before we know it. He'll have scars and that, but they say plastic surgery can do miracles.'

Mrs Bridges put her hand to her heart and sat down again before her legs gave way. 'Thank God for that. I shall go in a while to see him, while you get some sleep. One of you boys will drive me.' They all five nodded their agreement.

'Dad! I'm volunteering to take over from Gab at Beulah Bank till we get sorted.'

'I see, Josh. That's if I agree. Now what have you two to say for yourselves?' Billy Bridges turned to look at Megan. 'You, young filly, been enticing my boy, have you? Driving him out of his mind with your temptations?'

Indignantly Megan got to her feet. 'Indeed I have not. No.' She sat down as abruptly as she'd got to her feet. What else was there she could say? Talk about his obsession? His deliberate goading of Rhodri? Certainly not.

Mrs Bridges took hold of her hand and said sympathetically, 'I know what my Gab is like, once he's made up his mind, nothing will alter it. But you must be someone very special for him to have tried to . . . kill himself.'

Billy Bridges was beside himself. Fists clenched, face livid with anger he roared, 'He did not try to kill himself, it was someone else who shot him. I reckon there was a struggle and the gun went off, unexpectedly like. If Gab had fired it, he would have made a proper job of it. Him being trained to firearms.'

Mrs Bridges sprang to her feet with such speed she knocked over her chair and it bounced with a tremendous clatter onto the tiled floor, and small though she was, she battered his chest with her fists shouting, 'Do you want him dead? Is that it? *Dead*, to satisfy your pride? Eh? To want him dead rather than admit he didn't shoot straight? And to break my heart. Is that what you want?' She moaned in her anguish. 'He's so very precious to me. Oh! *Billy!* What are you thinking of? Shame on you.'

A shocked silence followed her outburst. No one knew what to say. The boys had never seen her like this. Then Mrs Bridges threw herself on Billy's chest and sobbed so painfully not one of them could bear it. Mr Bridges stood there helpless, as though this accusation was the last straw for his muddled exhausted mind. He was in such shock that he didn't even put an arm around her as she lay against him. Josh got up and went to take hold of her. He hugged her tightly and then sat her down on a chair and fished a tissue from a box on the kitchen worktop and handed it to her. He stood behind her and bent to rub his cheek on the top of her head. His father stood, head down, grieving.

Mr Jones, uncomfortable at witnessing such an intimate moment, cautiously got to his feet and said, 'We shall be more than glad of your help, Joshua, if your father approves. The lad's quite useful, just needs a kick up the behind sometimes, lazy, you know. We'll go. Billy, I'm sorry for all this and about Gab, but nothing Megan or I have done caused it. We are deeply grieved and we're grateful it isn't as bad as everyone first thought.'

Megan gave him her arm to hold on the way out. It was Josh who opened the door for them. Mr Jones said quietly to him, 'We're so sorry, believe me. You'll let us know about Gab?'

Josh nodded and closed the door behind them.

Chapter 15

Josh settled down to work at Beulah Bank as though he'd been there for years. He was the gentle one of the Bridges boys, at nineteen the baby of them all by five years, with the same height and colouring as them but an entirely different temperament from Gab. He worked hard, with none of the swagger and gutsy energy of Gab; he got through the work, and got the best out of the lad without even so much as raising his voice. Within a couple of days it was as if it had been him helping them out all these weeks and not Gab. What he refused to do was drink his tea or have his lunch in the kitchen. He and the lad had decided to eat together in the old tack room. They found a couple of old chairs in a barn and an old blanket box dumped in there years ago to use as a table and set themselves up very comfortably.

'No, thank you, Megan. I'll have mine with the lad. Keep an eye on him, you know.'

'I really don't mind, we'd be glad . . .'

Firmly Josh repeated his refusal. 'Thanks all the same.'

Megan hadn't realised until the pressure was lifted just how much Gab had upset her with his constant closeness. She'd never noticed that she was adjusting her behaviour all day to accommodate the vagaries of his moods and his working patterns, and to avoid at all costs being left alone with him, either in a barn or the cow byres or any of the stables. In fact her whole life had been governed by him and that didn't include trying to avoid those hot greedy eyes of his, nor the constant fear of his temper erupting. But she was grateful he hadn't succeeded in killing himself. That would have been one responsibility too far. She thought of Mrs Bridges and how she would have been slaughtered by his death. No, she had to be glad for that. It seemed as if a great load had lifted from her shoulders and as Josh's first week progressed and Gab too made progress, life suddenly took on a whole new aspect. She put her engagement ring on and wore it constantly, frequently pausing to admire it, much to her father's amusement.

They were sitting in the kitchen a week to the day of Gab's accident when her father said, 'I've got these plans.' He brought out a folded piece of paper. 'Writing's a bit shaky, but I think you can see what I mean.' He opened up the paper and showed her a rough map of the downstairs rooms. 'You see, I already have this room as a bedroom and the downstairs bathroom, and I thought if we broke through into the old dairy from the bedroom we could make the dairy into a bedroom and have my current bedroom as a sitting room. Then you could have the sitting room for yourselves and we'd still have a dining room too.'

Megan studied his plans and deep down inside her she was exceedingly grateful for his ideas and could see instantly that it had a great deal of merit, but she was afraid to show too much enthusiasm in case it looked as though she was glad to be done with him and have him shut away. This new considerate parent she'd unexpectedly acquired was taking some getting used to.

'It's very thoughtful of you, Da. It would obviously

268

work and we've never had any use for the old dairy, have we? Yes, that is a good idea, if you're happy with it.'

'Of course I am. We've loads of furniture so furnishing it would be no problem and if you and Rhodri wanted to buy new . . .'

'Well, there's not much of his we'd want to keep. He set up house when he first started earning so it's all a bit shambolic, nothing matches.'

'I'll find a builder. Rose has been having some changes made to their cottage, and she liked the chap who did it, so we could try him. There's another thing. I want him to change his name to Hughes hyphen Jones.'

'Da!'

'I mean it. Yours are going to be the only grandchildren I shall get and I want them to inherit not just the farm but the name too. I'm sure Rhodri won't mind.'

'And if he does?'

'We'll cross that bridge when we come to it.'

'But his parents might object. When we go down to see them next weekend I'll try to introduce the idea. It's a bit of a tall order, though, don't you think?'

'Why? When it means his children will be inheriting this place. When we bought it two years ago we got it for a song, it's worth twice what we paid for it. He'll be a wealthy man, and you'll be wealthy too.'

'No, Da, his children will be wealthy. Not Rhodri. He could take umbrage.'

'I don't see why he should, after all—'

'Have you had this planned all along? Let us get engaged and then catch us off our guard with this name scheme?'

'Now, now—'

'Well, you can tell Rhodri, because I'm not and you

can tell him soon because I'm not doing a thing about the wedding until it's been sorted. Honestly, Da! I can't forgive you for this.'

'But it's not much I'm asking. Just to add a name to his own. That's all.' Patiently Megan's Da protested it hadn't been in his mind all along, it was something that had occurred to him only the previous day.

'Just when I thought you'd had a complete change of heart. It's not fair, it simply isn't fair. You've got your own way about me being here to look after you, is there anything else you'd like to dictate to us about? Because if there is, let's have it out in the open right away.' Megan glared at him across the table and waited.

'It's just an old man's fancy, you know. I wouldn't like to die with no one carrying on my name.'

'They'd be of your blood line though, wouldn't they, any children we have?'

'It's not quite the same. I think it has quite a ring to it – Hughes-Jones. Yes, I rather like it. Hughes-Jones. Sounds quite distinguished. Or should it be Jones-Hughes. I can't decide.'

'It's not for you to decide – it's for Rhodri and me. I'm so disappointed.' Megan burst into tears.

'Megan. Megan.'

But Megan fled the kitchen and disappeared upstairs to her bedroom, broken-hearted by this new scheme to upset her and Rhodri. How many more hurdles did he intend putting in their way? She'd marry Rhodri and be damned. She would. She'd leave him here to rot and rot he would because he didn't lift a finger for himself. She did it all. He couldn't help that, she knew, because he was so twisted and crippled with arthritis, but just sometimes she had a suspicion that he could if he wanted. Only last week after

Gab, he'd gone into the kitchen and was making a cup of tea all by himself in the night. So he could do things if he wanted to enough.

There was a knock at the bedroom door. For one stupid startled moment she thought it must be Gab, because no one else had come upstairs since they'd lived there. 'Yes.'

'It's your da. Cup of tea ready for you in the kitchen in five minutes. OK?'

His words were the exact echo of what Gab had said that morning when he'd got into the house before milking. Da had got upstairs! He hadn't been up there since the week they'd moved in. Megan dried her tears, looked in the mirror, brushed her hair, tied it back with a length of ribbon and went downstairs, almost afraid to acknowledge that her da had kept her running about after him all these weeks and months when all the time he was capable of doing small things for himself. She saw him with new eyes when she entered the kitchen. He was just lifting the kettle to pour the boiling water into the teapot. Slightly shaky but not dangerously so. Just as he sat down at the table she said, 'I fancy a biscuit. Do you?'

'Yes, all right,' he said and got up to get the tin. He had to take his time but he did it, and when he sat down again, by dint of holding the tin to his chest he got the lid off and offered it to her.

'You said you'd been cruel to me and I denied it, but you have, haven't you? You've made me wait on you day in day out, every little thing, but look at you now. The times I've had to come in from the fields in the middle of doing something, taken my boots off, washed my hands just to get you your morning coffee, then gone straight back out again. You could have done it yourself, couldn't you?'

He didn't reply.

'Couldn't you?'

He still didn't reply.

'Well, I'm sorry, Da, but you're not pulling the wool over my eyes any more. I'm going out tonight, I've already put the dinner in the oven and I don't know when I shall be back.'

'There's no need to use that tone to me. I'm your father.'

'Really. The mood I'm in, I don't know when I shall be back, if ever. You've climbed the stairs, you've boiled the kettle, you've got the biscuit tin, and opened it. The milk from the fridge and not spilt a drop, the cups and saucers from the dishwasher. You've hurt me beyond anything you've ever done before.' Megan left the kitchen and didn't speak to or see her father again before she left.

Rhodri was surprised to see her at the Practice. He was just about to leave, regretting as he always did at this moment of the day that Harry Ferret wouldn't be there to greet him when he got home.

'Why! Megan, what a lovely surprise!'

'Footloose and fancy free I am, Rhodri bach. Shall we go out for a meal?'

'Of course, that would be lovely. Where shall we go?'

'We'll ask Dan for ideas. I expect Rose will have sorted somewhere good.'

Dan was about to leave and was standing talking to Mungo. They broke off their conversation and both said how pleased they were about the wedding and when was it to be?

'Soon. In fact very soon.'

Mungo kissed her on both cheeks and stood back to admire her. 'Good! You'll make a lovely bride. Lovely.'

Megan blushed, she couldn't help it, because he so obviously really meant what he said. 'Rhodri and I are going out for a meal tonight, do you have any bright ideas for where to go?'

Dan suggested the Italian restaurant in the precinct. 'Lovely food, and the staff are so welcoming. They'll be fighting to serve you. They love a good-looking woman.'

'The Casa Rosa?'

'That's right, it doesn't look much from the outside but the food is fresh, none of that microwave nonsense.'

'Right, we'll go there then. It seems funny here without Kate, doesn't it?'

Mungo nodded his agreement. 'It does, we miss her. Her stepmother rang yesterday to say that she's got settled at college and loving every minute.'

Dan said, 'She'll make a good vet, she has a large dose of common sense, no sickly sentimentality and a good brain. And she's hard-working.'

'I'll be off then.'

'How's your father, Megan? Keeping well?'

She didn't answer immediately. When she did all she said was, 'He's fine.' She knew if she said any more she'd burst into tears and look a fool.

Mungo said, 'Good, I'm glad. Be seeing you, Megan.'

Rhodri parked his car in the multi-storey and they walked to the restaurant hand in hand.

'The ring looks lovely.'

Megan held up her hand and admired it. Rhodri kissed it and said how proud he was that she was wearing it.

'Rhodri, I'm not ready to eat yet. Can we just sit somewhere and talk first?'

'Of course. I'll pop in and make sure of a table for, what? Half an hour or an hour?'

'An hour.'

When he came out of the Casa Rosa he said, 'The food smells marvellous. Let's sit by the fountain.'

This time he gripped her round her waist, sensing something was wrong. They found a seat by the fountain, and quite by chance there was no one else sitting around it so they were almost in a world of their own. 'There we are. Now what's the matter?' Rhodri put his arm along the back of the seat and held on to her shoulder, giving her a loving shake. 'There's something, isn't there? I know, so out with it.'

Megan told him about her father, how suddenly he found himself able to climb the stairs, to make a cup of tea and manage the biscuit tin. How he'd come up with the plan for making himself a set of rooms so they would have the sitting room to themselves. And . . . how he'd brought up the idea of Rhodri adding her surname to his.

It was such a startling idea that Rhodri couldn't reply immediately. He gazed instead at the fountain throwing the water about twenty feet into the air. He'd always liked fountains where the water shot straight up into the air before it came down. He didn't like those new-fangled ones that simply dribbled water over stones so the right sound wasn't there. 'Well, Megan, I don't want to make a mess of things, because it all appears to be going in the right direction. I feel like this fountain, as though my spirits are flying up into the sky, and nothing, nothing can stop them, but this . . .' He shook his head. 'This, I'm not sure.'

'I think he's gone a tad too far. I'm so angry with him, when I think of the times I've come in from the fields, boots off, coat off, gloves off, hands to wash, coffee to make, all because I thought he couldn't do it for himself, when all the time he *could have* if he'd wanted to.'

Rhodri went back to studying the fountain. It wasn't adding her surname to his, in truth it was adding *Mr Jones*'s surname to his. That was what he meant. The old sod. Did it matter in the great scheme of things? Yes, it did. Why? Because it meant Jones was dictating to him again. Getting the upper hand. Dominating him. And he wasn't having it. 'We'll have to think about that. I'm glad he's making an effort though. Won't do him any harm and I like his idea about the dairy. Good thinking, that.'

They sat a while longer, until Megan's stomach rumbled loudly and made them both laugh. 'Time to eat I think.' Rhodri took her hand and pulled her up off the seat, drew her close to him, and said, 'I love you. I can't wait for my parents to meet you. They'll both love you to bits. Anyway, lead me to the food, I'm starving.'

'So am I.' Megan smiled hesitantly and he knew why. She was so nervous about her da. Well, he was going to see to that for her. Tonight, in the old man's own house, he'd tell him where he stood.

They hadn't realised a sudden strong wind had got up while they'd been eating in the precinct, but as soon as they came out of the car park onto the main road the wind caught the car and Rhodri had to grip the steering wheel tightly to prevent it being pushed against the kerb.

'My word! Would you believe this? Some gale this is, Megan love.'

'Let's get home. I'm worried about Da.'

'No need. He'll be all right.' But perhaps he won't be when I've said my piece to him, Rhodri thought.

They battled their way to Beulah Bank, expecting any

moment that a tree would be down across the road. Up Beulah was a difficult road at the best of times, with all its steepness and twists and turns but now it was a nightmare.

Rhodri had to hold on to the door so Megan could get out of the car. They struggled across the yard and into the house. Megan's first words were 'Da! We're back! Are you all right?'

She'd no need to have worried. He was as cool as a cucumber, reading a book. 'I'm fine. Hello, Rhodri. Bad night.'

'It is. I was expecting a tree across Up Beulah, but there isn't, not yet.'

'Can I get you a drink, Da?'

'No, thank you. I haven't finished the wine I had for dinner.' Mr Jones picked up a wine glass from the table beside his chair and drank from it. 'Nice wine, this.'

'Would you like a drink, Rhodri?'

'I'd like tea, please. Don't want any more alcohol when I'm driving.'

'OK.'

Rhodri sat down on the chair nearest to Mr Jones. 'Megan has been telling me about your plans for opening up the old dairy as a bedroom for you. It sounds an absolutely splendid idea and very astute of you to have thought of it. It will be great for you to have a room where you can go when you're fed up with the two of us and great for us to have space to ourselves, and I reckon it's a very civilised way of going about it.'

'But . . . ?'

'You're right, there is a but. I shall come straight to the point because you're a man who prefers to look things squarely in the face and I admire that. You know where you are with a man like that. So . . . at the moment, I cannot see my way to changing my name. So that will have to be put aside for the time being. You're not, please, not, to make things difficult for Megan. She's had quite enough worry over Gab and your health without adding to it with this suggestion of yours.' Rhodri looked Old Man Jones straight in the eyes and didn't lower his gaze for a second.

But he didn't get a reply, so Rhodri continued the conversation as though he'd never mentioned the Hughes-Jones question. 'I hear you're going to stay with Dan and Rose while Megan and I are in Wales. You'll enjoy having the baby to watch, he's getting to look quite human. Smiling and such.'

Still there was no reply to his statement so Rhodri fell silent and watched the logs burning in the grate instead of talking. Megan came in with a tray and he got up and pulled a small table in front of the fire so she had somewhere to place it.

'You two are very quiet. What's the matter, Da? Cat got your tongue?'

'No, definitely not. Rhodri here has been telling me how pleased he is with the building work I've suggested, you know, breaking through into the dairy, and that he knows me as a man who likes to look things squarely in the face, and one who values honesty. So that's how he likes things too, and he's agreed to add Jones to his name, like I suggested. Jones-Hughes. Sounds imposing, don't you think?'

Rhodri's mouth dropped open in disbelief. Once or twice he'd used the word 'conniving' when he'd spoken of Old Man Jones, and he'd never been more right.

Megan looked amazed. 'Have you?'

Rhodri shook his head at her. 'No, I have not. I said, at

the moment, I can't see my way to changing my name. Not at all. At the moment.' He turned to face Mr Jones. 'You know full well that's what I said, and what I say I mean. If it is a prerequisite for marriage then I'm afraid it's just not on. We shall marry anyway and damn the consequences. You once said to me that there wouldn't be a penny of your money for Megan if we married, and I said we didn't care. We still don't care. We shall still marry whether you like it or not. We shan't starve, believe me.'

Rhodri got to his feet and put a cup of tea on his future father-in-law's table. Mr Jones dashed it aside and the tea spilt all over his table and on his bottles of tablets. Rhodri saw his hand stray towards his stick as he shouted, 'I said I didn't want tea.' His fingers closed as best they could over the handle of his stick, his intention only too obvious.

His voice fierce with anger and more Welsh than ever, Rhodri shouted, 'Pick up that stick and threaten me with it, and I shall walk out of this house with Megan and we shan't return. I will not be dominated by your temper and your wishes to the exclusion of everyone else's feelings. Megan comes first now and not before time.'

'I see. You can shout at me now, can you, now you think you've got your feet under my table?'

'I don't want to shout. What I do want is Megan's happiness. She's had little of that lately, at your beck and call seven days a week. I hear you've actually made a cup of tea, got upstairs without any help, served your own meal tonight while we've been out. That doesn't sound like the helpless man I've always thought you were. If ever it got out that you'd been *acting* helpless all this time, it wouldn't reflect very well on you, now would it?'

'Hmmph.'

Megan was silently crying, but, intent on their quarrel, neither of them noticed.

'Wanting me to change my name is your way of dominating me. Well, those days are done. Believe me. It is the most enormous sacrifice on my part to live here in this house. I so wanted Megan to live in my house, with me, away from all this, free from this slavery.'

Rhodri waved a hand at the invalid paraphernalia on Mr Jones's side table. 'I can just hear Rose tut-tutting if she heard about your behaviour.'

That stung Mr Jones. A picture of a smiling Rose came uppermost into his mind and he knew he didn't want her to know. Not Rose. No. Not all weekend knowing that in her eyes he'd behaved less than honourably. But, he asked himself, why did he feel able to behave dishonourably to Megan, then?

Ah! But if he was honest he knew the answer to that; it was because she was so like her mother in looks that he harboured a passionate desire, buried very deep, to get his own back on her. Her mother. His wife. Who'd despised him. Hated him even. He remembered how his behaviour had driven her to weeping bitter tears and he hadn't thought about those tears for a long time. Mr Jones looked about him. Saw Rhodri standing quite still, looking down at him waiting, waiting for an answer. Megan quietly crying so despairingly. There was an awful lot to lose at this moment. She wasn't to blame for what was happening now, simply because she reminded him of his failures. The bitter tears of her mother had to be laid at his door. And this Rhodri fellow was stout in his defence of her, a rock he was, a loving, devoted rock that's what – and a Welsh Nationalist too.

Old Man Jones took another drink of his wine, hoping

it would steady his nerves. The glass almost slipped from his twisted fingers as he put it down, but he mustn't let it, he mustn't show his weakness. 'The matter of changing your name can be left in abeyance. We'll have the reception at the George and I shall foot the bill like all brides' fathers do, and, if I can, I'll give the bride away but not from that damned wheelchair. I shall be upright on my own two legs.'

'Thank you. Thank you.'

The wind hammered at every window and door of the house, and howled down the chimneys. 'You must stay the night. It's too risky driving back in this gale. There's only Megan's bedroom aired so you'd better sleep in there.' He picked up his book, placed his reading glasses on his nose, and didn't look up to see their reaction. There was nothing like a magnificent gesture to impress everyone. He couldn't read a word, he was too confused. The lines wavered and waltzed over the page, so he had to pretend he was reading, till his head cleared.

He glanced up at the two of them. His daughter was sitting on a stool at Rhodri's feet and they were holding hands. He had an idea that Rhodri'd make sure Megan wouldn't be crying bitter tears, ever.

Megan must have forgotten he was still in the room. He watched her look up at Rhodri crouched on the edge of his chair, his arm around her shoulders, staring into the fire, and the look on her face caused her father's heart to lurch. He hoped Rhodri knew how blessed he was to have a wife who loved him like Megan did. But then he caught sight of Rhodri's face as he turned to her with a look full of love and adoration, and the dried-up, wizened core of him warmed to them both.